Murder on Bedford Island

Alex Trotter Mystery #1

Cheryl Peyton

ISBN-13 978-1483988009

ISBN-10 978-1483988007

This is a work of fiction. Names, characters, places and incidents either are the product of the author's imagination, or are used fictitiously. Government agencies referred to in this book are used fictitiously. Any resemblance to any actual persons, living or dead, events, or locales is entirely coincidental.

This book was printed in the United States of America.

Other Books by Cheryl Peyton

Six Minutes to Midnight

Walk on Through the Rain: A Polio Survivor's Story

Murder on the Bermuda Queen - An Alex Trotter Mystery

Murder in Margaritaville- An Alex Trotter Mystery

Available at www.amazon.com in soft cover and eBooks

In soft cover at www.barnesandnoble.com

Available through these websites:
www.cheryljpeytonn.com
www.authorsguildoftn.org

Murder

on

Bedford Island

Alex Trotter Mystery #1

Saturday, March 29

Chapter 1

Thirteen Sign Up for Bedford Island

ALEX TROTTER LEANED against the kitchen counter thumbing through the day's mail. She tossed aside the usual assortment of credit card offers, coupons, and advertisements; but the remaining envelope held her attention. It was hand-addressed on rag-content paper. Holding it up to the light, she made out the watermark of a high-end stationer.

Curious, she slit it open and pulled out the contents — a signed, completed travel contract with a check written to her business, Globe-Trotter Travels.

"I've got one more reservation for my Bedford Island trip," she announced to her apartment mate, waving the papers in the air. "A Lawrence Livermore – from *Charleston*, no less. Look at this formal handwriting on parchment paper. I thought it was a wedding invitation. I mean, who still uses a fountain pen?"

Seated at the dining table, Beth stopped typing on her laptop to squint up at the raised envelope. “Nice to see that somebody still can write in cursive, period.”

Alex shrugged. “Right. I just hope it doesn’t mean he's fussy. Bedford Island is a wilderness that won't appeal to someone who's real particular. Besides, he's almost too late. Today's the deadline, so now I have *thirteen.* He could be putting a curse on the trip.” Her gray blue eyes rounded in mock alarm..

Beth’s eyes rolled up to the ceiling. “Give the guy a break. He’s probably busy and happens to have nice penmanship. End of story. The phobia about the number thirteen is nonsense from the Dark Ages.”

Alex put down the envelope. “Tell that to the travel industry. Try booking a room on the thirteenth floor in a New York City hotel. Most of them don’t *have* a thirteenth floor. They think numbering the floors 'eleven,' 'twelve,' 'fourteen,' fools the guests.”

Beth chuckled. “Funny. Now that you mention it, there wasn't a thirteenth row on the plane I was on a couple weeks ago. I know I wouldn't like to sit in the thirteenth row on a Flight #13 taking off in a storm.”

Alex took a seat at the kitchen table. “In that case, your real problem is that the pilot is taking off in a storm, which they *don't do,* by the way. Besides, most airlines don’t have a flight number thirteen, either. People are still a little skittish of flying, so there’s no sense in making them more nervous.

“Speaking of scaring passengers,” Alex continued, “I wonder who the genius was who came up with *Amelia Earhart* luggage. Do you think that name inspires confidence in flying?” She made air quotes, “’Buy our luggage! It’s very attractive even though it’ll disappear after your first flight.’ Or, how about, ‘Buy our luggage. You’ll only lose it if you fly over the Pacific.’”

Beth laughed. “I never thought about that. It *is* a crazy name for a line of luggage.”

“I think the fear of the number thirteen comes from the biblical story of the Last Supper when Jesus was betrayed by Judas,” Alex segued. He was the thirteenth person to come to the table. I’ll have thirteen people eating together all week. Do you think that’s tempting fate?”

Beth held up her palms. “I don’t know about that, but I think I’ll count the people at Thanksgiving dinner this year. I might wanna move to the kids’ table.”

She looked down at her laptop. “Here’s what I found on Google for 'Friday the Thirteenth.' There was a ‘Thirteen Club’ founded in 1886 by a wealthy New Yorker who tried to dispel the Norse legend that if thirteen people dine together, one would soon die. The group met together annually for dinner, but disbanded in the 1920s.”

“Disbanded or *died off*?” Alex's eyes widened.

Beth scanned the screen. “Some of them died. But who can say that was due to the curse? People didn’t live that long a hundred years ago, you know. You can’t think there’s anything to this thirteen-eating-together curse. There must be groups of thirteen people eating together all the time. Besides, how can you give credence to people who named a frozen wilderness, *Greenland* and decided to live there. They could have kept going until they came here.”

Beth stood and brushed off her skirt. “Speaking of dining, I have to get going to meet John for dinner. Just the two of us, so I'll be safe.” She gave Alex a loopy smile and headed for the door.

Alex sat in thought. *I’m not foolish enough to put any stock in a Norse superstition. I’m just taking thirteen people to a quiet barrier island off Georgia to stay at a four-star inn. What could go wrong?*” The answer, as she quickly admitted to herself, was *plenty,* because that was the nature of the travel business.

Picking up Lawrence Livermore's contract, she scanned through it to read more about the man who might be hard to please and become a 'curse' on the trip. Hmmm. Impressive address. Broad Street in Charleston was home to international financial institutions and prestigious law firms. Probably his business address. Maybe he's a wealthy banker or lawyer.

Considering his tangible qualifications, as opposed to some ancient superstition, he looked like a desirable member of the group and free from all curses.

Thinking about the other twelve people who might not be either, she opened her file and reviewed their contracts. It was always entertaining, but rarely accurate, to picture the people based on the scant amount of personal information on the form. But still, you could draw a few inferences. Paging through them, she jotted down the names and a few notes by each one:

Mrs. Nadine Rodgers from Winnetka, Illinois— *wealthy widow? Could hook up with Lawrence Livermore?*

Mr. and Mrs. Conrad Pierce (Margaret) and daughter, Chloe Campbell, from Baltimore, Maryland — *second marriage. Prickly relationship between stepfather and stepdaughter?*

Ms. Rosemary Davis and Ms. Phyllis Hanover from Washington, D.C.— *two single women who live next door to each other in Georgetown. Also wealthy widows?*

Mr. David Albright and Ms. Jennifer Brown from Chicago, Illinois – *young professionals who live together. Probably attractive and sophisticated.*

Mr. and Mrs. Wade Kerley (Ronette) from Dunin, Florida — *young married couple from rural northern Florida. They're within a two-hour's drive from Bedford. Why would they want to spend a week there with a tour group?*

Mr. and Mrs. Johnny Berthold (Amanda) from Knoxville, Tennessee — *young married professionals. Could make friends with David Albright and Jennifer Brown?*

Looking back over the completed list, she hoped they would all be easy-going, cooperative and nice people; but, based on past groups, there were probably some prima donnas, pompous bores, inebriates, and complainers among them.

Even the most reasonable travelers could become out of sorts if there were too many disappointments, which was her job to minimize. Of course, there was a lot outside of her control; starting with the weather. Add to that: equipment failures, language barriers, rude waiters, hotel rooms that faced a blinking neon sign, and a thousand other frustrations that travelers faced. Some of the finest hotels in New York had recently battled an outbreak of bedbugs that had been nearly impossible to eradicate.

Not yet thirty, Alex had started her own travel business two years earlier after a brief, rather unprofitable stint as a painter.

As a young child she had traveled widely with her parents for their work. Her father was a nature photographer; her mother a free-lance writer. To pass the time, Alex started sketching and painting her father's subjects.

After graduating from college with a fine arts degree, she enrolled in the Chicago Art Institute to develop her skills into a marketable career. Completing the two-year master's program, she went on a few trips with artist friends to find subjects to paint. Her work was accepted by a gallery in Lincoln Park; but the income from sales was insufficient and too erratic to dependably support even a modest lifestyle and having a roommate to share costs.

Organizing trips with friends, she discovered she could travel for free by signing up enough friends and others for cruises and land tours. In time, she had enough clients and experience to design her own tour packages.

In making up itineraries for foreign travel, she offered what she called her Cultural Samplings in lieu of the usual fare of museums and cathedrals. In Italy, she enrolled tourists in a one-day cooking school to learn the art of pasta making. The sessions would end with the group dining on the results, supplemented by enough of the local wine to make everyone *contento.*

Touring large American cities, she devised "Get Down with Uptown" excursions, as she titled them. Her method for finding hidden places of interest was to befriend (and generously tip) a cab driver to take her around to the locals' favorite haunts. Thus she discovered a bar in D.C. that offered half-priced drinks to redheads. This was a hit with her Irish American Heritage group tour.

The upcoming trip to Bedford Island posed special problems as it was a National Wildlife Preserve that had little infrastructure and could only be reached by boat. There weren't any paved roads as cars weren't allowed, except for the few that belonged to the staff at the camp sites, the visitor center, and the Grover Inn.

Communication on the island would be virtually impossible: no internet service; no land lines or towers for cell phone reception. The Inn had some sort of two-way radio for emergencies. Alex had advised all her travelers of the lack of electronic connections, and assumed that those who signed up would welcome being cut off from the rest of the world for a few days.

The main attractions for tourists were the solitude, the natural scenery, and the wildlife, including a herd of two hundred feral horses whose ancestors were either survivors of a shipwreck or the descendants of stock abandoned by seventeenth-century Spanish explorers.

Lacking manmade development, the narrow seventeen milelong island was comprised mostly of salt marshes, inland lakes, and upland and maritime forests. The entire eastern side was edged in white sand beaches and the blue water of the Atlantic Ocean.

Activities would include hiking to view the many species of birds, and rarely seen wildlife, like armadillos, and tram tours from the hotel to see the horses and the few places of interest on the island, like the ruins left from earlier Indian and British occupation. Or the tram could transport them to the ferry to cross over the inlet to St. Annes to sightsee and shop. Swimming in the ocean might be limited as the waters around the island were known to have a high population of sharks.

Some might opt to spend the time relaxing on the hotel's wide front porch, getting massages and spa treatments, or sunbathing on the nearby beach.

Alex hadn't been to Bedford since the trip with her parents when she was a teenager but, since the island had been pretty much undeveloped since the Pleistocene Age, she figured there wouldn't be many changes in the last fifteen years. Besides, she had written Raymond Bean, manager of the Grover Inn, who confirmed the quality of the facilities still offered by the historic hotel.

Alex looked forward to the slow-paced schedule for the week. There couldn't be a more peaceful place, if you equated serenity with the lack of manmade facilities and human activity. The only disruptions to the tranquility might be the wild horses, the poisonous snakes, and the carnivorous sharks. She had never heard of a horse attacking anyone. To avoid snakes, you stayed on well- traveled paths in the woods, and sharks stay in the ocean.

Wednesday, March 12

Chapter 2

Mrs. Nadine Rodgers

THE EARLY MORNING SUN streamed through the French doors of the breakfast room, warming the white wainscoted walls and burnishing the pine cabinets in the adjoining kitchen. In mid-March, in the Chicago North Shore suburb of Winnetka, the rays of light provided enough heat to banish the chill in the air.

At eight o'clock, Nadine Rodgers came into her kitchen already dressed for her afternoon appointment downtown. She had decided on an olive green wrap skirt and a long-sleeved white cotton sweater that appeared "sincere" without being too "serious."

After putting up a pot of coffee, she dropped two halves of a whole-grain English muffin in the toaster. While waiting for the brewing and heating cycles to finish, she took a grapefruit out of the refrigerator, and sliced it in half. Checking her refrigerator calendar, she confirmed that her meeting was at three o'clock. *Good*, she thought. She still had some time to plan a few details at home. Her gardener Eddie should be coming soon to start work on the outside and he would expect to consult with her, first.

It was that time of year when the snow had melted leaving scattered twigs and brittle leaves caught in bare-branched bushes. In short, the yard needed a major cleanup to prepare for new shoots that would sprout in the coming weeks. Nadine didn't dare put off the work since everyone in her upscale community was expected to keep up appearances, in every way possible.

She glanced at her watch. Eddie was due in an hour. He would probably start with the last of the cold-weather pruning and then move on to raking and uncovering the back gardens, if there was time. Lawn care would be scheduled for a later date, sometime after the grass had a chance to emerge from its winter dormancy.

Sipping her second cup of coffee, Nadine had just gotten through the business section of the Trib when the phone rang. With a knowing smile, she rounded the corner of the kitchen to take the call in the sunroom where she could be comfortable for a long chat. Opting to sit on her wicker sofa, she plopped down and picked up the cordless receiver.

"Hello?" Her voice rose in a question.

"It's Lawrence, Nadine," the southern baritone voice drawled. "Lawrence Livermore," he clarified, his accent making it sound more like 'Lau-ance Liv-e-mo-ah.' "I trust I'm not calling too early."

"Oh, Lawrence. No, of course not. It's so good to hear from you." She leaned back against a cushion and crossed her slim legs.
"This is the perfect time, actually. Couldn't be better. Did you read my email from last night, then?"

"Yes, of course – that's the reason for my call. Your description of your upcoming trip to Bedford Island gave me an idea that I wanted to pass by you. To come right to the point, what would you say to my joining up with the tour so that we could meet in person? I'm only a couple hours' drive from there, or I might pick up a local flight."

She sat up straight. "I'd love it if you did. I confess that was in the back of my mind when I wrote, knowing the island's proximity to Charleston."

"It's about 150 miles from here—an easy drive on the interstate, although I've never been there before, which is another reason I'd like to sign up. Of course, I wouldn't expect to monopolize your time — or even talk business, if you didn't want to," he added.

"Don't worry about that. I feel we know each other pretty well by now these past few months since the Bradfords put me in touch with you. I wouldn't mind talking a little business in person so we could better discuss your financial strategies. I need to finally make a decision about whether to invest in your hedge fund.

"Of course we'd both be free as to how we spend our time," she continued. "I've traveled quite a bit on my own in the last three years since William, so I'm not in need of company while vacationing. You probably feel the same, having been single for so long."

"That's true, Nadine. On the other hand, I have quite enough solitude in my life and in my work. I would enjoy having your company, I assure you."

"Well, that's very nice. I'm sure we can work out our time to our mutual advantage. Why don't you go online to read more about the island and the Grover Inn? Make sure it suits you. The island's a pretty wild place, but I think you'll find the hotel is very comfortable. There's a contract on the website you can print out to send or fax back to Alex Trotter, the tour operator."

"I'll take care of it today, Nadine. Incidentally, last week I sent your friends an excellent first-quarter statement on their investments. I don't know if you've talked to them lately, but I assure you they've very pleased with the result I've gotten for them, and I'll do the same for you, should you decide to go ahead and invest with my fund."

Nadine sat up straighter. "Actually they *did* mention it to me. Again, as in your previous reports, you managed to outperform all the major indices, and by fifteen to twenty percent. I must admit that I'm tempted to sign up, but it's a major decision. Anyway, we'll talk more about your financial plan for me when we're together on the island. I have some other friends with substantial net worth who could qualify to invest in your fund, as well. If you can convince *me*, I'll see if they're interested, too."

"I would be most grateful, my dear. As with you, I'd need to thoroughly discuss with them their asset picture and financial goals. I make some pretty gutsy moves. A lot of people don't have the stomach for the risk level I accept. I can only tell you that I sleep like a baby every night."

"Well, I hope that doesn't mean that you wake up crying every four hours," she responded with a chuckle.

"Ha! That's a good one! I'll have to remember that. I'm really looking forward to meeting you in person, Nadine. I feel like we've signed up on a singles' dating site, don't you?"

Nadine flushed with a mixture of pleasure and embarrassment. "I guess it does. Of course, we've seen each other's pictures, and we only have a business deal riding on our gettogether, but still ... "

Lawrence cleared his throat to bridge the awkward moment. "Well, listen, it's been nice talking to you, Nadine. I'll let you get back to whatever you were doing. Thanks for telling me about the tour – believe me, I could use a little vacation. I'll email you later with my travel plans after I'm signed up. Maybe we can meet in St. Annes before we go over to the island."

"Good idea, and thanks for joining me in this, Lawrence. I'm looking forward to our adventure. Bye for now."

* * *

ANSWERING THE DOORBELL a half hour later she found Eddie on the stoop ready to work, dressed in a plaid wool shirt, jeans, and brown cotton garden gloves.

She grabbed a jacket off a hook in the mudroom and joined him outside to discuss a plan of attack on the gardens, the pool area, and the shrubbery along the walkways.

* * *

A LITTLE AFTER ONE THIRTY, Nadine backed her silver Mercedes coupe out of the garage of her Tudor-style home. Catching sight of Eddie in the front yard, she waved before heading south to make her way over to Sheridan road. Stopped at the first light, she quickly rechecked the papers in her briefcase on the front seat. Yes, she thought that she had brought with her all the documents that she needed. She only hoped she was doing the right thing – and not getting carried away, or causing an unnecessary fuss. By two-forty, she had parked her car in a public lot on LaSalle Street and was in an elevator of a high-rise office building on Jackson. Getting out on the ninth floor, she followed signs to lead her down the marble hallway to Suite 950. Standing outside the closed door, she hesitated long enough to read the gilt-edged transfer letters on the glass: "Offices of the United States Securities and Exchange Commission." Shrugging her shoulders and sighing deeply, she turned the ornate bronze knob, opened the door and went inside.

The simply-furnished waiting room was empty except for the gray-haired receptionist who sat behind a sliding frosted glass window. Her mouth was puckered in concentration as she studied something on her desk. A couple seconds later, when the door latch clicked back into position, the woman first looked up, peered over her half-glasses at Nadine and frowned.

“May I help you?” the still-pursed mouth asked, sounding like a suspicious floorwalker talking to a loitering teenager in an electronics department.

“Yes, I believe you can,” Nadine responded, nonplussed. "I'm Nadine Rodgers and I have a three o’clock appointment with Agent Burke. Michael Burke. He should be expecting me,” she added, a little forcefully.

The unsmiling receptionist looked unconvinced. “I’ll see about that,” she cautioned, consulting a calendar book. After a moment – “Yes, I’ve found your name here,” she admitted, still grim-faced. "I’ll buzz his assistant. Have a seat. You’ll have to wait since you’re early,” she advised with the first note of pleasure in her voice.

Nadine looked at her watch: five minutes to three. She nodded, turned and selected a chair halfway across the room. *Not much of a welcoming from a greeter,* she thought. *Good thing she doesn’t work for a business that needs to make a profit.*

After waiting about five minutes, a door opened and a soft, throaty voice asked, “Mrs. Rodgers?” Nadine looked up at the speaker, an attractive young woman with a stylish blunt haircut. Her short black skirt, paired with a classic pin-striped shirt, qualified as business dress, but had been cannily selected to enhance her good figure, as well.

When Nadine nodded her assent hearing her name, the woman introduced herself with a smile. “I’m Katie, Agent Burke’s assistant. Please follow me.” Turning, her stilettos clicked on the tiled floor as she led the way down the hallway until they came to a closed glass paneled door. The secretary knocked softly. "Agent Burke? Your three o'clock is here.”

"Come in, come in. Mrs. Rodgers, is it? Michael Burke." The shirt-sleeved agent half stood, extending his hand over piles of papers on his old-fashioned wooden desk.

As they shook hands, the agent's strained face relaxed into a pleasant smile. “I know it doesn’t look like it,” he said, cocking his head toward his littered desk, “but I’m ready for you." His face was sculpted with a smooth broad forehead, high cheek bones and a strong jaw. *Typical G-man,* Nadine thought, inanely.

"Please have a seat," he said. Nadine pulled out a straight-backed chair and sat down. "I'm sorry it's not comfortable, but it's not supposed to be. Would you like coffee or tea?"

"No, thank you," she replied, a little too sharply, thinking of the accident potential in trying to maneuver Styrofoam cups of hot liquid around foot-high piles of classified records.

"Okay, fine. Katie would you close the door, please? And I won't need you for a while. Thanks.

"Now, let's get down to business, Mrs. Rodgers." The agent's voice had hardened. "I understand you're here to report a securities' fraud. Is that right?"

Nadine's eyes widened. "Uh, no. I'm not in any position to identify a securities' fraud," she clarified with fervor. "In fact, that's why I'm here. Let me explain. I have wealthy friends who, for the past year, have invested in a hedge fund managed by a man named Lawrence Livermore from Charleston, South Carolina. I've never met the man, but my friends referred him to me as a potential client, and Mr. Livermore and I have been emailing back and forth for the past few months. We've become friends, I would have to say. I haven't invested with him, but the couple I mentioned has put *two million dollars* at risk with the man and have not yet received any money, although Mr. Livermore has furnished them with quarterly statements showing profits that far surpass the market performance."

"Okay, now hold on a minute right there, Mrs. Rodgers," Agent Burke cut in. "Just so we understand each other — not every highly successful hedge fund manager is another Bernie Madoff, you know."

Nadine nodded knowingly. "I understand. But, speaking of Bernie Madoff, I heard about the private investigator from Florida who notified the SEC in 1995 that Madoff's hedge fund was a fraud; and the SEC didn't find any evidence of it for another *thirteen years.* Finally, it was discovered that Madoff had been operating a Ponzi scheme since the '70s, as I don't have to tell you."

"Okay. Okay." The agent held up his hands in surrender. "That case was a black eye for us. It's also true that hedge fund managers have operated without much regulatory oversight up to now, and that there are some who have no doubt engaged in questionable trading practices, and some in outright frauds. But what are your particular concerns with this Livermore guy? Just that he's shown a greater profit than other funds?"

Nadine leaned forward in her chair and spoke in a confidential tone. "He has outpaced all the indices by 20% for the *past four years — in a down market.* Yes, that's one red flag that concerns me on behalf of my friends, who have only seen paper profits; and for myself, should I decide to invest the required two million dollars.

"But what I hoped to accomplish here was to obtain some evidence that Mr. Livermore is *legitimate*, and that his fund management strategies are sound, to exercise my due diligence as a potential investor. For instance, I understand that the recent Dodd Frank Act requires hedge fund managers to be registered with the SEC for the first time. I wonder if you can tell me whether Mr. Livermore has done so since the March deadline is almost here. It would be reassuring to me if he has."

The agent nodded in agreement. "Based on your inquiry, I checked on Mr. Livermore's status as a hedge fund manager, and I can tell you that he *has* registered. Now, he wasn't one of those who voluntarily registered before the Act, but he has now, as of a couple of weeks ago."

Nadine sat back. "I'm relieved to hear that. Thank you."

"As to reviewing his strategies," the agent continued, "that's a complicated procedure. Do you know his investment approach—like, for instance is it 'global macro,' or 'directional,' or 'event-driven,' or 'arbitrage'. Does he deal in futures?"

She shrugged. "I know he's a 'global-macro' strategist, as you say, and that he's discretionary, I believe, but that's about all I know. That's what I tried to explain when I first sat down — I'm not so well-versed in hedge-fund management that I can evaluate his strategies. I've brought his prospectus, which has some key information about his fund, along with his leverage limit, and I hoped that you would take a look at it. Is a 'global-macro strategy' a good one?"

Agent Burke held his open palms up. "I can't tell you what is the best approach to investing. I'm only interested in what's legal. And his approach is legal, assuming that he is actually investing as he claims, and not just taking money to support a Ponzi scheme, which is a different matter, altogether. I *can* tell you that a global approach makes sense as there have been extreme uncertainties and activities in the global market that could offer opportunities to the sharp investor. I'm talking about long and short positions in currency markets, and other things that get pretty technical."

Nadine crossed her ankles. "Okay. I understand that's it's all very complicated. I guess one of my concerns is that my friends, the Bradfords, have not yet received any money from their investment, as it's been reinvested, according to Mr. Livermore. They're paying him a *small fortune* every month for his services. He charges 4% of their investment as a management fee. In addition, he takes a performance fee of 20% for his profits."

Burke tapped a pencil on his desk. "That's the highest percentage allowed legally, but as I say, it's *legal.* Are your friends in agreement that he should be investigated? The Bradfords?"

"No, they don't even know I'm here. And I don't want them to know at this point, if that's possible. There was an interesting development today concerning Mr. Livermore. I had emailed him last night to invite him, in effect, to join up with a tour group I've signed up for, spending a week on a small

Georgia island. This morning he phoned to say that he would like to go. I know that once we're there, he'll try harder to convince me to sign over two million dollars to invest in his fund. My plan is to get a better feel for his integrity by talking to him in person, and maybe getting more particulars about how he's able to make a greater profit than anybody else. Are you willing to look over the prospectus and financial information he's given me?" She held up a sheaf of papers.

Burke reached for them and placed them on a pile. "Yes, but all that I can do is to check on whether I can duplicate on paper the profits he claims from the particular financial maneuvers that he's made. But you shouldn't make any accusations directly to him. If he's operating an illegal money-making scheme and not investing, or making the profit he claims, he could be dangerous. He'd want to keep you from reporting him, he might even –"

"Agent Burke," she interrupted, "I can't believe Laurence would resort to violence; but don't worry about me in any case. I'll have the security of a group of people, and we're staying in a very safe, historical old Inn."

"Okay, you probably know best," Burke agreed. Indicating Nadine's stack of papers he asked, "Are those copies of reports that I can keep?"

"Oh, those are all for you." She patted the pile. "So, you're taking the case?"

"I'm not 'taking any case,' because there's no official complaint being made. We have a separate department for that, should it become necessary. As an SEC agent, I'm willing to look over the figures you brought me, and see if they hold up against the numbers I can get from the same investments, as I said. In the meantime, I still think you should hold back. Maybe not even go on the trip that could expose yourself to trouble."

Nadine pushed back her chair. "Thanks for your interest, but I'll be careful. My hope is that Lawrence is on the up and up, of course. I was reluctant to even bring this to your attention as he seems like a fine gentleman, I must admit."

"I'm not challenging that sentiment right now," Agent Burke said, standing. "But I'll tell you that the only successful con artists I've known are the ones who are charming, and don't appear to be crude or dishonest."

"Yes, of course. That makes sense," Nadine agreed. "I'll leave you the information about where I'll be staying, and the dates I'll be there." She stood and picked up her purse and briefcase. "Please contact me at the Grover Inn if you come up with anything suspicious, and I'll do the same. I hope I have a nice quiet vacation in the company of a financial genius who will make me a lot of money for security in my old age." Extending her hand which he shook she added, Thank you so much for your time, Agent Burke. I feel so much better for just having come to see you."

After Nadine left his office, Agent Burke started looking over the financial reports that she had left, his brow furrowed as he made penciled notes in the margins.

Saturday, March 15

Chapter 3

Margaret, Conrad, and Chloe

"CONRAD, WILL YOU COME HERE and help me with my dress?" Margaret Pierce couldn't keep the impatience out of her voice. It was a half-hour before their dinner guests were to arrive and she was feeling irritable and anxious. She held out little hope that her husband would stay sober long enough to get through the evening without wearing a lampshade on his head, so to speak. And this wasn't just any dinner. They were entertaining her daughter's future in-laws for the first time. The Pierces had only met Richard and Judith at the engagement party the Worthingtons had hosted at their D.C. town home two weeks earlier.

Chloe, a senior at Goucher, and Tom, in his last year as an undergrad at Johns Hopkins, were planning a late-summer wedding. That was enough to worry about without having to ward off any trouble that Conrad might make for the couple. He had already voiced his disapproval about his step-daughter's upcoming nuptials.

Calling him again, he finally sauntered into the bathroom, dressed casually in a brown jersey shirt and tan slacks. She had to admit that he was still darkly handsome, although he had softened around the middle in recent years.

"You look pretty sexy tonight, Marg," he flirted, eyeing his wife up and down.

Unsmiling, she turned around for him to finish zipping her up. The bathroom mirror reflected the slim attractive woman holding up her silvery blond hair to better expose the neckline of her bright blue dress, as her husband peered down from his six-inch height advantage.

"You look nice, too," Margaret managed, not entirely trusting her husband's good mood.

Turning to face him, she ventured, "We both have to make sure that the evening goes well, for Chloe's sake, all right?"

"Don't you mean that *I* have to *behave* so that the evening goes well?" he smirked.

"Please don't start. You can be most charming when you want to be, but we both know what happens when you drink too much. We've been over this often enough. Richard and Judith were very welcoming to us in their home, especially when you consider how awkward it was for us to meet *after* our children had decided to make us a family."

"They were okay," Conrad replied, brusquely. "That's not the point. Chloe is too young to be getting married. She's never been out on her own – never even had a serious relationship before. And we don't really know Tom. He could be a monster underneath his clean-cut facade. In any event, she should take her time to travel and live on her own."

"She's been lucky to have traveled quite a bit already," Margaret replied evenly, ignoring his criticisms and other advice.

"She's coming with us to Bedford Island. We all need to relax and take a breather. She and I can talk over wedding ideas. Let's not worry about everything right now and spoil things for her. She's a good girl, and Tom seems like a fine young man. You've no reason to think otherwise. "

Margaret patted his cheek. "Anyway, let's go down and get ready for dinner. Chloe's helping me in the kitchen, but I still have a lot to do." She brushed past him on her way out of the bathroom.

"Well, don't worry about *me!*" Conrad said, mockingly, making faces to her back as he followed her downstairs. "I'll be the life of the party!"

You mean the death of it, Margaret thought glumly.

* * *

TWO HOURS LATER the party of six was finishing their chocolate mousse pie. Margaret's face was drawn with tension, dreading the next social faux pas from her intoxicated husband. The evening had started off well enough, she reflected. Richard and Judith, arriving with Tom, had brought a bottle of fine wine, complimented the "lovely home," and made comments as polite guests who don't know their hosts well.

Tom and Chloe had each made contributions to encourage conversation by relating some interesting facts about their parents:
"Mom grew up on a farm in Pennsylvania," — from Chloe. "Dad has been researching his family tree," — from Tom, which led to Richard's explanation that the surname, "Worthington" came from the Saxon words of "wreath in ton" meaning "farm in town," noting that they were originally farmers, too, going back to the Middle Ages in England.

Expanding on the subject, Richard said that the name was often thought related to nobility. "Believe me, that image is misleading," he advised. "I have discovered that several of my ancestors were anything but noble – even came up with a couple who were hanged for thievery."

Conrad, who had been quietly sucking on his martini, came to life. "Hah! I'm not surprised to hear that! People with sordid pasts can often disguise the fact by seeming to be well-bred. You never know what people are really like. Look at Ted Bundy."

No one knew quite how to respond to a serial killer being compared to relatives of the guests, so there was silence for several moments.

Judith rescued them all by walking over to the bookshelves and inquiring about several framed family photographs, asking Margaret to point out who the people were, other than the Pierces and Chloe. Margaret took her time identifying each image to Judith and Richard who had joined them.

Appetizers and dinner had gone well enough, Margaret thought, marred only by a few more inappropriate remarks by Conrad, which were pretty much ignored. Each topic of general interest that had been raised was taken up with animated talk by the rest of the party, until Conrad said something negative and offputting, so that the subject was changed.

Now that they were coming to the end of the meal, Margaret grimly noted that Conrad was helping himself to another strong drink. When he offered more wine or cordials to the company, Margaret waved off having her glass refilled, as though her own sobriety could somehow deter her husband from further imbibing.

This evening can't last too much longer, can it? she wondered, dying to look at her watch to see if it was getting late enough to politely end the evening. She knew that Conrad had now passed the point of no return and was capable of losing all inhibitions. Hopefully, there wouldn't be any more triggers to set him off.

Conrad hadn't said anything *ruinous,* she tried to convince herself. Maybe the others had taken little notice of his comments, being more concerned with the impression they were making. That's how it always is; people worried more about what others were thinking of them, she reasoned.

While Chloe was telling a funny school story, Margaret relaxed for a moment to consider the positives to take away from the evening. Certainly, the meal had been a success. The roast had been tender and juicy, and was complemented by the creamed potatoes and the asparagus, and everyone was enjoying the richness of the dessert – nothing like a little chocolate and whipped cream to make people feel good. There couldn't be too much chocolate and whipped cream for this group, she thought, giving a sideways glance to her husband.

While she watched her pretty, fair-haired daughter telling her story, she thought of a new topic of conversation that her husband couldn't be negative about – their upcoming trip. It had been Conrad's idea after he had read an ad in a travel magazine.

"Richard and Judith," she began. "I wanted to tell you about a little trip that the three of us are taking next month."

"I don't think the Worthingtons are interested ..." Conrad blurted out, but stopped when he caught Margaret's murderous glare.

"Oh, go ahead," he groused.

"As I was saying," Margaret continued in a brittle voice, "We're going to Bedford Island for a week. I don't know if you've ever heard of it." She paused as her guests shook their heads. "Well, it's a barrier island just off the southern coast of Georgia. It's quite remote – it's only reached by boat from St. Annes. The island has very little development. It's basically a wildlife refuge, although it does have a beautiful old inn, and a white sand beach along its length.

"The most unusual attraction is the herd of 200 wild horses that runs free. Can you imagine? We thought that would be something to see, and the island will be a nice place to relax for a few days. Chloe will have finished her exams and all."

"Sounds great," Judith said. "Richard and I saw the wild horses of Chincoteague and Assateague when we drove over from Ocean City. They call them 'ponies,' and they're separated by a fence that runs between Maryland and Virginia; so they don't mingle. Each herd is protected by the two different states.

"What really surprised me," Judith continued, "is that they're truly *wild animals*. I had thought that wild horses were just like other horses except they hadn't been broken to a bridle or a saddle. But the ranger warned us not to go near them because they'll kick you, bite you, or knock you down if they can.' And it happens a lot, apparently, when visitors get too close."

"That will probably happen to Chloe. She doesn't have any common shense!" The Worthingtons stared at him, open-mouthed as Margaret gripped the edge of the table.

"I don't mean that she's shtupid. She's schmart. But she does shtupid things. For instance, here she is, just becoming an adult, when she should be going off on her own and finding her way, and what is she doing, inshtead? Getting married! That's pretty shtupid." "Wait a minute, Pierce," Richard started.

Chloe slapped down her napkin and stood up "That's enough, Conrad. This isn't the time for this talk. Anything you have to say to me, can be said in private. You don't mean all that you're saying right now, anyway, so I won't argue with you. And you don't have to worry about me getting too near the horses, or doing anything else stupid, as you call it."

Tom got up too, and joined Chloe as she headed for the living room. Everyone but Conrad then stood and followed them out.

"Wonderful meal, Mrs. Pierce, — Margaret," Tom said, smiling a bit too broadly as he stood by the front door with Chloe.

.

Standing nearby, Richard and Judith thanked Margaret for the meal and the evening. Richard explained that they needed to start back, as they had an hour's drive ahead of them. Chloe and Margaret promised to get in touch with Judith in the coming weeks to find a time to shop for a wedding gown.

As Conrad ambled out of the dining room, the visitors quickly hugged Margaret, called out goodnight to him, and started out the door.

Chloe stepped outside with Tom and his parents, leaving Margaret and Conrad alone. Margaret turned to her husband, her face stormy with rage. “You know, there are times when I could just kill you!” she hissed.

Monday, March 17

Chapter 4

Rosemary Davis and Phyllis Hanover

"YOO-HOO, ROSEMARY! Are you there? Rosie!" Phyllis Hanover was in the backyard of her Georgetown row house, calling over the boxwood hedge.

"Yes, I'm here, Phyllis!" Rosemary Davis answered, impatiently, as she was finishing sweeping up her patio for the first time after the winter. Putting down the broom she walked out into her yard, shielding her eyes from the sun that was low in the sky. *Free-spirit Phyllis,* she thought, as she caught sight of her friend in a turquoise-flowered muumuu, waving with one hand and holding a glass of wine in the other.

"Oh, there you are, Rose! It's so nice out today, I was sitting on my patio when I heard your back door open and close, but then I didn't see you. I wanted to tell you that I'm having a glass of wine." "I see that, Phyllis," Rosemary said, smiling.

"Oh, of course you do," Phyllis laughed, raising her glass.

"Anyway, why don't you come next door and join me? I want to hear more about that wild island that you're going to visit, dear! Sounds like something I might like, for the adventure."

"Bedford Island, Phyllis. Remember, I've told you about it before when I've gone there on school trips. I don't think it's your kind of island. It's a wildlife preserve, you know, not a tropical resort. Think New Guinea more than Maui. You'd have to count the alligators and armadillos to take the census. Not exactly you're cup of tequila."

"Oh, don't be so sure! I've been thinking about it the last couple of days since you showed me the travel brochure. Since all this fuss with the stepchildren contesting their father's will, it occurred to me that I could use a quiet week to be incommunicado. And I love the sound of that divine old inn. You hadn't told me about that before. Anyway, come over for a few minutes for a drink and
give me some more of the details of the trip."

"Sure. I'm happy to tell you about the island, but I haven't been to the hotel before, which probably is the only thing you'd like about the place. Just let me finish bagging my sweepings on the patio. I'll be over in five minutes."

After collecting all the debris into a dustpan and depositing it in a yard waste bag, Rosemary retreated into her comfortable Edwardian home, smiling at the mental image of her friend hiking in sling-backs on the sandy trails of Bedford Island. On the other hand, from all reports, the historic inn offered the level of amenities that would satisfy her.

A few minutes later both women were seated on cushioned wrought-iron chairs on Phyllis's brick patio with a half-empty bottle of Chardonnay in an ice bucket on a nearby table. The two friends were of a similar age, but oddly matched, otherwise. While Rosemary had eased comfortably into middle age, accepting gray hairs and laugh lines as being well-earned and distinguished, Phyllis appeared to have fought the signs of aging tooth and nail (the former, capped, and the latter, sculpted).

Tucking salon-tanned legs under her, Phyllis rearranged the folds of her Hawaiian dress around and rested her head on the back cushion. "I know that you've been to this same place several times, *camping,*" she started, saying the word 'camping' in the same tone someone would say, 'being held hostage.' "Why is it again that you've done that so often, dear?"

"I took a group of seniors there for research projects to study wildlife in its native habitat. Sometimes we had to make a second trip as you're limited to a maximum of seven days' stay at a camp site. That's six days too long for most people, considering the primitive conditions. You have to understand, Phyllis, this is one of the most undeveloped places in the United States."

Phyllis put down her wine glass and sat up straight, her eyes widened in alarm. "But what about the four-star hotel? It's nice *there,* isn't it?"

"Yes, but when I took the students, we were roughing it in the back-country, and in the summer, yet. There aren't any facilities, including running water. You're not even allowed to have a campfire, so food preparation is greatly limited."

"Oh my stars! But why didn't you eat at the Inn?"

"Their dining room is only for their guests. Staying there is the main reason I've decided to take this tour, so I can experience the island in comfort. I was probably sent the brochures because I've been a camper so often. The travel agent must have figured that anyone who had stayed at a wilderness camp site would be pre-sold on staying at the Inn."

"That would be my marketing strategy," Phyllis agreed. "What did you study when you were there — the wild horses you told me about?"

"No. Everyone likes the horses, but I was there mostly to study the birdlife and the fish in the marshes and tidal creeks.

Since there's so little interference from man, you can study their natural interaction. There are over three hundred species of birds, some endangered, like the Least Tern, the Wilson's Plover and the Oystercatcher.

"On a couple of trips, we studied the loggerhead sea turtle that's also endangered. They come ashore between May and September to make nests for the hundred eggs they lay at a time. After they hatch, the adults leave them to fend for themselves – not exactly over-protective parents. Only a few of the babies survive the land predators to attempt the scramble across the beach, and then they must avoid birds of prey. When, and if, they get in the water, they're met by hungry sharks."

"Sounds like mid-life dating, to me," Phyliss put in.

"Hah!" Rosemary barked. "Anyway, that's enough of a lecture on the wildlife of Bedford Island."

"Oh,I think it's very interesting," Phyllis protested, unconvincingly, "but I have to admit I'm more interested in the civilized life inside the Inn. But, tell me the truth, would it be all right with you if I went along? I don't mean that we'd share a room, or that I'd expect you to do everything with me. I'm thinking it would be a good chance to unwind, walk the beach, have massages, facials — that kind of thing. Is that what you were thinking of doing?"

"Not exactly, but it sounds good to me. I know I'll be hiking some with my niece Amanda, and her husband Johnny who'll be there. They live in Knoxville and have liked to camp out in the Smokies. But I want some pampering, too. Like I said, I'm going on this tour so I can explore Bedford at my leisure and in comfort."

Phyllis leaned over and refilled her wine glass, then held the bottle up to Rosemary who shook her head. "That's nice that you can spend time with your niece and nephew, and having them there, you won't feel you need to entertain *me*. I'll find my own amusements. Actually, I'm looking forward to sitting on the front porch and reading a book or two."

Rosemary leaned back and stretched out her legs. "If you're sure you'd enjoy an uneventful week on a primitive island, you're welcome to come along. You'd make it more fun for all of us. There'll be others in the group you can get to know, too. Who knows? You might even meet a nice, eligible man. These groups usually have singles, like us, who like to socialize with people they meet traveling. But, it'll be a pretty small group. The inn has only thirteen rooms, total."

"Actually, I prefer being with just a few people in a nice, quiet setting," Phyllis responded. "I'm certainly not going there to meet anyone. I've been married often enough, God knows. I haven't even had a date since George died last year. Right now, I'm just trying to deal with the four stepchildren who are livid over the terms of the will. I mean, it wasn't *my* idea to put the man's assets in a generation-skipping trust. But you wouldn't know that from the kids. I'm suddenly the wicked stepmother who wants them to live on the streets."

"Why *did* George set up his will that way?" Rosemary asked, unable to contain her curiosity. "There could be other grandchildren born after he's gone that he wouldn't even know — that he might not like, if he were around."

"You're right. And the ones he *did* know might grow up to be wastrels. It's crazy, but he never asked my opinion. I know he avoided paying estate taxes by setting up his 'Dynasty Trust.' Of course, the other terms that his children object to are that even the grandchildren won't come into their inheritance until after I die or remarry. Hell, I'm the one who should be worried about them!"

"I thought you were pretty close to George's children. You were their stepmother for twelve years, right? I noticed they liked you well enough to often come over for dinner."

"Yeah, well now they like Benjamin Franklin more. I gave them wonderful Christmas presents to soften their disappointment, but I'm not chasing after them for gratitude. I'll treat them the same as they treat me. Right now that means just not running them over with my car.

Phyllis set her chin firmly. "The more I think about it, the more I want to go away for a complete rest. Maybe if I get away from everything – you said you can't even use a cell phone there – I can think of a resolution to this whole business. Not having kids of my own, I'd like to have a decent relationship with George's, if they're willing to meet me halfway. I just wish he had explained his estate planning to them years ago instead of leaving me to deal with it."

Phyllis hoisted the wine bottle out of the cooler and held it above her friend's glass. This time Rosemary nodded, and Phyllis refilled both glasses, emptying the bottle.

"It's amazing how relationships are affected when money is in the picture," Rosemary mused aloud. "Maybe that's why my niece seems to be so fond of me. I should let it drop that I'm thinking of changing my will to leave everything to the Anti-Cruelty Society – just to see what happens. Good thing you'll be with me, in case she tries to do me in."

"Oh, Rosemary, really! We needn't imagine everyone wants to kill us for our money."

"I know. I think it's just the wine talking," Rosemary agreed. "But do feel free to join us on the island. I think we'll make a good foursome. Just keep in mind that there won't be much to do. Who knows, maybe you'll want to go hiking with us. Why don't you throw in at least one pair of shoes that you can actually walk in?"

Phyllis held up her sandal-shod feet. "Are you kidding? Me, hike? I've taken more walks down the aisle than walks in the woods. Like I said, peace and quiet is fine with me. Anyway, I'm hungry and you must be too. Let's go rustle up something to eat."

Friday, March 21

Chapter 5

David Albright and Jennifer Brown

DAVID LOOKED INTENTLY at his fiancé across the table. "Jen, I don't see the point in your chasing this guy down again. What do you hope to accomplish by showing up on this Bedford Island to surprise him?"

Jennifer twirled a finger around a curl of mahogany-colored hair on her shoulder. "I don't know. I just need to see him once more
– to get him to admit he's my father. Maybe — to admit he's sorry he's been such a jerk, but that's unlikely. It sickens me that he could just *walk away* from my mother when she was pregnant with me, and years later shut the door in my face. He couldn't even *acknowledge* that I was his flesh and blood, much less help out my mother with child support. I won't let him get by with that without at least confronting him again!"

David put his hand over hers. "Look, I understand your anger and your need to vent to the guy. I do. I just don't think that you can change the way he feels. And no good can come from it. He's had *four years* to reconsider and get back in touch with you, and he hasn't."

"Hell, he's had *twenty-five years* to get in touch with me!" Jennifer corrected him.

"Okay. Right. Obviously, he wants *nothing* to do with you, and while that's disgusting and a great loss for him, there's not much you can do about it. But if you insist on going to this island to blindside him, I'm going with you. There's no telling what this guy could do when he's cornered.

"David, I'm not asking you—"

"No, I'm serious. He could become violent if he feels trapped. You already know that he's heartless. He could be dangerous, too."

It was a Friday night and David Albright and Jennifer Brown were seated in a cozy booth at L'Angostino's on Dearborn Street in downtown Chicago. This was their weekly "date night," which usually meant meeting for dinner at a Loop restaurant to unwind before going home to their hi-rise condo on the Drive.

This evening relaxation didn't seem possible, in spite of the low-lighting, background jazz and comfortable seating. As soon as they were shown to their booth, David noted Jennifer's agitation as she tossed her purse on the upholstered banquette and slid in, without smiling at the waiter who had angled out the table for her.

Once seated, she had nervously scanned the room before she brought her attention back to him. "I have something important to tell you," she had said, her hazel eyes flashing, "but let me collect my thoughts, first."

"Yeah, sure. I'm not going anywhere. Take your time, hon. Oh, good, here's your wine."

After she had taken a couple of sips of her cabernet, David ventured to ask what could have gotten her so upset. Her response had shocked him, taking him back four years to when she had first told first about having located her "real" father, who didn't know of her existence, and that she had planned to go to Baltimore to look him up, without giving him any advance warning.

At the time, he hadn't been so involved with her that he felt he could have argued against it. Besides, Jennifer had been determined to go through with her plan. Tonight, she was telling him she was planning to surprise Conrad Pierce a *second* time. But now there was no doubt what her father's reaction would be.

Four years earlier, the man had denied her claim that she was his daughter, although he must have realized that she couldn't have tracked him down without her knowing about his relationship with her mother.

Back then, Jennifer had filled in David on her family history: Conrad Pierce and her mother, Katherine, had lived together two years after their graduation from Northwestern. Katherine had supported them on her income as a caseworker, while Conrad had continued on as a graduate student at the business school.

Seven months before Conrad was due to graduate, Katherine was shocked to discover she was pregnant. Fearing Conrad's reaction, she kept her condition secret for the first couple of months. When she finally had to break the news, he flew into a rage, calling her "stupid" for allowing it to happen. He made it clear that he didn't want children, especially then when he was about to start on his business career. In fact, he argued, there was no proof that the child was even *his*. He had been away from home a lot — in class or in the library studying -- and didn't know *what* she had been up to.

Katherine was outraged by his insinuation, answering back that if anyone was unfaithful, he was the one with the opportunity, as she was either at work or at home. The argument had continued, on and off, for a few days until there was a stalemate of silence. At that time, Katherine made a few phone calls to find an affordable apartment for herself without telling Conrad.

Soon afterwards, Conrad appeared to have a change of heart, telling Katherine he was sorry for the things he had said; that he had been in shock. He was close to graduating and was nervous about taking his finals. Of course, he was excited about the baby coming and he was happy to be living with her in their apartment she had made so attractive. Things would work out, somehow, if they met each challenge together. They were a team. Katherine tore up her list of apartment addresses.

Two weeks after his graduation, Conrad was gone without a word. Once Katherine got over the shock, she wasn't even surprised. She hadn't really been fooled that Conrad loved her and had accepted the new life inside her. She had only hoped that she had been wrong about him.

She gave him one week to contact her. When he hadn't, she went to the placement office at the university to find out where Conrad was working. She was shocked when the counselor advised her that she wasn't entitled to such confidential information as she wasn't a relative. Even her advanced state of pregnancy wasn't persuasive, as paternity hadn't been established– as though Katherine might be chasing down all recent MBAs with good jobs to find one who would support her child.

Looking for other ways to track down Conrad, Katherine realized that she had very few contacts. His friends that she knew were either good liars, or hadn't been told of his plans. He had told her that his family was back east, but hadn't given her their full names or their addresses. She *had* been stupid: that was one thing Conrad got right. She couldn't take him to court if she couldn't find him, and paternity couldn't be proven, anyway. There were only tests to eliminate candidates.

When her daughter was born in the nearby hospital, she named her Jennifer Marie Miller. Father's name on the birth certificate: Conrad William Pierce. She wasn't having a child whose father was "unknown." Dammit.

For the next several years Katherine was the sole provider for her child, until she married Joseph Brown when Jennifer was in the seventh grade.

After Jennifer turned twenty-one she started thinking in earnest about looking up her biological father. What kind of a man would never bother to make contact after deserting her in utero? She and her mother had stayed local and wouldn't have been hard to find. It galled her that not only had her father deserted her mother, but that he had failed to send support money, and hadn't even been curious enough to learn anything about her existence.

In the space of one afternoon spent on the computer, she found him. It hadn't been that hard knowing his full name, birth date and social security number her mother had saved. There he was: Conrad William Pierce, on Estes Road in Baltimore, Maryland. Her father. Or, rather, her sperm donor who had never become her father.

A few weeks later, she drove up to his substantial colonial home on the winding, tree-shaded street. After parking in the driveway, she stiffly walked up to the door, and stood there, frozen in place. She had thought about the "pitch" that she would make, but doubted that she'd have the words when she needed them. She only had a first line nailed down, anyway – "It's taken me twenty-one years to get here."

When the man opened the door to her, she found herself looking at the masculine version of her own face: the same turnedup nose, the same flecked hazel eyes; the same full lower lip.

Shocked to see her and to hear what she had to say in rapidfire delivery, Conrad Pierce had cruelly played dumb, even denying any knowledge of her mother. Starting to close the door on her, he demanded that she leave immediately, or he would call the police; like she was a crazy person. But she had made her case, and had been seen and heard by his wife and a teen-aged daughter, (her halfsister?) who had come up behind him.

Jennifer had looked both women in the eyes to convey her truthfulness.

The wife, Margaret, had run out of the house to stop her from driving away, telling her that she thought her story was believable, noting that the young woman's resemblance to her husband was undeniable. Taking Jennifer's business card, Margaret promised to encourage Conrad to contact her in the future; that she would keep in touch with her, at least, and send along any pertinent medical information about her husband's family.

Over the next four years, Margaret had sent Jennifer Christmas cards, and the occasional note. Yesterday, in the mail, came a letter with news of Chloe's engagement to a Tom Worthington. As a sort of a post script, Margaret had added that Conrad, Chloe, and she were going to Bedford Island on a group tour with Globe-Trotter Travels in mid-April for a quiet rest to make wedding plans.

Jennifer had gone online to research the destination and, on a whim, decided to contact Alex Trotter to request an application for the tour. Telling her mother her plan, Katherine had advised against it, reminding her that Conrad had made it clear he didn't want a relationship with her; and showing up out of the blue, again, wasn't a good strategy to change his mind. She thought it wasn't really fair to Conrad, or his family, to interrupt their vacation this way.

Jennifer had argued that the meeting this time would be in a more relaxed setting, and that Margaret and Chloe already considered her a member of the family. Jennifer ended the conversation by promising that if Conrad objected to her presence, she would leave him alone, and would never contact him again.

Sipping her after-dinner coffee, Jennifer was feeling more confident in her decision, especially since David had agreed to go with her. If things didn't work out well with her father and his family, she and David could go off by themselves and enjoy the natural beauty of the island, and spend some time relaxing on the beach.

Friday, March 2

Chapter 6

Wade and Ronette Kerley

THE DAY'S END TRAILER COURT in Dunin, Florida, is not as restful and serene a place as its name implies. In fact, the residents always refer to it as "Dead-End" Trailer Court; possibly because it's located where the dirt road stops, but, more likely, because the shabby trailers house those who are down on their luck and have little hope for a future.

This particular morning, Ronette and Wade Kerley sat on their front steps loudly arguing, adding to the usual cacophony of blaring television sets and bawling babies coming from several nearby trailers.

Ronette waved a colored brochure in Wade's face."I don't understand why you had to sign us up with some high-falutin types to stay in a fancy hotel! If you think you're gonna pull somethin' off there, you're crazy! You know what's gonna happen? You'll get caught, and then I'll be hauled in for being an accomplice. You can go by yourself!" she declared, jumping up and glaring down at him from her full height, which included at least six inches of teased yellow hair.

Although it was early in the day, Ronette had already applied her bronze-toned makeup, heavy black eyeliner and false lashes that she always employed to enhance her appearance and "bring out" her eyes. To a more conservative observer, the embellishments only served to obscure her youth and natural beauty.

Wade recognized her familiar ploy of bolting when she was upset, and grabbed one of her hands to keep her from walking away. "Ronnie, baby. Sit down and just hear me out, and then you can do what you want. I promise."

On cue, his wife paused, sighed loudly, and slowly sank down on his step, but at the greatest possible distance that the stair width allowed; keeping her eyes on the ground.

"Okay," he said, satisfied with the concession. "That's better. Here's the deal. This travel group will give us cover. We can blend in with those rich people who won't bother us as they'll be gettin' massages and drinkin' cocktails with umbrellas in them all day. No one else will be around cuz the island's deserted 'cept for a few campers in the woods. If we play our cards right, we can blend in as just another couple on vacation."

"You've never taken me on any va-ca-tion. I hope you don't think that living here with you is a day at the beach. But this Bedford Island trip don't even sound like a vacation, not with what you probly have in mind. What is it, anyway? Lifting wallets from the men's locker room? Or boosting jewelry and Rolex watches? I'm not helping' you, I'll tell you that."

Having spent her anger, Ronette stopped to take a breath for a minute. Finally, having come to a decision, she said, petulantly, "I'll only go if I can have massages, too, and sunbathe on the beach." She spread out her hands to admire her new lavender-pink nail color.

Wade's pock-marked faced relaxed into a smile, revealing the spaces of two missing teeth. "Babe, you just leave everything to me. You don't have to do nothin' but enjoy yourself and make me look good. When you clean up, you look like any other snotty bitch." "Gee, thanks," Ronette muttered, shooting Wade a dirty look. "You're too kind."

"I'm just sayin' you're hot, and as good as anybody. You should have nice things, too. I promise that this plan's a winner. Don't give up on me now, Ronette." Wade put one tattooed arm around his wife, who tried to wriggle out of his grasp. "C'mon Ronnie, aint I still your lovin' man?" he cooed, squeezing her shoulder and kissing the top of her head, but only coming in contact with her lacquered hair.

Letting out a long sigh, Ronette turned and peered at him under a fringe of lashes, and shrugged a reluctant acceptance. "All right, all right. I guess I'll give you one last chance. I know you love me — in your way. Tell me what your plan is — but I'm warnin' you, it better be good, or I'm not goin' along with it. And if it don' work out, I'm leaving, even if I have to go back to maw. I probably make enough at 'Hands Down!' to find my own place," she declared, referring to her place of employment, 'Best Nails — Hands Down!' nail salon.

"Okay, okay. Hold on for a minute and let me explain the plan," Wade interjected, seeing that he was losing her confidence, again. "First of all, you know that Cuba is a Commie country, right?"

"What?! What the hell does that mean?! You're not gettin' mixed up with some Commie goons, are you?"

"Of course not! I'm just sayin' that it's a Commie country. Why that's important, is that it means you can't get a lot of Cuban things here, like their cigars, cuz it's against the law. You can only get them if you're in Cuba, but no Americans can go over there. But since they make the best cigars, everybody wants 'em. The dealers here *who claim* to have them are sellin' fakes.

"I got this Cuban friend – Jose – who can get a reg'lar supply from another Cuban who shuttles a cargo boat between

Florida and Cuba. If I buy all these illegal cigars, cheap, I can make a friggin' fortune selling them to dealers, here."

Ronette blinked hard. "Cigars? That's your big idea? Like you could find cigar dealers or would know a real one from a fake in the first place!" she snorted.

"Jose's showed me the real thing and told me all about them. You kin ask me anything. Go ahead. Ask me something,"

Ronette folded her arms. "Okay, I'll ask you something — are you out of your fucking mind? For starters, where are you gettin' the money to buy enough cigars to make 'a fortune'?"

"I borrowed some from my old man for a down-payment. Before you say he stole it — he won a trifecta at the track. And Jose's workin' with me on this. He needs an American connection – I don't think he's got papers--and he sez he knows a big-time dealer who'll buy 'em from me, no questions asked."

"Oh, great," Ronette groaned. "Your dad finally picks a coupla nags that aren't running to the glue factory, and it causes me trouble. Anyway, you're probably talking two crimes here — smuggling and helping an illegal. Yeah, I'm feeling much better now." She jammed a cigarette in her mouth, and struck a match off the sole of her shoe.

Wade pulled up his "I'm a Hog" tee shirt and wiped his forehead with it. "Listen, Ronnie. I got it all figured out. The best real Cuban cigars, Ramone Allones Gigantes, go for like five hundred bucks for a box of twenty-five on the black market. Jose's take will be thirty a box, and he pays a little to his guy with the supply boat. Jose brings his small boat up to Bedford Island and meets me there to drop off the cigars. You got that so far?"

"Yeah. This illegal alien, Jose, makes out big-time peddling cheap cigars to suckers like you." She took a deep drag on her cigarette and blew out a long slow stream of white smoke.

Wade shook his head in exasperation. "Wrong! One hundred percent wrong! I told you, I know a *real* Cuban cigar. And I know that I can sell 'em to this hotshot dealer for two hundred fifty bucks a box. I figure we can get forty boxes in a suitcase. With four suitcases, that's a hundred and sixty cigar boxes, and at a profit of two-hundred twenty bills a box, we can make over thirty-five thousand in profit. I did it on paper with Jose, so I know it's right.

"And that's only for this one run," Wade quickly went on, since Ronette hadn't interrupted him. "I picked up this brochure for

Bedford Island in town and read that it has *no police force*, *no phones,* and *no patrolled harbors.* Hell, forget about cigars, I could smuggle in illegal *Cubans* in a place like that! Except that I think they might attract attention as bein' the only dark-skinned people on the island. If this works out the way I think it will, we can go up there again in a few months."

Ronette pursed her glossy pink lips in thought. "That *is* a lot of money," she observed, impressed. "But why doncha take the cigars out of the boxes? We could make twice that much. We could move out of this tin can and into a real house."

"I can tell you *why,*" Wade answered back. "Remember when I said that almost all of the Cuban cigars here are fakes? The real ones come in specially-marked boxes with the factory sticker with the Spanish word 'Habanos' on the cover, with a solid black tobacco leaf. The box has to be sealed with the government official seal." Wade leaned back on his elbows, pleased that he had remembered the foreign word and the other details. Plus, he had been able to get the better of his wife, for a change, he thought.

Ronette tossed her cigarette butt down on the bare dirt ground and stubbed it out with her sandal. Rounding on Wade, she poked him in the chest with her forefinger. "Okay, wise ass, what about *clothes*? What about *money* to travel with this group of rich people? How do you think we're gonna fit in the way we are? Look at us. You think *they're* all tatted up, wearin' biker rags?"

“They won't see much of us, first of all. We'll go off on our own during the day. When we come back for dinner, I'll put on a shirt and my brother Billy's jacket, and you can maybe borrow a dress or two from your tight-ass cousin.

“You read all those women’s magazines at your nail salon, so you can do most of the talkin’ about world events, when necessary.”

“What about the freakin’ money we'll need to stay there?” Ronette boomed. “Have you thought about that, genius?”

“I made a coupla scores. Just tell me, are you in or out?”

“I told you," Ronette replied speaking slowly through clenched teeth. “I’m going along with this, but I’m leaving you if it don’t work out. Now that’s all I have to say on the subject. I’ll call Sherrie and see if I can borrow a few things. She’s actually been on a vacation and has some nice things to wear. She’ll know somethin’s up, that you’re not really taking me to some fancy resort for the fun of it, but she’ll keep her mouth shut. She don’t wanna make trouble for me. Everybody knows that’s *your* department.”

Friday, April 12

Chapter 7

Johnny and Amanda Berthold

"JOHNNY! YOU'D BETTER get up here and pack!" Amanda called down to her husband watching TV in the den. No response. "Johnny! Can you hear me?!" she called again, louder this time.

Johnny half-turned away from the screen. "Just a minute! I'll be up when my show's over!"

Ten minutes later, her lanky husband strode through the doorway of their bedroom as she was pushing down on an over-packed suitcase.

Johnny flipped through the pile, shaking his head. "What're you gonna do with all these good clothes? This place is a nature preserve, isn't it? You've packed something besides dresses and heels, right?"

"Of course. That's why I have to pack so much. I need old clothes and gear for hiking in the woods, and cocktail clothes for dress code at the hotel at night, plus all the suntan lotions, moisturizers, make-up, hair products, jewelry, and shoes. I could go on." She took a deep breath.

"Please don't – I get the idea. The island is natural, but the Inn is pretentious, so we need more than usual." He picked up a platform shoe, looked at it quizzically, shrugged, and replaced it in the suitcase.

"I hadn't really gotten into the details, I guess," he murmured. "If I need to wear a jacket every night, I'll probably need a larger suitcase than this bag." He picked up an empty soft-sided case from the floor.

Amanda stared at him. "That?! I thought that was your carry-on."

Johnny held up his hands in mock surrender. "All right, all right, I'll pack more clothes. Don't have a stroke. I'll take whatever you want. Tell me again, what's the schedule going to be? It's only seven days, I know that."

"Here, I've got the booklet the tour guide sent us," Amanda held it up and flipped through some pages. "Okay, it says we'll be with the group for breakfast, lunch and dinner." Johnny let out a low moan. "Just listen. A full breakfast will be served in the dining room. Lunch will be picnic-style, eaten while we're exploring the island. Cocktail hour starts at five-thirty when we'll be served hors d'oeuvres in the bar area. At six-thirty, we'll go into the 'candlelit dining room' for a gourmet dinner."

She looked over at him. "I think you stopped reading when you got to the part about the hiking trails." She reached for a glossy brochure laying on the dresser. "Look, this is where we're staying -- the Grover Inn." She held out the flyer folded to show a photo of the four-story brown shingle cottage-style hotel. Don't you love the big porch all the way across?"

"Oh, yeah. Love it. There's nothing I like better than sitting on a porch."

Amanda ignored his sarcasm and continued. "It says here that 'it dates from 1900 and is furnished entirely in family heirlooms and antiques. Every guest room has its own unique décor and has its own name.' The public rooms are even grander."

"Do 'heirlooms and antiques' translate into 'small beds,' 'no TVs,' and 'no air-conditioning?'" Johnny asked, looking over his wife's shoulder.

"The bedrooms have queen and king-sized beds, and TVs. And those rooms are air-conditioned," Amanda answered.

Johnny noted his wife's dodge. "So, there's no air-conditioning in the 'public rooms,' as you called them — like the *rest* of the hotel."

"No, but they all have ceiling fans, and it cools down at night, *and* we'll be there in mid-April, not mid-August. But you might as well know that we can't use any electronic devices on the island or make or receive a phone call. There aren't land lines, and cell phones don't work."

Johnny blinked. "What? No wi-fi? No phones? We'll have gourmet meals, but we can't make a phone call? I hope we don't have an emergency that can't be handled by a maître d' or a wine steward."

Amanda but kept reading. "It says here that the hotel has a radio-phone – whatever that is. Anyway, that's what they have for emergencies." She shrugged and smiled, uncertainly. "It *could* be fun to be isolated from the world for a week, don't you think?"

"How would we know? We've never been out of touch for more than a couple hours when we're at the movies. That means *you* won't be able to get a call from your mother every other day, unless you can convince them it's an emergency."

She made a face. "My mother calls to find out how you're treating me. Anyway, there's a private ferry service the hotel provides to take people over to St. Annes, if we need to contact the rest of the world."

Johnny pulled his hands down his face. "Great."

Amanda brightened. “I’ll have my Aunt Rosemary there to gossip with, if I need to talk to someone else. I’m glad she encouraged us to sign up, aren’t you? I mean, this place sounds like it’s really different.”

“*Different?* Odd, is more like it. Bizarre. But, yeah, I'm glad your aunt will be there. I don’t really know her, but she seems nice enough. Hell, who else would we talk to? We’ll probably be the youngest people there. I don't want to sit on the porch hearing all about the Depression.”

Amanda chuckled. “They’d have to be in their *nineties* to remember the Depression, and not likely to sign up to hike in the wilderness. Rosemary will be great to hike with. She’s camped on Bedford with her students to study the wildlife. You know she teaches biology at American in D.C. Her friend Phyllis is coming with. She’s probably like Rosemary – studious and down-to-earth. Maybe a little too serious.”

Johnny walked over to the closet and pulled out a couple shirts on hangers. “I don't really mind the dress code. After hiking around marsh lands or in the woods all day, I’ll be ready for a hot shower and a decent meal. Beats our usual camping trips to Big South Fork where we have a cold creek for clean-up and dry-packed food for dinner.”

“Right.” Amanda sat down on the bed. “I think I’m packed. I’ll leave you to it. Remember, we can't have any suitcases that weigh over thirty pounds since they might have to be carried up four flights of stairs.”

Johnny smacked his forehead dramatically. “Oh, of course. No elevators. Four flights of stairs? How are all those old people going to go up those?”

Amana got up off the bed. “I don’t know, but you can bet we’ll be on the top floor. We *are* probably the youngest. Anyway, just get finished, so we can get some sleep. We have to leave early for McGhee-Tyson. We can relax tomorrow on the porch with all the 'old people.”

"That's what I'm afraid of," Johnny said grimly. "I'd better post something on Facebook so our friends don't think we've been in an accident when we're not heard from next week."

Saturday, April 13

Chapter 8

Flying High

"WELL, I'M OFF TO BEDFORD ISLAND. Wish me luck." Alex called out to her roommate as she staggered into the living room pulling two suitcases. A satchel and purse hung heavily around her neck.

Beth jumped back. "Whoa! From the look of it, you couldn't have forgotten anything. Why so much for one week?"

Alex dropped the handles of the luggage, plopped down on the chenille chair and blew out a stream of air. "It's not that much, really. I had to pack two week-enders rather than my usual because the bags have to be carried up the stairs in the hotel."

"No elevator in a hotel?"

"I told you it isn't modern; unless you consider electricity as being up to date. Its appeal is that it's authentically vintage and isolated from the rest of the world.

"Sounds perfect for people who are running from the law– or the mob," Beth offered.

Alex sat up. "Don't say that even in jest. I'm already nervous about this group. I just hope they get along — they don't appear to have much in common. They're from all over the country; from urban areas and small towns; they're in different age groups; half are single, half are married."

She wiped her brow with the back of her hand. "The island itself is a lot to deal with. People will need to tolerate some discomforts. Besides being hot, humid, and swarming with insects, it's overrun with wildlife. I hope everyone paid attention to my 'Suggested Clothing and Supplies' list. We'll be hiking some days and then we need to dress up for dinner."

"And you call that a *vacation*," Beth said with a smirk. "Sounds more like spending time on Devil's Island, except for the fancy dinner part."

"Yeah, well gourmet dining *does* distinguish it from a no-escape penal colony. That, and not being chained to the walls. And stop suggesting these people are criminals!"

Beth held up her hands. "Fine. They're all model citizens. We hope. By the way, if they're from all over, where are you going to meet up with them? Do they have to make their own way to the Island?"

"They have to at least make their own way to St. Annes, the small town across the inter-coastal. I've told everyone that the hotel ferry will pick us up on the main pier at three o'clock. I know already that half of them can't make that. They'll come later by water taxi or the public ferry and the hotel van will pick them up. It's not ideal, but the main attraction of Bedford is its solitude, so that's what you have to expect."

"Should be interesting to see if they all make it," Beth commented. "Are there still thirteen people coming? I know that had you rattled."

"Yeah, but I'm over that. Like you said, I'll be happy that all of them can find their way there. Nothing is scheduled until this evening when the group will get together for cocktails at five-thirty. I should have met everyone by then, and I'll make the introductions. They'll have an hour to get acquainted before we go in for dinner. And after that, we'll adjourn to the lounge where I'll be the evening's entertainment."

"What are *you* going to do — sing?"

"No, I'm juggling knives." Alex paused. "What do you *think* I'm going to do? I'm giving my usual first night talk on local history and the attractions. It should get very cozy sitting around the large stone fireplace."

"It'll be cozy, all right, without air-conditioning," Beth joked.

Alex smiled. "We won't make a fire, that's for sure. Anyway, the island has a long history. It's been inhabited for at least 4,000 years, starting with the indigenous Indians to the English who set up a fort and renamed it for the Duke of Bedford."

"What had it been called before — Wild Kingdom?"

"Hah. No, it was Santa Anna, a name kept by the town, but anglicized." Alex stood up and took hold of her suitcase handles. "Anyway, I've got to get going to O'Hare to catch my flight to Jacksonville where I can get a shuttle to St. Annes. There's one couple from Chicago and a woman from Winnetka who could be on my plane, but, of course, I don't know what they look like."

"As I told you, I won't be in touch since there's no cell phone service on the island, so I'll just see you next Saturday, God willing."

Beth picked up the satchel. "I'll help you get downstairs at least.

* * *

BY TWO-TWENTY that afternoon, Alex was standing on the dock of St. Annes trying to spot anyone who might be on her tour. After a few minutes in the hot sun, she was annoyed to feel her hair frizzing up, and sweat running down her arms under her long-sleeved shirt. Her clothes had been appropriate in Chicago and in the thin atmosphere on the plane, but now she felt like her mother had dressed her.

Wilting in the heat, she let her sign, "Globe-Trotter Travels" slip down by her side, deciding that she would hold it up only if she saw people with luggage. No use calling any more attention to herself if she didn't have to. So far, everyone passing by were carrying only bags from souvenir shops. No one seemed to be looking for a tour director.

After ten minutes, she began to feel uneasy. Had she been clear about where and when to meet? True, she was still almost a half hour early for the hotel ferry, but someone from her tour group should be coming along soon.

To distract herself, she turned her attention to a bow-rider boat coming into port. Two bikini-clad young women and a young man in swim trunks were standing and shouting docking instructions to the pilot. Looking at them in their abbreviated swimwear made Alex feel even more overdressed.

As the young man at the controls steered the sleek boat close to the pier, one of the women neatly lassoed a pier post. Pulling the rope taut, she jumped onto the dock and tied the line to a cleat in front; then grabbed another line to secure the back of the boat. *Expertly done,* Alex thought, impressed.

"Excuse me, are you Alex Trotter?"

Alex spun around to find herself looking into the clear blue eyes of an elegant older woman she recognized from the plane.

The passenger smiled at Alex. "I saw the sign. Is this where we get the ferry to Bedford Island?"

Alex took in the smart yellow polka dot dress and sandals, thinking how much cooler the other woman looked than she felt.

"Yes, of course, I'm Alex, and you're —?"

"Nadine Rodgers – from Winnetka." The older woman extended her right hand, causing her gold bangle bracelets to jangle.

"I'm so pleased to meet you. I've been looking forward to this week."

Shaking her hand, Alex thought she had lucked out with her first tour member. Hopefully, Mrs. Rodgers was only the first of thirteen who were just like her.

"I'm supposed to be meeting another member of our tour," Nadine continued, "A Mr. Livermore. He and I had originally arranged to meet in town, but he called to tell me that he was delayed, and I should come directly to the dock. I'm wondering if he might have checked in with you?" She glanced around, nervously. The only other people on the pier were families.

Alex felt a momentary shock hearing that her 'fantasy couple' had already gotten together. "No, you're the first one to arrive." She tried to keep her face expressionless. Glancing at her watch she added, "But it's not yet twenty minutes to three, so we're still a little early."

"Actually," Nadine said in a low voice, "I'm embarrassed to say that I hoped you would have seen him first because I don't know him on sight. We've only corresponded and exchanged pictures. Oh, look, here are several people coming now."

Alex turned to see three women and a young man crossing the street with their luggage. As the foursome approached, one of the women spoke up. "Your sign's helpful — we saw it from down the street." She set her carry-on bag on top of her suitcase. "You must be Alex Trotter. I'm Rosemary Davis from D.C."

Alex liked her assertive manner and approved of her simple cotton outfit and sturdy shoes.

Gesturing toward the other three, Ms. Davis continued with introductions. “This is my friend and neighbor Phyllis Hanover, my niece Amanda Berthold, and her husband Johnny, from Knoxville. We all met up at the airport and came over on the same bus, and with no time to spare, I might add.”

Alex waved dismissively. “Oh, you’re in plenty of time.” Glancing around at the others she said, “It's nice to meet all of you, and thanks so much for coming. This is Nadine Rodgers, another member of our group. We’re only waiting for a Lawrence Livermore who contacted Mrs. Rodgers that he was running late. Several others are getting to the island by other means, but we’ll all be together for cocktails at the Inn at five-thirty.”

Hearing a motor, Alex looked out to the water to see a flat-bottomed boat with rows of seats partially under roof approaching the dock. “I think that's the hotel ferry coming now. We still have a few minutes before it’s scheduled to depart, if you need anything before we leave. The ferry ride will take about forty-five minutes.”

Phyllis Hanover, dressed flamboyantly in a colorful printed silk blouse with slacks approached close enough for Alex to take in her expensive smelling perfume. “Let me ask you something, dear. Have you been to this Inn before?”

Alex nodded hesitantly. “Yes, I’ve been there.”

Phyllis’s face relaxed. “Good. I hope it’s as nice as it appears in the brochure. You know what they can do with photographs these days – even put things in that aren’t there at all.”

“I haven't been there in quite a while — Mrs. Hanover, isn’t it? But I’ve checked out their present operation, and I’ve talked to others who’ve been there recently, so I'm pretty sure you have nothing to worry about. It doesn’t look like the place has changed much since I saw it years ago, and I hear it's been well maintained."

Phyllis smiled broadly showing small white teeth. "Oh, I'm so relieved to hear that. I'm not much of a hiker, you see, so I'm planning on finding my enjoyment at the hotel."

Alex hadn't thought Ms. Hanover was 'much of a hiker.' The clues were everywhere, from her freshly coiffed hairdo, her carefully applied makeup, her manicured fingernails, her silk pants outfit and, especially, her high platform sandals.

Phyllis's face lit up as she pointed behind Alex. "Miss Trotter, look at that distinguished looking gentleman over there. He could be joining us."

Alex turned to see a trim, well-dressed man hoist a suitcase and garment bag off the back seat of a cab, close the door and signal to the driver to move on. After adjusting his luggage, he started towards them, taking long strides. As he drew near, Alex could see that he was graying at the temples and was older than she had first thought from his fit appearance and athletic moves.

Glancing around, Alex noted that all eyes of her little tour group were riveted on the newcomer, and that conversation had ceased. The only sound was Phyllis Hanover's audible sharp intake of breath behind her raised hand as she took a step closer to the new arrival.

Nadine stepped forward to stand next to Phyllis.

Nadine smiled tentatively at the man. "Lawrence?" she asked, uncertainly. "Lawrence Livermore?"

Phyllis shot Nadine a baleful look before turning to ogle the new man, while holding her place next to Nadine.

"Nadine," the man answered, taking her outstretched hand in both of his. "How *are* you? I'm so sorry to be late." Becoming aware of everyone staring at him, he flashed a brilliant smile and addressed them. "I had to change my plans to drive down from Charleston. I hope I haven't held anyone up."

Alex broke in at this point. "Not at all, Mr. Livermore. I'm Alex Trotter, your tour director, and these are others in our group who have all just gotten here as well. I'll let them introduce themselves as we get going. As you see, the ferry is just tying up. We should be able to board as soon as they put down the gangplank.

Everyone nodded and greeted Livermore, except Phyllis, who appeared to be in a trance, staring at the charismatic man whose attention was focused on Nadine who smiled contentedly, raising her face to whisper to him while he bent down close to her face, laughing lightly, in response.

As Alex pulled her suitcases over to the ferry she thought, *another example of being careful what you wish for. I hoped that the group would be able to find something in common, and now they have: two women are interested in the same man.*

Chapter 9

Crossing the Rubicon

AFTER THE FERRY HAD BEEN TIED UP, Alex watched as the bent older man in a nautical cap and a plump, balding man with a comb-over in a tan uniform shirt, stood by the gangplank to assist passengers. Walking over to introduce herself, she read their name tags: "Captain John Bauer," and "Raymond Bean, Manager of Guest Services, Grover Inn."

"We're ready for your passengers to board, Miss Trotter," Raymond Bean said, bowing his head which caused strands of hair to fall forward over his eyes. "Captain Bauer and I will assist your people with their luggage," he added, resettling his band of hair.

Oh, brother! Who's going to assist whom? Alex wondered, making a jaundiced assessment of the would-be porters. But, complying with the manager's request, she walked back to the passengers and repeated his offer.

Johnny Berthold cast a disparaging look over at the two hotel employees before saying as an aside to her, "I'll take care of all the luggage, okay? There's not that much. Just have everybody get on the boat."

"Yeah, that's a good idea," Alex agreed, nodding. "Thanks." Turning towards the captain and manager she called out, "We've got the luggage situation covered, and everyone's ready to board."

Nadine and Lawrence, still engrossed in conversation, hadn't seemed to notice what was going on, but they moved forward to be the first to step up and onto the boat. Nadine gracefully swung into the first open-air seat and Lawrence dropped smoothly into the seat next to her, without breaking off their conversation.

Next to board were Phyllis and Rosemary. Phyllis started down the deck first, but stopped dead next to Lawrence. After a few moments, Rosemary gently nudged her to move along.

Phyllis turned to respond. "Sorry to hold things up, but I feel something sharp in my shoe. Mr. Livermore, would you be so kind as to let me put a hand on your shoulder while I check what's bothering me?"

At the sound of his name, Lawrence looked up and smiled quizzically at Phyllis. "What's that? Oh, sure. Let me help."

Putting out his arm, Phyllis took hold of it while deftly lifting her left foot and ran a finger along the insole of her shoe. "Ah! That's much better. Thank you." Giving his arm a little squeeze, she turned back to her friend, smiling triumphantly. "Now, where would you like to sit, Rosemary?"

Amanda called out to her Aunt, signaling for them to move to the back of the boat where she had spotted four seats in a row across the stern. "We can all sit together there!"

Alex waited to be last to get on after Johnny Berthold had capably loaded the luggage. While waiting, she had amused herself watching the boarding maneuvers; especially the little tableau of Phyllis Hanover's, when the woman managed to eavesdrop on Lawrence Livermore's conversation, *and* hold onto his arm.

Alex took a seat under the roof near the Captain's helm and Raymond Bean's chair as co-pilot, so she could ask any questions that occurred to her. But, as they got underway, she just leaned back against her seat, tilted her face up to catch the refreshing breeze, and thought about how nice it would be to get to the hotel, shower, and change clothes.

Thinking about the Inn, she wondered when the other people would arrive and what they would be like. There had already been intriguing interaction among the early arrivals. Nadine and Lawrence were still absorbed in each other, she noticed, which was probably getting Phyllis's attention, as well.

It would be most interesting to see what developed between Nadine and Lawrence, who had just met face-to-face. And how aggressively Phyllis would pursue the man. Phyllis couldn't be blamed for being attracted to Lawrence. After all, he *was* very handsome and elegant. And single; although it had to be understood by Phyllis that Nadine had the first claim to his affections. Both women seemed respectable and wouldn't engage in any cat fights. But, in matters of the heart, you could never predict what anyone might do.

It was a good thing that Phyllis was in the company of friends who could distract her and occupy her time. Rosemary Davis, for one, seemed very level-headed and full of common sense. She would certainly discourage the infatuated Phyllis from making any indiscreet, unwanted advances. And the helpful young couple, Johnny and Amanda Berthold, would keep Phyllis entertained and on the go.

All in all, it was a decent group, so far, she thought. And, really, she needn't worry about imagined complications. Besides, every group could use a little spice, like a harmless flirtation or two. What if she were leading an all-singles group? There would be all sorts of romantic entanglements among the people who signed up for that kind of tour. This was hardly anything to be concerned about. Adults could work out their own relationships without needing any help from a tour guide.

Having mentally relieved herself of responsibility for interpersonal relationships, Alex stretched out her legs and relaxed. The ferry moved through the harbor to the mouth of the St. Annes River, which it would follow for several minutes until the river opened onto Bedford Sound.

When they came into open water, Alex felt like they had gone out to sea. The lower edge of the blue sky melted into the water so that it became one expanse without limits. After several minutes, a tree-covered island rose up out of the mist as though someone thought to paint it on the solid background to give the scene more interest. As they drew closer, Alex noticed several wading birds in the tall grasses, and realized that the boat was approaching the island further up in the marshes, rather than behind the hotel, as she had anticipated.

Turning to Captain Bauer, she shouted to be heard above the noise of the wind and the engines, "Why aren't we arriving at the pier behind the hotel?"

"Our pier is under reconstruction to make some repairs!" Raymond yelled back. "What's nice is that gives us a chance to show our guests a little of the island right after they get off the boat!"

Alex nodded vigorously to indicate she had heard him. She had to stifle a giggle as the poor man's hair was now standing straight up on one side of his head. *Mine probably doesn't look much better,* she thought, having been blown about in the same wind and sea spray for the last forty-five minutes.

As the ferry approached the pier, Raymond Bean stood up to prepare for their docking. Leaning towards Alex, he said, "Have everyone disembark with their personal effects and wait for me by the hotel van while Captain Bauer and I see to the luggage. If Mr. Berthold wants to assist, that would be appreciated."

Alex moved to the stern to give the foursome the message, sharing a meaningful look with Johnny Berthold. "I really hope the week will be all that you anticipate," she added. If you're dissatisfied with anything at the Inn, just tell me. I know they'll do their best to accommodate you."

"Oh, I'm sure I'll be most satisfied," Rosemary responded, heartily. "You don't know, Ms. Trotter, but I've camped on the island before; in the back-country. I've never even been inside the hotel. I had to stay in proximity to the natural habitat of the wildlife I was studying with my students. Now, I'm here to relax and be pampered. I don't think it'll seem like the same island to me without mosquito netting over my face at night," she added, chuckling.

Alex smiled to herself on having figured Rosemary Davis for a down-to-earth sort which turned out to be literal in her case. Camping on Bedford Island was as primitive as it gets. At least she had one tour member who wouldn't complain about any amenities or services.

The ferry was pulling up to the dock, so Alex hurried towards the bow to deliver the same message about the luggage to Lawrence Livermore and Nadine Rodgers. Again, they were all smiles, thanking her and expressing pleasure at being at the island. Alex wondered if they had even looked at the place yet.

Chapter 10

Arriving on the Other Side

THE GROUP QUICKLY DISEMBARKED with their small bags, purses, and cameras, eager to get to their destination. Awaiting them in the parking lot, stood a dark green van with the Grover's crested logo on the side; an unnecessary identification as it was the only vehicle in sight.

After Johnny Berthold had brought the luggage over and stowed it in the back of the vehicle, the six tour members climbed in and sat in pairs in the three rows behind the driver. Captain Bauer stayed behind at the dock, while Manager Bean stepped up into the driver's seat, and Alex sat in the passenger's seat.

Turning around, she advised the others, "Mr. Bean told me that we didn't dock behind the Grover Inn because their pier is being rebuilt. We'll be driving about five miles to get to the hotel, so you'll be able to get a preview of the island. Just sit back and enjoy the ride and we should be there in a few minutes."

Having politely waited until Alex finished speaking, Raymond started up the motor and pulled the van out of the parking area.

The vehicle rolled softly on the sandy road, past the salt marshes with their waving grasses, continuing upland to pass under gnarled limbs of live oak trees draped with Spanish moss. Redheaded woodpeckers swooped between the trees, landing on trunks they battered looking for tasty insects under the bark.

As the group rode along, Alex was pleased to overhear positive comments as they took in the scenery. Moving through the lush foliage of palmetto and loblolly, the van entered the maritime forest where the canopy of trees muffled all sounds and blocked out most of the light.

Alex thought about how you could view the island through different lenses: it was both a calm, unspoiled wilderness, and a wildlife habitat, full of predators. Where the group would be staying was a sanctuary, built to keep out the dangerous elements; a place of refinement, offering some of the most desirable comforts of civilization.

"Mr. Bean," Alex said, getting the manager's attention, "Are there other people staying at the Inn this week, besides our group?"

"No ma'am, there aren't. Y'all are takin' ten of the thirteen rooms. As you know, a few of the rooms need to share bathrooms, so it's sometimes difficult to accommodate individual needs," he said, giving a diplomatic explanation for the few vacancies.

"There are cottages on the property, as well. Most of them are occupied by staff, and then we have a couple for guests during busy seasons."

"How many people are on staff?" Alex asked.

"Twelve all together. Let's see -- Howard and Mary Dunkirk live in 'Beechwood.' Howard's one of our maintenance men, and Mary's one of our housekeepers. Our dining room waitress, Edna Butz, and our head housekeeper, Irene McCool, share Thornberry. Tina Wrenn, our receptionist, lives in 'Wildwood,' and I live in 'Pine Cottage.' Our chef has his own place, as does our bartender, and housekeepers share two others.

Oh, and our nighttime janitor and maintenance man, Virgil Grimm, lives in a room in the basement of the Inn, by choice. I'll introduce you to everyone after we arrive."

A few minutes later, the van turned off the road and onto a long, curved drive that offered a sweeping view of the four-story hotel. The brown shake shingles trimmed in white was perfectly poised at the top of a gentle slope, anchored in place by symmetrically placed spreading live oaks on each side, with a glossy-leaved magnolia tree in front.

Pulling up to the broad steps that led up to the front porch, Raymond stopped and turned in his seat. "Again, take only your personal effects with you. Ms. Trotter will get your room assignments inside from Reception."

Alex quickly exited the van and bounced up the several stairs to be first into the hotel. Inside, she approached the cherry wood front desk. Perched on a stool behind the counter was a young dark-haired woman, concentrating on some documents. Alex read her name tag as: 'Tina Wrenn.' *Well-named,* Alex thought. The petite receptionist, with her hair pulled up into a topknot, looked like a little bird as she plucked at her pile of papers, making rapid, jerky movements as she worked.

Alex waited several seconds to be noticed. "Uh, Miss Wrenn?"

"Oh! I didn't hear you!" Tina Wrenn squeaked, her dark eyes darting around the room before focusing on Alex.

"I'm sorry to have startled you. I'm Alex Trotter of Globe Trotter Travels, and I have a group–"

"Oh, of course! I've been expecting your party, Miss Trotter, but no one has arrived yet!" The woman seemed to be in distress.

"I was about to tell you that six are here now – seven with me – and the remaining seven should be arriving soon. Everyone is expected to be here by five-thirty at the latest."

"Oh, I hope so," Tina Wrenn said, placing her hand over her heart. "Here, I have the group's room assignments with the locations of each one." She handed over a plasticized sheet. "We didn't have to put anyone on the fourth floor," she added, leaning forward and speaking confidentially to emphasize how truly undesirable those placements would have been.

Scanning the list and the floor plan, Alex was relieved to see her request that only members of the same party would have to share a bathroom had been honored. "Thank you, Ms. Wrenn; this looks fine. Just ring my room when the others arrive, if you will. Oh, that's right," she waved off her remark, "you don't have phones here. It'll take a little time for me to adjust to not being 'plugged in' twenty-four hours a day."

Tina Wrenn blinked twice, but otherwise didn't respond.

As the others made their way in, Alex directed them to check in with Tina Wrenn first, and then to come to her for their rooms and locations.

After everyone had reassembled, Alex started reading names and rooms off her sheet. Amanda and Johnny would be in the "Jackson" suite on the third floor overlooking the backyard and the inter-coastal, and had their own bathroom. Hearing they were on an upper floor, Amanda and Johnny exchanged knowing looks and smiled. Rosemary and Phyllis were assigned to second-floor adjoining rooms, the "Magnolia" and "Camellia," at the north end of the building, and were to share a bathroom. Nadine was given the "Crape Myrtle" suite on the second floor, facing the front. Lawrence would be alone in the "Live Oak" suite on the same floor at the south end of the hallway, facing the back.

After all the assignments had been made, Phyllis asked Alex if she could take a look at the second floor layout. With the sheet in hand, she held it up for a closer inspection, explaining to the others, "I just want to see where the linens are on our floor; that's all."

"There's the linen closet -- right across from *my* room, and not far from yours," Lawrence said, cheerfully, pointing to the plan. "That's convenient. I like to make sure I have fresh towels available after a hot shower, don't you?" he asked Phyllis, causing her cheeks to flush as she nodded mutely.

"Uh," Alex broke in. "I just want to remind you all that cocktails will be served in the bar lounge in about an hour and a half, so you have plenty of time to explore the main floor, or walk outside, or rest a little in your rooms before you need to change for the evening. Dinner will immediately follow cocktails. Someone from the hotel will probably have brought your luggage to your rooms by the time you get upstairs, or they will soon be brought up. If you're missing anything, let me or Tina Wrenn at the front desk know.

"Okay? Anything else? If not, I'll see you in the bar area at five-thirty when, hopefully, we'll meet the other seven members of our group. See you then."

As the group started up the stairs to their rooms, Alex turned down the hallway towards the south end of the building to tour the public areas. The sign on the first door she came to read, "Library." Stepping inside, she looked around the high-ceilinged room, at the elaborate plastered moldings that framed the walls. Overhead were two large bronze fans, whirring quietly. The room seemed reasonably cool.

All the walls were lined with books, many of which were bound in leather with gold lettering on their spines. Antique chairs, upholstered in various faded tapestry fabrics, were scattered around on a frayed Oriental-style rug. The room's lighting was supplied by several glass-shaded lamps that stood on polished cherry tables.

Next, she visited the Study, across from the Library. It was a relatively small room furnished with an old-fashioned sofa that appeared to be stuffed with horsehair, some mismatched pull-up chairs, a wingback chair, and a tall secretary desk. Several fine oil paintings hung on the grass-cloth walls.

The next room down was the Billiards Room that contained a namesake table, as well as a couple of card tables. In addition, Alex noted that there was a cabinet against the far wall that held stacks of boxed board games.

Walking back along the hallway, Alex again approached the reception area where Tina Wrenn was still busy with papers, her head bobbing up and down. This time she looked up, and stared quizzically.

"Uh. . . hi, Tina. I was just familiarizing myself with the public rooms so I know what all is available. I see the decor has been kept pretty much like the original. Doesn't the place date back to just before the turn of the last century?"

"Eighteen ninety-six," Tina answered. "That's when it was built as a private residence. It was first named Grover House in 1908 to honor President Cleveland after his death. The president and the first lady had been guests here a few times in the last two years he was in office." She rattled off the familiar information without a pause.

"Some of the furnishings are original," she continued. We can't afford to be replacing things all the time," she added, defensively. "Our housekeepers work very hard to keep everything well maintained."

"Oh, I didn't mean that I don't like the antique style, or that the rooms aren't taken care of — they obviously are," Alex said, apologetically. "It's just unusual to see so many antiques in actual use in a hotel, that's all. It must be very difficult to keep them in repair. Well, anyway, I'll just be on my way and look at the rooms in the other hallway. See you later."

Alex turned and started down the hallway leading to the north end of the hotel, grateful for the escape. Tina Wrenn seemed very sensitive on the point of the interior decor. Of course, everyone in the Inn must be proud to live with so many valuable pieces and didn't want to see the place updated, Alex thought. She shouldn't have suggested that the place was looking shabby. After all, the signs of wear were part of the charm.

The first room Alex came to was the Main Lounge, immediately identifiable by its generous size, the amount of seating and, of course, by the massive limestone fireplace that dominated one end of the room.

The walls were wainscoted in walnut that set off large oil paintings that hung from moldings in the Victorian manner. The upholstery appeared to be real antiques, consisting of a variety of chairs and sofas, some very low to the floor with deep seats to facilitate sitting in a hoop skirt. The room felt more comfortable and less formal due to many printed fabrics, as well as the visible wear and tear on the furnishings and the sun-bleaching.

Crossing the hall, she looked in at the bar and its lounge which were painted in deep vanilla and furnished with dark-stained wood furniture. Behind the bar were glass shelves stocked with liquor bottles, goblets, tumblers, snifters and beer steins. A half dozen burgundy leather stools were pulled up to the hammered copper bar that gleamed under pendant lights.

The lounge area was softly lit by brass fixtures that were suspended from chains over the heavy pine tables and the booths along one wall. There was not much natural light as the windows had been covered with stained-glass panels.

Walking through the bar, she came to a small hallway that led to the "Dining Room" which she entered. In contrast to the lounge areas, this room had several small-paned windows that were set into the walls at regular intervals. Light streamed in on the white linen cloths causing the glassware and silverware to sparkle.

Four of the rooms' tables had been pushed together to make one long table with thirteen chairs, she noted with a slight chill, remembering back to her conversation with Beth, but shrugged it off. She felt that it was a good idea to have a group seated at one table for the first meal, if size allowed. It served as a sort of kick-off banquet to celebrate the start of their time together.

Leaving the dining room, she made her way down the back hallway to the staircase and was about to ascend when she heard voices at the front desk. She looked over to see a young couple talking to Ms. Wrenn. Tina, spotting Alex, motioned her over. "Here are two others in your group, Ms. Trotter!" she said, as though surprised. "David Albright and Jennifer Brown," she announced, breathily.

"Oh, yes, of course," Alex said, walking over to shake hands with the attractive dark-haired couple. "Nice to meet you. I know that Miss Wrenn must have welcomed you to the Grover Inn, and I'm very pleased you've joined my tour. You're still in time to catch your breath before you need to change for dinner. Cocktails will start at five-thirty. Feel free to come down whenever you can – just be sure you're down for dinner at six-thirty. I'll go get your room assignment."

"Thanks," David said. "You must have gotten the earlier flight from Chicago. It takes a while to get here, but I like the look of the place," he commented, glancing around approvingly. "I hope things work out."

"Yes, of course they will," Jennifer broke in. "I'm really looking forward to being here this week. Has everyone else arrived?" she asked, anxiously.

"No," Alex answered. "We're still waiting for five others, but I'm sure they'll be along soon."

"Let me just come out and ask, are the *Pierces* here yet?" Jennifer's question startled Alex. *Just how many people in this group know each other?* she wondered to herself.

"No, they aren't," Alex said. "Then you *know* the Pierces," she added, stating the obvious. "I wasn't aware until today that *any* in our group were acquainted, but I've learned that three of the people who came over on the ferry with me are related, and two others have corresponded over the internet."

"Well, I'm related to Conrad Pierce," Jennifer confided in a low voice, "but he doesn't know I'm here, so don't tell him if you see him first," she warned, her face taut. "In fact, I should get out of sight right now, just in case the family comes in soon. We'll see you in a little while for cocktails." She turned to go up the stairs.

“Okay, fine,” Alex said. “Just a sec — let me see where your room is.” Walking over to a console where she had left the room chart, she looked down and found the couple's room. “You're on the third floor, in the ‘Palmetto’ suite with your own bath, of course. Can I help you with your luggage? Our guest, who acted as temporary porter, is upstairs in the room across from yours, and I'm not sure where anyone from the hotel is right now.”

“Oh, we can manage,” David responded. “Don't worry about it.”

As the couple started up the stairs, Alex doublechecked the room chart and felt a sense of relief that they weren’t on the second floor where the Pierces were. Somehow, she was uneasy to hear about Jennifer Brown’s “surprise.” Tour guides never liked surprises – they were almost always unwelcome, she thought to herself.

Before she had a chance to follow the latest arrivals upstairs to her own room, she heard a commotion at the front door. Looking in that direction, she saw a bony young man in jeans with long stringy hair coming in with a woman in short shorts whose brassy hair was teased high on her head. Both were loaded down with suitcases and garment bags, and were arguing with Raymond Bean, who had suddenly appeared.

“I told you, I kin take ‘em upstairs, myself!” the man shouted. “We don’t need no he’p — but thanks jus the same,” he added, suddenly more polite as he caught sight of Alex coming over.

“Hi, there,” she greeted them. “Are you with Globe-Trotter Travels? I’m Alex Trotter,” she continued, not offering her hand to the overloaded pair.

“Uh, howdy, ma’am, and yes’m, we are. I’m Wade Kerley and this here's my wife, Ronette Kerley. We were just comin’ in with our stuff and then this this –”

"I only wanted to take their luggage upstairs for them, Ms. Trotter," Raymond Bean explained. "Perhaps I wasn't clear about my intentions," he offered, differentially.

"They're not too heavy, and I've got 'em in hand," Wade Kerley insisted.

"Okay, that's fine," Alex said, standing back to clear a path. I'll check you in at the reception desk and you can go upstairs. Everything is taken care of, and I have your room here on my chart. Pointing over to the staircase, she said, "You need to go up to the third floor, down the hall to your left, to the 'Rhododendron' suite. You'll have your own bath."

"Well, I should *hope* so!" Ronette Kerley bellowed. Wade Kerley bumped her with one of the suitcases as a warning. "I'm not sharing a bathroom," Ronette protested. "I've had enough of that.

By the way, we know we need to dress for dinner," Ronette said, speaking to Alex in a normal tone, "so don't be concerned about our travelin' clothes," she added, throwing back her head. Her hair didn't move.

"You're fine," Alex said calmly with a smile. "I need to go up and get changed, myself. I had been looking around the Inn a little, waiting for everyone to get here. You go ahead. Cocktails and beverages will be served in the bar lounge starting in about half an hour, and dinner after that. See you later."

With that dismissal, the Kerleys rolled their cases and bags over to the stairs and lifted them up, seemingly without effort, as they started up the steps.

Alex let out a little sigh as she watched them go. *A little rough around the edges. Well, more than a little, and more than just the edges, but they'll add a certain grittiness to the group, that's for sure.*

Checking her watch, she saw that it was now 5:00. She needed to go up and get ready for cocktails and dinner, although she'd like to be on hand to greet the Pierces, who were the only ones of her group who hadn't yet arrived. Since her room was across the hallway from the family, maybe she would be able to hear them when they got in. She had to admit that she was curious about this family who was related to Jennifer Brown; although Jennifer hadn't told them that she would be here, for some reason. The secrecy still made Alex uneasy. She could only hope that Jennifer Brown's big surprise would be an unexpected treat, and not an upsetting shock.

Chapter 11

Settling in at the Grover Inn

BEFORE HEADING UPSTAIRS, Alex looked around for Raymond Bean to help her carry her bags. Seeing he had disappeared again, she threw her carry-on over one shoulder, and picked up her two suitcases, which seemed a lot heavier than earlier in the day. Each step became an exertion, and by the time she reached the second floor, she felt like she was ready to collapse from hyperthermia and muscle fatigue.

The stress of travel had caught up with her, she thought. The people in her group must be tired, as well. She'd try to gauge everyone's mood and energy level during cocktails and dinner to decide whether to announce her history lecture or put it off until tomorrow night.

Stopping momentarily to catch her breath, she set her small bag onto one of the cases and then started down the hallway until she came to the room with the "Bougainvillea" sign on the door. Turning the key in the lock, she pushed her way inside. As she pressed back against the door, she was shocked to feel a rush of cool air. *Air conditioning!* She had forgotten that the bedrooms had window units — hallelujah!

Dropping her bags on the floor and kicking off her shoes, she flipped on a wall switch to get a better look at the place. As she took it all in, she was pleased with the style and comfort of the room that was a mix of old and new – like the vintage cheval mirror in one corner and a flat screen TV in another.

Contributing to the room's Victorian character were architectural details like multiple moldings, custom woodwork and tall, deeply recessed windows; as well as the furnishings, which included a chest of drawers with carved acorn pulls, and a velour overstuffed chair that sat between the windows.

The drapery fabric was printed in a feminine floral motif in the room's namesake flower in shades of magenta and green. By contrast, the bed was hefty and muscular; a queen-sized Colonial, topped by a substantial comforter and several plump pillows.

The floors were of dark-stained oak, set off by leaf green rugs on each side of the bed for barefoot comfort. The mauve of the chair, and the grayish lavender paint on the walls, updated the space and made it feel more sophisticated.

Between her bedroom and her bath was a short hallway furnished with a useful upholstered bench placed next to the small closet. The ceramic-tiled bathroom had been modernized to include a vanity cabinet under the sink, a shower stall, and good lighting over a full-sized mirror.

Back in the bedroom, Alex opened one of her suitcases on the luggage rack and rifled through it to find something to wear. Seeing an edge of the blue fabric she was looking for, she pulled out her favorite cocktail dress Holding it up, she was chagrinned to see the straight skirt was now pleated after being scrunched under all her other clothes for a day and a half. Well, she'd hang it in the bathroom while she took a quick shower. If that didn't work, she'd run a damp washcloth over it.

Fifteen minutes later, she was stepping into the reasonably smooth indigo dress. Reaching behind herself to zip it up, she thought, not for the first time, that designers who used back-zipped dresses should be locked up alone in a room and be forced to get into them without any help. After wrenching her arm to pull it up, she only made a stab at connecting the miniscule hook and eye at the top before accepting defeat. To finish her outfit, she slipped into a pair of high-heeled silver sandals and draped a long silver necklace over her head.

Standing in front of the cheval glass, she thought the result was quite acceptable, considering that she had been traveling most of the day and had been stressed out about the tour group. Of course, the shower hadn't helped her hair, which now looked like she had been shocked by a stun gun, but still . . .

Looking at her watch, she saw that it was 5:25. Not bad, but she'd have to go downstairs right then to be there to greet her group and make any needed introductions. She hadn't heard the Pierces moving in across the hall, but the thick walls probably provided good sound-proofing. Picking up her grey silk evening bag, she gave one last admiring glance at her room, closed the door behind her, turned the key in the lock and set off down the hallway. There was no one else around.

Waiting for her at the bottom of the stairs was a shined-up Raymond Bean, dressed in a dark suit and tie. "Miss Trotter, I'm sorry to interrupt you, but I thought now would be a good time to take you around to meet some of the staff; before the evening gets underway."

"Well…" she said, hesitating, while she scanned the area to see if any members of her group were nearby. "I'm not sure that I have time before my people come down to the lounge. I hoped to be there in time to greet them at the door."

"There's just one party in the lounge, Miss Trotter," Raymond advised. "A gentleman is at the bar who's waiting for his wife and daughter to come down to join him.

"We'll just go to the kitchen and I'll introduce you to Chef

Kasmarek. The Chef is European-born – he got his culinary training in Hungary, I believe, but I think you'll find that his menus are broadly Continental."

"A gentleman waiting for his wife and daughter," Alex repeated mostly to herself, making synapse connections. "That must be Conrad Pierce. The man who's in for a big surprise," she added, to the blank-faced hotel manager. "I'm sorry, Mr. Bean – it's just something that I heard earlier. Yes, it'll be fine to go to the kitchen now. I probably have a few minutes before Mr. Pierce's family and the others come down. It's really okay if I'm not the first one there, anyway."

"Fine. Just follow me." With that, the manager started off for the back hall.

When they arrived at the kitchen, the room was filled with savory smells and bustling with activity, presided over by a rotund, mustachioed man in a toque. From the fragrant aromas, the man apparently knew what he was doing, Alex thought.

When the chef looked up to see Raymond and Alex in the doorway, he held up a finger to let them know he'd be with them momentarily. Putting down a ladle, and wiping his hands on his apron, he gave a last order to an employee before walking over to join them. Raymond Bean made the introductions, presenting Alex as the owner of Globe-Trotter Travels who had brought thirteen hotel guests for the week.

"Yes, yes, of course!" the genial cook exclaimed in a Germanic accent, upon hearing Alex's name. Bowing from the waist, he took her hand. "I've got all the menus worked out, my dear. If you have any special requests— – someone's birthday or anniversary, perhaps, just let me know."

"Thanks, I will. I'm not aware of any up-coming celebrations. I always ask about dietary restrictions, too, and I advised the hotel that no special diets had been requested."

"Yes, so they informed me. Thank you."

"Well," Alex smiled and nodded, easing backwards out the door, "it's been nice meeting you, but I see you're very busy and I have to join my group for cocktails. I know we're all looking forward to excellent meals, especially tonight when we're all tired from traveling and very hungry. See you later."

Back in the hallway with Raymond Bean, Alex saw a stooped man in a grey workman's uniform coming towards them. As he shambled along with his head down, he kept brushing against the wall. When he was abreast of them, Bean put a hand on the man's arm. "Hold up a minute, Virgil. I'd like Miss Trotter to meet you. She's in charge of the group that's staying in the hotel this week."

Raymond turned to Alex. "This is Virgil Grimm, our nighttime janitor and security man. He'll be around in the evenings to take care of the public areas. He's on call if there are any problems; even late. I'll give you a pager that has his number in memory."

The janitor had backed up against the wall, only once glancing at Alex while he was being introduced. "Virgil," Raymond said, again, to be sure that he had the man's attention. "I want you to be available if Ms. Trotter needs anything in the evenings after I've gone back to my cottage." The janitor didn't show any sign he had heard.

Alex thought, *God help me if I need anything in the evenings! I can only hope if there's a problem, it's on Raymond Bean's watch.* "Nice to meet you," she managed, as Virgil Grimm brought his head up, fastening his watery blue eyes on her face, "But I hope I won't need to call you." She smiled, getting a dead-eyed look in return. "I mean, I hope I don't have to bother you."

Virgil Grimm wiped his nose with the back of his hand.

Raymond Bean nodded to the janitor in dismissal. "Well, okay, Virgil, that's all." Turning to Alex, he continued, "You can get into the back of the bar lounge, right across the hall, here."

Virgil Grimm moved on, sliding back down the hallway. When he had moved out of sight, the manager explained in a low voice, "Virgil's all right – just a real quiet sort who sticks to his own business. He does a good job for us, though. You know, I think you have to be a bit of a loner to be a night janitor."

"Maybe so," Alex allowed. "Well, thanks for taking me to meet Chef Kasmarek. I hear voices inside, so I'd better get in there. I'll see you later."

Raymond nodded with a bow."Right. I'll stop by the bar and check on things in a few minutes. I'm staying around this evening for dinner, just to make sure everything is going smoothly the first night." He turned and walked away.

Saturday evening, April 13

Chapter 12

Meeting and Greeting

WALKING INTO THE LOW-LIT BAR, Alex looked across to the lounge area to see Rosemary, Phyllis, and Johnny and Amanda seated at one of the tables.

Phyllis smiled briefly, then turned her attention towards the open doorway on the other side of the room.

Glancing at the bar, Alex noticed a silver-haired man in a navy blazer, sitting alone, hunched over and tapping his empty martini glass.

"I'll have another one of these," she heard the man say in a raspy voice to the curly-headed young bartender, whose name tag read, "Tim Williams."

Alex thought the martini drinker must be the man Raymond Bean had seen earlier, whom she assumed must be Mr. Pierce. Apparently, he was still "waiting for his wife and daughter to come down." She went over to introduce herself.

"Excuse me – you must be Conrad Pierce, one of the travelers in my group. I'm Alex Trotter." She extended her hand, but it wasn't taken. Instead, the man slowly swiveled on his stool to face her, locking reddened eyes on her for a couple of seconds before moving his gaze slowly down her body, coming back up to her face. He gave her a sly smile, barely parting his lips.

Tim Williams unobtrusively delivered another martini to his only customer, setting it down on a napkin without leaving a bill.

"I *am* Conrad Pierce, and you're someone with beautiful blue eyes," the man intoned, close enough for Alex to smell the gin on his breath. "Who'd you say you are, again?" he asked, frowning in confusion.

"Alex Trotter. *Your tour guide.* I heard you were waiting for your wife and daughter to join you," she said, to redirect the conversation and discourage his flirtation.

"*Step*daughter," he corrected her. "Yeah. They both wanted to primp a little before they came down. I decided to get a head start. I guess those other people over there are from our group, too." He cocked his head in the direction of the table with the foursome. "Like that sexy brunette with the old ladies and the guy," he added, by way of identification.

"That's Amanda Berthold with her *husband* Johnny," Alex clarified, stiffly. "The woman in the green linen dress is Amanda's aunt, Rosemary Davis, and the woman in the floral print is Rosemary's friend, Phyllis Hanover. Would you like to go over and meet them? I'll introduce you," she said, forcing an hospitable tone.

"Nah, that's okay. I'll meet 'em later. Oh, look! Here come my loving wife and my s*tep*daughter now." Catching his wife's eye, he raised his glass in mock salute.

Alex turned to look in the direction where he was gesturing and saw a slim, attractive woman, smartly dressed in a black and white cocktail dress followed by a willowy younger woman with flaxen-colored hair.

Alex overheard the older woman say to her companion in a derisive tone, "There's Conrad; at the bar, of course."

Jeez, saved by the belles, Alex thought, amusing herself with her double entendre.

Margaret Pierce darted a scornful look at her husband before directing her attention to Alex. "And you're . . ." she started, in an accusatory tone.

"I'm Alex Trotter, Mrs. Pierce." She held the other woman's probing gaze. "Your tour director," she said, giving each word emphasis and time to sink in. "I was just talking to your husband while we waited for you and your daughter."

Margaret Pierce visibly softened. "Oh, Miss Trotter. Of course. So nice to meet you – and this is my daughter, Chloe Campbell." Alex couldn't help but notice the bemused smile on the girl's face. This was not an unfamiliar scene to her, Alex thought.

"Well, I'm glad you're all here," Alex responded, more politely. "Since you're the last ones to arrive, why don't we go around the room and meet the others? I see a few more people have come down, now." Without waiting for an answer, she turned and strode over to the foursome at the table.

While introducing Margaret Pierce and Chloe Campbell, Alex became unnerved when Conrad Pierce suddenly appeared and stood over Amanda Berthold, ogling the young woman. After several seconds without breaking his stare, Amanda started squirming in her seat, apparently embarrassed at the attention she was getting from the older man.

"Excuse me, Mr. Pierce," Johnny spoke up. "Did you want to meet my *wife*? Her name is Amanda. Amanda Berthold, and I'm John Berthold. We both just met your *wife* and daughter."

Alex grimaced at the defensive tone; not that it wasn't warranted.

"Yeah, I know," Conrad mumbled with his half-closed eyes still trained on the young woman. Bending down, he took Amanda's hand and murmured, "I'm glad to meet you. You're very pretty."

"Okay, let's move on," Alex advised, grabbing onto his coat sleeve and pulling him away from the table.

As he was being escorted, Conrad stage-whispered to Alex, "So, who's the skank coming in with the mullet-head?"

Where had Margaret Pierce and Chloe gone? Alex wondered, needing them to exert some control over this man. "Uh, I see that the Kerleys have come down," Alex announced, a little too loudly, to talk over Conrad. As the new arrivals approached, Alex couldn't help her but make her own critical judgment of the pair.

Wade Kerley was wearing an ill-fitting plaid sports coat with sleeves that hung down over his hands; although, in fairness, he had changed out of his tight jeans and into a more reasonable pair of wash pants, she was glad to see.

Alex thought Ronette had attempted what could kindly be called a "show-girl" look with her low-cut, form-fitting red dress and spiked heels. To create a "formal" evening hairdo, she had pulled up her hair into folds and swoops to a staggering height which bore a striking resemblance to an extra-large cone of soft-serve ice cream.

Alex quickly went through the introductions and tried to pull Conrad away from Ronette before he made suggestive remarks, but she was too late; he was already peering down her ample cleavage and patting the top of her hair.

Turning towards Alex, sensing her disapproval, Conrad explained that he just wanted to "see how much there was," without being specific as to what he had wanted to quantify. Ronette giggled appreciatively, before Wade grabbed her arm and jerked her back.

Glaring at Conrad, Wade snarled, "You put your hands on my wife, again and you'll be picking your teeth off the floor."

With fortunate timing, Nadine Rodgers came floating into the room in a long pale green caftan, followed closely by Lawrence Livermore, looking suave in a beige linen sports coat with a blue shirt and blue and brown figured tie. The couple stopped to greet acquaintances at the table.

"It's nice to see both of you looking so well," Phyllis gushed. "I love your caftan, dear. Very flattering on you. You're so fortunate that green doesn't reflect up onto your face as much as it does on some women."

Alex had to wonder just how many times she would be needed to run interference with this group. As she looked around, Jennifer Brown and David Albright were making their appearances in the doorway. Alex reflexively waved them over, before she remembered that Jennifer was about to spring her surprise on the inebriated Conrad Pierce.

As Jennifer walked in ahead of David, Alex heard, and then felt, sudden movement behind her. As she turned, she caught sight of Conrad Pierce lurching forward.

"What the hell?!" he bellowed, causing everyone to gape, slack-jawed. "What the hell are *you* doing here?!" he bawled, pointing at Jennifer who had stopped dead in her tracks, the blood draining from her face.

"What the hell is *she* doing here?!" he screamed again, looking around wildly for someone to give him an answer. Locating Margaret Pierce, he fixed her with a baleful stare.

"Is this *your* doing?!" he demanded, at the top of his voice. "Or yours?!" he asked a scowling Chloe Campbell, standing next to his wife.

Margaret Pierce appeared to be shell-shocked as she slowly shook her head in disbelief, unable to speak. Chloe put her arm around her mother, presumably trying to shield her from further verbal assaults. Patting her mother's back, Chloe whispered in her ear as Margaret nodded in agreement.

Without getting more of a response from his wife and stepdaughter, Conrad Pierce wheeled around to focus his attention on Alex. "Did *you* arrange for this little set-up? You must have *known* about this, at the very least. How dare you trick me into coming here so that I could be sabotaged. I'm getting out of here, but you haven't heard the last of me!"

For several seconds, the others remained frozen in place; seemingly mesmerized by the spectacle in front of them. Even Conrad Pierce just stood there, swaying, and staring daggers at Alex, while he waited for a response to the last words of his tirade that still hung in the air.

Before anyone else had a chance to react, Alex stepped forward, grabbed the unsteady man and propelled him back towards the bar, away from the lounge seating. Margaret Pierce and Chloe quickly followed. The others who were left behind, looked after them, spellbound, wondering what could possibly happen next. In fact, they wondered what had already happened since the scene had made no sense. Why had that man flown into a rage when he saw the pretty young woman?

Chapter 13

Bar Fight or Flight

WITH MARGARET PIERCE and Chloe Campbell backing her up, Alex steered Conrad over to the bar and hoisted him up onto a stool. Firmly grasping his lapels, Alex stared at him for a long moment; not trusting herself to say anything until she had gotten her thoughts together. When she did speak, her words tumbled out in a steady stream; not seeming to take a breath that would allow for any interruption.

"Mr. Pierce, I've had it up to here with you," she hissed, her hand slicing the air under her chin. "And we're still in the first hour of our acquaintance. That doesn't bode well for the rest of the week — if there is a 'rest of the week' for you. But I have a few things to say to you before we even talk about that.

"First, you accused me, along with your wife and stepdaughter, of secretly plotting to bring you and Jennifer Brown together on Bedford Island. I can't speak for them, but I can assure you *I* had no prior knowledge that any of you"— she angled her head to indicate the rest of the group — "knew one another before coming here. I've been surprised to learn just today that several people did, and that some are even related. As you're aware, there is no place on the travel contract to give information about another party.

"Secondly, while I can't imagine why Jennifer would *want* to come here when you're here, I don't know why *she shouldn't be here*. She's a paying guest, just like you. And, although I don't know her well, from what I've observed, she's a respectable young woman who did nothing to provoke your outburst."

"You don't know what you're talking about!" Conrad snarled. "She's out to cause trouble for me, and I've given her fair warning before to leave me alone."

"Thirdly," Alex went on without acknowledging that he had spoken, "you may leave this island if you wish – in fact, I have half a mind to *ask* you to leave since I'm responsible for everyone here, and I can't have one guest be so disruptive. But, if you leave on your own, or not, keep in mind that you won't be entitled to any refund. The facility and I have lived up to the terms of the contract, and, if you were to pursue legal recourse, you would find that I have the law on my side.

"Lastly," Alex went on, quickly, before Conrad Pierce could protest again, "I offer you a couple of suggestions. I don't know what your problem is with Jennifer, and it isn't my business, but I can ask you to deal with it *in private.* And, whether you leave or not, you owe me and everyone else in this room an apology for your tirade we all had to endure. Then, and only then, in the interest of maintaining the integrity of the group, I'd actually prefer that you stay on— provided that you can keep your temper in check for the rest of the week."

Margaret Pierce broke in. "This whole incident was totally unnecessary, Conrad. You've disgraced all of us, not to mention poor Jennifer."

'Poor Jennifer! What about poor me?!" Conrad Pierce bellowed. 'I'm the one who got blindsided when I should have been left in peace to enjoy my vacation!'

'I didn't know Jennifer planned to meet up with you here," Margaret shot back. "I did send her a note to let her know that Chloe was engaged and, I think, mentioned something about our trip, but not as an invitation to join us. But to tell you the truth, I'm glad she's here. You never gave her a chance when she came to our house— or in the four years since then. You owe her an explanation for your behavior; for your denial. You know she's your daughter. Hell, *I* know she's your daughter, and she doesn't want anything from you but recognition. She doesn't need any money from you, if that's what you're worried about."

Alex was shocked by Margaret's declarations, but that explained a lot that had happened, while leaving many questions unanswered. Why had paternity become an issue now? Jennifer Brown was a grown woman with a good job and was in a committed relationship. And why here?

As Alex sat listening to the drama unfolding, she noticed that Raymond Bean was motioning to her. Leaving the Pierces, she went over to him.

"Sorry to interrupt, Miss Trotter, but I wondered if you've been able to take care of the, er, 'situation,' or if I could be of some help? These things happen."

What things? Alex thought. *Putative fathers pitching fits when their estranged adult children show up out of the blue? This happens here often?*

"Oh! I hadn't even realized that you were here, Mr. Bean. Thanks, but I think we're working out the conflict. I'm sorry it got out of hand."

Returning to the Pierces who were still at the bar, Alex noticed Virgil Grimm nearby cleaning up the area, putting used napkins and other waste in a plastic bag. Alex took a stool next to Chloe, as Tim Williams came by to wipe down the bar, giving

Chloe a sympathetic look before handing Conrad Pierce a tab, apparently cutting him off for the evening.

"Come on, Conrad," Chloe was saying. "You owe it to us. We don't want you to spoil everyone's time here and make us look like fools in the process. Why don't you just apologize to the people? It's not a lot to ask. And, while you're at it, why don't you agree to talk to Jennifer? In fact, I'm going to set up a meeting with her tomorrow morning, after breakfast."

"All right! All right," Conrad huffed, but his shoulders were sagged in defeat. "Just don't expect anything from me. I'm only agreeing to this to get it over with, and then I want to be left alone on that subject."

"What about your apology?" Alex cut in. "It's about time to go in for dinner and I'd like to get this settled before we eat."

"Fine! I'll say some kind of bullshit to the mopes. If I hadn't been blindsided, I wouldn't have had to act like I did. But, what the hell. I suppose other people didn't see it like I did so . . ." his voice trailed off as he stood up and got out his wallet to pay his bill. "Let me get this shit over with," he mumbled under his breath, shaking his head before making his way over to the lounge.

Looking at Margaret Pierce and Chloe, Alex shrugged and got up to follow Conrad the other two women got up to go with her.

The rest of the company was sitting and quietly conversing; but seeing Conrad Pierce in the center of the room, the talking stopped in anticipation.

Clearing his throat, Conrad stared at the floor, appearing to be unsure of why he was standing there. After an audible sigh, he spoke in a low voice. "I was caught off-guard this evening, but I shouldn't have lost my cool in front of all of you. My family and I will deal with our problems privately. You can go about your business," he finished, holding up his hands as though asking 'what more could be said on the subject.'

Ronette scanned the group, her bronzed face creased in bewilderment. "What's the big deal? It's not like he *killed* someone. I get honked off with Wade wors'n that most of the time!" Wade rolled his eyes up to the ceiling, uncomfortably shifting in his chair and pulling up the sleeves of his plaid jacket.

Lawrence Livermore half stood in place. "Ahem," he started. "Yes, well, I hope that *everyone* will behave in a civilized manner. We're practically in each other's pockets here, so we don't need any more drama. But I'm willing to not take any further notice of this incident."

Nadine followed him. "I agree with Lawrence. It's in everybody's interest to get along to enjoy the week. Let's just move on."

"No one wants to have our time spoiled while we're at this charming inn," Phyllis chimed in.

Pierce said under his breath, "*Whatever,*" and took a chair near the door, away from the others.

Margaret and Chloe went over to Jennifer and David's booth. Jennifer sat scrunched up against the wall sucking on a mixed drink, her face darkened in anger. Chloe sat down next to her, giving her a bright smile. Margaret and David shared a look of resignation, as Margaret sank down next to him.

"I think I know what you had in mind, Jennifer," Margaret offered in a sympathetic tone. "But, as you found out last time, you won't get a good response from Conrad when you surprise him — especially when he's been drinking. I'm not excusing him by a long shot, but I know right now he feels he's on the defensive. I'm hoping he still comes around. At least he made some effort to smooth things over with the rest of the people," she added, halfheartedly.

Taking a big swallow of her drink, Jennifer grimaced at Margaret. "I'm sorry now I ever decided to come here. It was an impulsive decision after I got your note. I thought it would be a good opportunity to confront my father, out in the open, with enough time to work through his objections. I didn't *think* about other people getting involved. That's my fault. What a disaster. He acted like a mad man."

"Oh, it wasn't the first time, and it won't be the last," Chloe said, sighing. "He'll just have to get his act together and grow up."

"Chloe's right," added David. "It is *Chloe*, isn't it? he asked, looking across at her. "I think our introduction got lost in the melee. Anyway, I'm David. I think you know that Jennifer and I live together."

"Oh, right," Jennifer interjected, "You've never met each other. That's the problem – we don't even know one another, and yet, we're a family, connected by way of Conrad Pierce."

"Don't worry — we'll spend time together this week." Chloe responded. "We're going to stay on. By the way, Conrad's agreed to meet with you, along with Mom and me, tomorrow after breakfast. Is that okay with you?"

"Yeah, sure — if the two of you are there." Jennifer looked from Margaret to Chloe for confirmation. "What about David? Should he be there, too?"

"If he wants to be," Margaret answered. "It's fine with me. He might be a calming force for Conrad — if anything will be."

"I'm willing to be there, although just as an observer; for support," David responded. "Jennifer will feel more confident with me there, right, Jen? I wasn't in agreement with her plan to come here, but I'm backing her in whatever she feels she needs to do to connect with her father."

Jennifer reached across the table to put her hand on David's. "Thank you, honey. You were right in the first place, and I'm sorry I dragged you into this, but maybe we can still salvage some good out of this mess. Who knows?"

"Okay," Margaret said. "The five of us will get together after breakfast. I saw the study across from the library. Let's meet there at, say, nine o'clock. I think there's a tram tour of the island at ten. Maybe we'll all want to go on that, together? And, maybe, not," she quickly added in response to the dubious looks around the table.

Alex checked her watch, relieved to see that it was finally time for dinner. "Well, it's 6:30, folks. We should go into the dining room. For tonight, some tables have been put together so that we'll all eat at one long table. Just take any seat.

"Anyone who's ready, let's go." She stood and went over to hold open the door to the dining room, thinking, *I should have my head examined taking this group into a room where there are a lot of knives at hand. And I think we'll forget about the cozy fireside chat after dinner. Let's see if we can just get through a meal without a complete breakdown of civilized society.*

Chapter 14

Thirteen Dine Together

THE GROUP SILENTLY FILED into the candlelit dining room, eyeing one another suspiciously as they approached the long table. Jennifer and David hung back while Conrad, Margaret and Chloe selected seats first. Nadine reluctantly took the seat next to Conrad, and was joined on her left by Lawrence. Phyllis quickly slipped into the chair next to him, while Jennifer and David dashed to claim chairs directly across from them. That left the other five to scurry around until they had each pulled out a chair and pounced on it in unison, as though the music had just stopped in a game of musical chairs.

Alex crossed her eyes in exasperation as she watched the group jockeying for "safe" seats. She, in turn, opted to sit at a nearby table with Raymond Bean. The less-than-exciting manager seemed to be the ideal dinner companion by comparison. Besides, she needed to get the details about the tram tour of the island he would be leading the next morning.

As everyone sat expectantly, the swinging kitchen doors crashed open and out stomped a thickset woman with a pencil stuck in her iron-gray bun, carrying a pile of menus. As she crossed the room, listing from side to side, her stockings made a whistling sound as each thick leg created friction with the other in the labored effort. Arriving at the table, she planted her feet apart to give herself balance as she scrutinized the group, shifting her squinty-eyed gaze from person to person around the table, frowning all the while. Finishing her inspection, she seemed more displeased with the diners than before, but, having apparently not found disqualifying violations, she handed out the menus.

"I'm Edna Butz, your waitress, and I'll be serving youse all your meals, but I wanna give you a word of caution – there's a dress code in the dining room. If you dunno what it is, it's posted. Just ask at the front desk, or check out the 'Welcome' booklet in your room."

Yeah, that's very welcoming, Alex thought to herself. *Where did they get her? Must have put in her twenty years with the Army before she retired to work here. What's with these employees? One's weirder than the next?*

"We got three entrees each evening," Edna continued, interrupting Alex's thoughts. "I wouldn't recommend exchanging a side dish. The menu has been put together the way it is for a reason," she added, shooting a warning look around the table.

"There's a regular menu for breakfast with one special every morning. Lunch will be sandwiches and fruit that're boxed. You can eat 'em on the beach or wherever.

"If anybody's got complaints, tell your tour director. You kin look over the menus, then I'll be back." With that, she toddled back to the kitchen, disappearing behind the swinging doors.

"Well, looks like somebody's got a burr up her butt!" Ronette offered after the door had closed. "Or should I say, Butz!"

Phyllis laughed out loud. "That's getting right to the *bottom* of things. I certainly hope the food is more appealing than the staff!" Two minutes later the door banged open and Edna Butz reappeared, in no better a mood. When she got to the head of the table, she whipped out an order pad, pulled the pencil out of her bunched hair and barked, "So, whaddya want?" to the startled company.

The drink and meal orders were called out by everyone in rapid succession, with no one making substitutions on side dishes. Edna took it down without comment and then shuffled out through the other door, presumably to get the drinks at the bar.

"Well, I'll be," Rosemary exclaimed. "Looks like they don't waste any time on social amenities around here."

"I'm sorry about that," Raymond Bean apologized to the group, rising from his seat. "Edna's worked here for several years, and is more dedicated to being efficient than personable, I'm afraid."

The fearsome waitress soon returned with drinks on a large oval tray which she balanced on one of her ample hips as she set down each glass, while removing any extra glassware.

Following her departure, this time the table broke out in conversation, with everyone joining in. Alex could only overhear snatches of the talk, but the bits she caught indicated polite social interaction. *Maybe there's hope for this group yet,* she thought, optimistically.

Johnny Berthold, in a transparent ploy to promote camaraderie, suggested that they go around the table and each person tell a couple of things about themselves; like where they were from, and what they did for a living.

It seemed to be working as each person offered up some personal information. When it was Lawrence Livermore's turn, he briefly described his hedge fund management. Conrad Pierce said he might investigate the profits in view of possibly making a future investment.

Phyllis Hanover was next, and commented that she, too, would like to hear more about investing with Lawrence.

Nadine Rodgers volunteered that her friends had put money in Lawrence's fund, and they had encouraged her to contact him, so she and Lawrence had emailed and talked over the past several months.

Phyllis Hanover leaned forward. Turning towards Nadine and Lawrence, said, "So, you two have never met before today?"

With that, Rosemary Davis quickly jumped in to introduce herself and described her previous trips to the island. She then invited others to join her and the Bertholds on a hike in a couple of days' time.

Next, was Ronette Kerley. "I think I can speak for both Wade and me," she began, darting a warning look at her husband. "We live in the Day's End subdivision in lovely Dunin, Florida. It's like Paradise, you know? A lot of the people there just sit around and enjoy it since they don't have no jobs. I myself am a cosmo-tol-o-gist at a spa. And ole Wade here, you could say is an on-tra-pen-oor. He invests in different, whaddycall 'em —co-mod-i-ties,' like Mr. Livermore was talkin' bout." Wade's jaw had dropped open. Seeing that, Ronette pinched him under the table that made his eyes tear up.

Continuing her narrative, and clearly enjoying having the spotlight on her fantasy description, she continued, "We're only a couple hours away from here, but we're not on water so we thought it'd make for a nice change to stay on an island. Wade has a good friend with a boat, and he may stop by and take us out for a spin," she finished.

Several of the others looked at her quizzically, but nodded and smiled politely. While Ronette was talking, Edna Butz brought out dinners and set them down in unerring order. No one started to eat, either out of fear of what Edna might have done to their food, or out of politeness. When the table had been served, Rosemary took the first couple of bites, looked around and nodded reassuringly, and the rest followed suit.

Jennifer Brown was next to speak, but, before she started, she cleared her throat and paused, scanning the diners that caused David Albright to hold a forkful of potatoes in the air mid-way to his mouth.

"I think you all deserve some explanation for what transpired during the cocktail hour," she began.

David was still frozen, not daring to move. On the other side of the table, Margaret Pierce clamped a hand on her husband's arm.

"While I don't want to get into any details," Jennifer continued, "suffice it to say that I came to the island to see the Pierces, although they didn't expect me to be here. It would have been better if I had let them know beforehand." She glanced over at her father who was looking down at his plate, moving his beans around with his fork. Everyone had stopped eating, to better focus their attention on Jennifer.

"But I had a good reason not to," she continued with more fervor.

"I don't think you want to go there," warned Conrad Pierce, putting down his utensils. Margaret thumped her fist into his ribs, making him wince.

"Hush," she hissed.

"Yes, I *do* want to go there," Jennifer asserted. "This isn't earth-shaking. The simple truth is that Conrad Pierce is my biological father whom I've seen only once before. He chose not to invite me into his family circle; although Margaret Pierce and Chloe have been very accepting of me."

Murmurings broke out around the table in response.

Raising her voice, Jennifer went on, "And the Pierces and David and I are getting together tomorrow morning to talk. I'm just saying there shouldn't be any more said on the subject in front of you, but I felt I needed to say something now."

"Is *that* what this fuss is all about?" Ronette's shrill voice was heard above the commotion. The room went silent as Ronette continued. "Where I come from, 'who the daddy is' gets settled real easy—with a shotgun. Then there's no misunderstandin'. Everybody knows what's expected after that. Hell, it wouldn't be a family reunion without sortin' out daddies for some of the younguns!"

"Thank you," Alex called out before Ronette could go any further into family relationships. Putting her napkin aside, she stood up. "I think Mrs. Kerley makes a good point that we've talked enough about a private family matter that doesn't concern the rest of us. Let's just enjoy our meal and the balance of the evening. We won't get together later for my talk on the island's history. We'll do that another night. Tomorrow morning, Mr. Bean will be conducting a tram tour of the island, leaving from the hotel at ten o'clock. This will be the easiest way to see the ecosystems of the island and some of the area's wildlife. For sure, we'll see some wild horses. You don't want to miss it."

There was a smattering of subdued applause, followed by a mixture of conversation and the clinking of silverware on plates as people responded to Alex's suggestion to finish their dinners.

Let's hope that all the wild life is on the outside of the tram, Alex thought as she sank gratefully onto her seat and returned Raymond Bean's wan smile.

***

AN HOUR LATER, PEOPLE started getting up from their chairs and moving away from the table asking one another what to do next. Ronette said she was going to the smoking area at one end of the front porch, if anyone was interested. Conrad Pierce said he'd like to join her, but first he was getting a cordial from the bar, and he'd get her a little something.

Phyllis turned to Lawrence and asked if he might have time to talk to her about his hedge fund, unless he had a previous commitment, of course. Looking over at Nadine, who nodded curtly, he turned back to Phyllis and said he'd be delighted to sit on the porch with her for a few minutes, and why didn't they get another glass of wine to take with them?

Rosemary suggested to Johnny and Amanda that they explore the public rooms on the first floor—perhaps they'd like to play a game of pool in the billiards room, or select a couple of books from the library. Amanda was enthusiastic about visiting the Library, in particular, as she had noticed some antique leather-bound volumes she'd like to see; and maybe, she'd pick up a novel to read.

Margaret Pierce offered to walk outside with Chloe who said she'd like that. Jennifer asked if she and David could join them, and was warmly invited to come along.

Alex decided she'd go outside for some air by herself before she went upstairs to watch a little television and go to bed early. As she approached the front door, she heard the whirring of a distant vacuum cleaner that was being used in one of the first-floor rooms off the porch.

Outside, Alex noticed that only the front path was lit in the darkness. At the bottom of the stairs she noticed she was behind the others who had left for a walk, so she turned off to the right onto the lawn. Behind the dense magnolia tree, she was shocked to see Wade Kerley, who didn't notice her, peering out from behind the tree's large leaves.

She crouched down to see what Wade was looking at. She could make out Conrad and Ronette sitting on a swing, kissing, as Conrad moved his hands up under Ronette's tight red dress. Ronette leaned back, moaning.

Embarrassed to be looking at the intimacy, Alex turned to leave, hoping not to be seen or heard by Wade. Silently stepping out from behind the tree, she made her way back to the path and mounted the staircase to go back inside.

At the front door, she noticed Lawrence and Phyllis sitting on one of the benches with their heads close together, laughing. As she walked inside she thought to herself, *what was in that food, anyway?*

Sunday morning, April 14

Chapter 15

The Morning After and Other Headaches

THE NEXT MORNING sunlight woke her early as it sliced between the drapery panels in Alex's room. Sitting up in bed, she had an uneasy feeling about the day ahead; then she realized why— the sexual encounter between Conrad Pierce and Ronette Kerley last night. Wade probably had seen the whole thing; however it had turned out. Did Margaret and Chloe see them, too? It seemed that Conrad was bent on making everyone miserable.

It had been a trial just to get through cocktails and dinner last night; and today was only their first full day on the island. At this rate, how would they make it through a whole week?

An hour later when she walked into the dining room and greeted those who were there, she picked up on tension in the room, noticing there wasn't much conversation. Looking around, she observed the Kerleys, seated by themselves, didn't appear to be on speaking terms; Phyllis, Rosemary, the Bertholds,

Lawrence Livermore and Nadine were uneasily sharing a table. Dirty looks flying back and forth between Phyllis and Nadine.

Alex sat at a small table by herself where she could read over some island history and look out the window.

After breakfast had been served, Alex overheard Rosemary attempting to lighten the mood at her table by talking about the tram tour that morning. "You'll be amazed at the different species of birds and animals here on the island. I wouldn't miss the tour. You could say wild horses couldn't keep me away." She rolled her eyes at her lame play on words. Johnny groaned in mock disgust, which got everyone smiling.

Nice going, Rosemary, Alex thought. *This is a tough crowd. You're lucky they're not throwing fruit. Speaking of throwing things, I wonder how the Pierce family is doing in the Study talking things through.*

If she had been there, she would have seen Jennifer barely controlling herself *not* to throw something at Conrad as she pleaded with him. "Maybe we'll decide there's no good reason for us to see each other, again," she said, reasonably. "But all I'm asking is that you admit you're my father. Half my genes are from *you,* which means something to me even if it doesn't to you. And, by the way, I'm considered to be a nice person and quite successful – one would think you'd be proud to claim me as a daughter," she finished, tears welling up.

"Okay, Jennifer." David had stood and put his arms around the distraught young woman. "I think you've said enough, honey. *I'm* proud of you and your mother and stepfather are proud of you. You don't need this guy's approval of who you are and what you've accomplished."

Conrad jumped to his feet. "Hold on! I'm not the 'bad guy' here! You came from out of nowhere, with, 'Here I am!'" he mimicked her in a falsetto voice. "Your beloved daughter you've never heard of.' What would anyone think? She could have been some psycho who wanted to kill me and my whole family!"

Jennifer bore down on him. "What are you talking about? You *knew* about me. 'I'm some *psycho* who wanted to kill you?'"

Margaret pulled her husband down onto the sofa, then held up her hand like a traffic cop. "Okay, let's everybody calm down. When you first showed up, Conrad didn't know he had a *daughter*, which is *his fault,* but it was a shock, nevertheless. Now he knows. Conrad, if there's any doubt in your mind, submit to a blood test for DNA analysis. Otherwise, accept that Jennifer is your daughter. She's the only offspring of the woman who became pregnant while you lived with her, which should be proof enough for you, so let's get on with it."

"Okay!" Conrad groused. "I'll say it. Jennifer is probably my daughter. Is that what you all want to hear?" Conrad's face was contorted with rage. "She's also a *stranger* who has grown up without my knowing of her existence, and it's too late now to change that. So, if all you want to do is to find me guilty of not living up to my responsibility as a father, fine. You've proved your point. But if you think I'm going to somehow turn into a doting parent now, you've got another 'think' coming.

He ran his fingers through his hair. "I'm glad you've grown up to be such a *big* success. Hooray for you! Hooray for your mother! And good luck to you in the future. Now, let's just go our separate ways, okay?"

"I can't *believe* you!" Jennifer keened. "I'm just glad I inherited your eye color instead of your character."

During the exchanges Chloe had sat mutely without expression. Now, looking at Jennifer, her eyes filled with tears as she spoke in a small choked voice. "You're the lucky one. You could have *lived* with him, and he could have done to you what he did to me."

Jumping up, Conrad's face was red and puffy. "Shut up! We don't need to hear from you, too. I've had just about enough from all of you! I hope you're happy, Miss Jennifer Brown. You may be proud of yourself, but I'll tell you one thing – you don't have the sense of a goat to set up this little trap. *I'm outta here* and I don't wanna ever see you again!"

After slamming the door behind him, everyone sat, stunned. Finally, breaking the tense silence, Margaret said, softly, "Why don't you two go along, now? I'd like to talk to Chloe in private."

Sunday, April 14

Chapter 16

Experiencing the Wild Life on the Island

JUST BEFORE TEN O'CLOCK, Manager Bean drove the tram up to the front door of the Inn. Inside, he found Alex and the group waiting for him in the lobby.

"There you are, Mr. Bean," Alex greeted him. Looks like you got a late start today," she said in a friendly tone.

"No, I've been in the building since eight-thirty," Raymond responded. "I've had tasks to take care of. I just went around to the garage and got the vehicle. Is everyone here who's going on the tram tour?"

"Well, there are eleven so far, so we're missing three people. Maybe we can wait a couple of minutes to be sure we don't leave without anyone who wants to come?"

"Fine with me," Raymond responded. "The ones who are here can board now. In the meantime, I'll go get the lunches to take with us."

Alex relayed the information to the group. Once outside, Johnny and Amanda stood back from the tram to let the older people get on. Neither Nadine nor Phyllis, who were closest, made a move. Lawrence remained behind the women.

David Albright took Jennifer Brown's elbow and urged her to board to break up the log jam and get people moving.

Ronette Kerley, wearing large dark sunglasses and a halter top with short shorts, stayed back from the tram with her chin puckered and her lower lip stuck out in a pout. Turning away from Wade, he roughly grabbed her arm and dragged her over to the vehicle, then pushed her up the steps. On board, he shoved her to a rear seat where she sank down with a protesting "hrumph!"

Rosemary nudged Phyllis who reluctantly started up the tram steps. Nadine followed, as did Lawrence. Nadine turned back to Lawrence and said, "Here are two seats for us!" pointing at a row behind Phyllis and Rosemary, on the opposite side of the tram.

Alex got on last, taking a seat behind the driver that had been left unoccupied. Looking back at the mostly unsmiling faces, she said, "While we're waiting for Mr. Bean to come back with our lunches, does anyone know if the Pierce family was planning to come on the tram tour?"

"Not if Conrad knows what's good for him," replied Wade Kerley, under his breath, but loud enough for everyone to hear.

Jennifer responded out loud. "I don't think they'll be coming. They had some, er, things to do."

"Okay, we'll get going as soon as Mr. Bean returns," Alex said. "Let me tell you a few things about our outing this morning. We'll spend about four hours touring the northern end of the island, making stops to visit landmarks as well as getting off to take pictures from time to time. Mr. Bean will be using a microphone to comment on the sights, so you'll all be able to hear. We'll stop for lunch at the wharf, which is at the half-way point. Also, it has the best facilities on the island.

"Let's see. Oh — be sure you're seated when we're moving because the roads are unpaved and rough; maybe even hang onto the seat in front of you, and secure any loose items." Several blank faces looked back. *Where is Raymond Bean when you need him?*

After a minute or two, she was relieved to see him outside the tram, carrying white bakery-style boxes tied with string and a couple of grocery bags which he took to the back of the tram. Alex jumped out to assist him as he opened the rear door to store things in coolers.

Once on their way, within minutes they approached a broad green meadow where a dozen shaggy brown horses were quietly grazing.

"There they are! Our first sighting of the wild horses!" Amanda exclaimed. "Can we get some pictures?"

Raymond brought the tram to a stop, turned in his seat and held up one finger up to ask for silence. Speaking low, he cautioned them, "Leave the tram quietly and take your pictures; but be sure you don't spook them as they're unpredictable and you don't want to get in their way. Believe me, they'll run right over you."

Off the tram, they all crept into the trees for cover except for Ronette who stomped off in the other direction, in tall grass toward the horses.

"Ronette!" Wade squeaked in a hoarse whisper. "Get back here!"

Ignoring him, Ronette continued walking, her eyes fixed on the horses that hadn't yet noticed her. Getting within a hundred feet of them, she crouched down into the weeds and lifted her camera. As she did so, the herd's stallion jerked up his head and flicked his ears back and forth several times as he looked around, wildeyed. Flaring his nostrils, he let out an ear-splitting whinny and reared up, pawing the air with his forelegs.

This appeared to confuse and frighten the mares and colts as they started running around in circles. After a few moments, the large steed brought down his front legs with a thud and charged forward, his hooves pounding into the ground sending dirt and debris flying. The other horses crowded together behind him, snorting and bumping against each other in confusion until they took off after the stallion at a gallop.

Once they had crossed the road, within seconds the herd became just a distant rumble, out of sight.

Slowly and cautiously everyone in the woods got up and looked around, dazed. After a few moments, Wade called out his wife's name and ran out into the flattened meadow to where he had last seen her. Alex ran after him, fearing the worst, but unwilling to let him face it alone.

Not seeing any sign of Ronette where they thought she should be, they paused and ooked at each other. "What the. . . . ? " Wade started.

Alex shook her head in puzzlement and started walking around to inspect the area. Her attention became drawn to boulders off to one side. Approaching them, she tentatively called out Ronette's name. After a moment, a small shaky hand rose up from the pile of rocks.

"Ronette!" Alex called out, running now, along with Wade, who had also seen the sign of life. Arriving at the spot, they crawled over the boulders and looked down where they had seen the hand. Wedged between two of the largest ones, Ronette lay, bloodied and disheveled, but alive and conscious. Looking up through lopsided broken sunglasses, she asked in a quavering voice, "Are they gone, now?"

"Oh my God! Ronette!" Wade reached out to take her hand.

"Don't move her yet, Wade," Alex warned. "We need to check out her injuries, first." Alex lay down on her stomach to better talk to the injured woman.

"Ronette, can you tell me what happened? Are you badly hurt?"

"I don't know, When I saw that big ole horse rear up I knew I was in trouble, so I crawled over here to hide and hope he dint see me. I'd wedged myself in 'ere when I heard the horses comin' and then the ground moved. They were jumpin' over me and runnin' past me!" She broke down sobbing.

"Go on, Ronette," Alex urged. "You weren't hurt by their hooves, then, right? They didn't actually come down on you, did they?"

"I don't think so, but I was hit with stones and dirt. I had my face down, but that was all that I could do to protect myself. Honest to God, I thought I was gonna die!" The last words were choked out as she dissolved into tears.

"It must have been terrible, Ronette, but you're going to be all right," Alex said reassuringly. "Just try to move a little so we can make sure that nothing is broken. It looks like the blood is coming from scratches where you scraped against the rocks."

"My poor baby!" Wade cried. "I wish I coulda helped you!"

Ronette glared up at him, her scarlet lips tightened into a thin line. "Just remember, Wade – this trip was for *your* benefit!"

The rest of the group had gathered around the three of them, gaping at the scene. Raymond Bean brought over a bag of ice, a couple bottles of water and some cloth napkins. Alex soaked a few napkins in water and began gingerly patting Ronette's bloody face.

"From what I can see, the wounds are superficial, Ronette." Alex said, continuously turning the napkins over as she wiped off the blood. "Just some scratches and a few nicks. You're very lucky. Well, not really lucky," she smiled, apologetically. "But lucky, considering."

Ronette cautiously moved her limbs to convince herself and the others that she was still intact. "I just don't understan' why those horses started up to stampedin'. There wasn't nothin' to spook ‘em like that. They couldna seen me. I was way down in the grasses. Unless . . .” she stopped. “Do you think the flash of my camera went off and spooked ‘em? I kin never tell if the flash is on or off, y’ know?”

“We’ll check that out,” Alex assured her. “For now, let’s just see if you can stand. It doesn’t appear that anything is broken.”

Holding onto Alex, Ronette stood on shaky legs. The other members of the group let out a cheer, which made Ronette smile.

“Good going!” Alex said, enthusiastically. “How do you feel?”

“I - I - think I’m okay. I’m gettin’ over the shock. Yea, I think I’m okay,” she added, more firmly, nodding.

“That was a close call,” Raymond Bean said, sounding relieved. “There’s no doubt about that. I try to tell people that the horses are like other wild animals and can be dangerous if you get too close.” Turning to Alex he said, “What we need to decide now is should we go back to the Inn? Or would you like to continue? Or what?”

“I think it’s up to Ronette. What do you want to do?” Alex asked, looking at the young woman.

“I’d just as soon keep goin’. Mebbe I won't get off at every stop — not if we see any more damn horses, that's for sure.”

“That's like the old Ronette,” Alex commented, gently squeezing her shoulder.

Walking back to the tram, Rosemary drew Alex aside. “Miss Trotter, I’m really puzzled by what happened here. It’s not logical for horses to have been spooked like that, just by our presence. I’ve never seen anything like it, and I’ve been around those horses many times. I can’t believe a flash going off on a sunny day would have frightened them. You know how often those same horses have been photographed?”

"Well, I don't know *how* or *why* it happened," Alex answered, "but we all *saw* it. They *did* get spooked. I'm just glad Ronette had the presence of mind to get between those rocks when she did, or she wouldn't have had a chance. I'm still shaking just thinking about it."

"And I made some silly joke at breakfast about 'wild horses' being more than just an expression," Rosemary mused, shaking her head.

Alex laid a hand on her shoulder. "Oh, don't worry about it. No one could have imagined that this was even possible, except maybe for Raymond Bean, who warned us."

Everyone got back on the tram, still talking about the stampede. Alex sat in the back with Ronette, offering her ice in a plastic bag to put against her face. It couldn't be determined if her face was puffy from crying or from being injured; but Alex thought ice should help in either case.

The tour continued past the site of where two British forts had stood and the remains of the 17th century cotton plantation and cemetery, before the tram came to its next stop: Raymond Bean picked up the microphone. "This is Englewood. It was a 22,000-square foot mansion built in 1898 as a wedding gift to the scion of a railroad tycoon."

The group followed Bean inside for a guided tour while Alex stayed on the tram with Ronette.

"I wanted to talk to jest you" Ronette confided when they were alone. "Do you believe in, whaddyacallit—karma?"

"You mean the belief that peoples acts results in good or bad fortune? I don't know, but why do you ask?"

"Well, I'm just wonderin' if I was gettin' payback for what I did last night. Not that Wade hadn't already taken care of me on that score," she muttered ruefully. "But, when I was having a ciggie and a drink last night with that Conrad Pierce he — well, he 'took advantage of me.' You know what I mean? I think he put somethin' in my drink—and that ain't no lie! But, maybe, I'm under some kinda curse, you know?"

"I don't think so, Ronette," Alex answered seriously. "If anything, what happened gives you reason to believe in Guardian Angels, not curses."

"Well, I dunno about that, but I'm thinkin' that I dint start nothin' last night, so if I'm cursed, so's that guy."

* * *

AT NOON, the group sat to eat their lunch at picnic tables under the twisted branches of live oaks in view of the water. While they ate, Rosemary pointed out various birds she sighted: the oyster-catchers, ring-billed gulls, plovers, terns and sandpipers, that were active along the water's edge.

"Wait! What's that funny-looking little fellow?" Phyllis asked, indicating a needle-nosed mammal with a hard-shelled back that scurried into the marsh grass.

"That's an armadillo," Rosemary answered. "You don't see them very often. They're shy. Not dangerous at all. If you were to come upon one, he'd crawl back into his armored shell and play dead. They're a recent arrival on the island."

"My friend Rosemary knows the most interesting things about birds and animals," Phyllis remarked to the group. "It's wonderful to have deep knowledge about a subject, like you, Lawrence, about investing. I learned so much talking to you last night. As I told you, I have a complicated financial situation that I need to work out to mend my relationship with my step-family."

Nadine held up her wrist to make a point of looking at her watch.

"Oh, yes, look at the time," Raymond Bean said, reflexively. "We should get going if we want to stay on schedule. Our first stop will be the Rocky Bluff that overlooks the water. It's the best place to see dolphins, but we can't guarantee it, of course."

* * *

TWENTY MINUTES LATER, they pulled over. Everyone got out and climbed a gritty promontory above an expanse of deep blue water. Rosemary and Johnny had binoculars they offered to share if something interesting was spotted.

"I see a pair of dolphins!" Amanda Berthold cried out. "Look, over there, swimming from left to right!"

"How come you're always the first one to see the wildlife?" Johnny asked. "Although the last time it didn't turn out so well. Here – you look first and then let me see, okay?"

Everyone crowded together passing the binoculars around while exclaiming over the sight of the two grey mammals, glistening in the sun, diving through the water.

Suddenly, there was a surge of movement in the group and a woman screamed. Everyone's attention became drawn to the edge of the cliff where the sound had come from. Peering over, they saw Phyllis dangling above the surf clinging to a branch growing out of the side of the rock. "Help me! Please! Somebody help me!"

"Hold on! I can get you. Just hold on!" Johnny yelled as he flattened himself on his stomach and stretched out his hand. "Two people should sit on me, or something, so I can pull her up!" he ordered.

Lawrence and Wade were the first ones to get down and each grabbed one of Johnny's legs. "Go ahead!" Lawrence cried. "We've got you! You can move forward to reach her!"

Johnny squirmed ahead until he was hanging off the ledge past his waist and grasped her by one hand. He shouted back, "Pull! Good! Pull, again! She's coming! Everyone else, get outta the way!"

The group moved aside in one unit. With two more good yanks by Lawrence and Raymond, Johnny was able to drag Phyllis back over the edge on her stomach. Turning her over,

Johnny pulled her up to a sitting position. "Are you all right, Mrs. Hanover?" he asked.

Phyllis turned towards him and took hold of his arm. "Thank you, young man. You're wonderful to have saved me. Just let me catch my breath. I think I'll be okay, but I can't believe what just happened."

"What *did* happen? Johnny asked. "How in the world did you fall off the cliff?"

"I didn't really fall. I felt someone pushing me from behind and I lost my footing on the crumbly surface! I was just fortunate there were a couple of branches sticking out that I could hold onto. A few inches on either side of those and I would have landed on the rocks below."

Alex joined Johnny, sitting on Phyliss's other side. "We must have been leaning on you while we were watching the dolphins, not realizing where we were standing," Alex suggested, sympathetically. "When you look through binoculars, you get a distorted idea of distance and where you are. I'm sure no one meant to cause you to lose your footing." She tried to sound convincing. *Was it even possible that someone could intentionally push Phyllis over the edge? Why would anyone want to hurt her?*

After giving Phyllis a few moments to get her breath, Johnny and Alex helped her to her feet and Lawrence put his arm around her to support her. "You have a lot of pluck, Phyllis," he said, giving her a squeeze, "but I can feel that you're shaking. I think we better get you back to the Inn. You've had quite a shock to your system."

"Yes, I think it's time we went back," Alex agreed wholeheartedly.

Everyone quietly re-boarded the tram and took their seats. Before Raymond started up the vehicle, Alex stood to address the group: "We've had an eventful trip today, but not the one we planned. Thankfully, Ronette and Phyllis didn't come to even more harm. Those were both bizarre accidents – I can't imagine that they could ever happen again in the same ways. Anyway, we'll be getting back earlier than we expected, so they can have a much-needed rest before cocktails.

Alex glanced around the group. "I was going to give my talk on island history tonight, but in view of the traumatic events today, I think it would be better if we had some fun this evening. You've all played the board game *Clue*, right?" Everyone nodded, but looked quizzical. "Well, I've thought of a way that we could play it in live-action, using our own Library, Study, Billiards Room, Dining Room, Kitchen, Entry Hall, and Lounge like on the board of the original game. We're only missing the Conservatory and the Ballroom."

"Oh, that sounds like fun!" Phyllis exclaimed, rousing herself. "We could use an entertaining distraction. I'll be Mrs. Plum. Isn't that one of them?"

"I believe it's *Professor* Plum, Phyllis," Alex said. "How about if you're Mrs. Peacock?" she suggested, as others chimed in with names of "suspects" they recalled. "I'll explain the rules of the game when we get together after dinner; let's say about eight o'clock in the Entry Lounge, okay?"

* * *

Later, as Alex walked past the front desk, she was startled by Tina Wrenn who hopped out from behind the counter looking wide-eyed and anxious, as usual. "How did the tram tour go?" she asked, intently.

"It didn't go well at all, I'm afraid," Alex replied, grimacing. "Two of our people had accidents that could have been very serious, or even fatal. They were lucky to escape with just a few scratches and bruises. I think they're going to be fine, though."

Tina put her hands up to her face. "Oh! I'm sorry to hear that! I mean, I'm not sorry they'll be fine. I mean . . ."

"I know what you mean," Alex said, smiling at the befuddled young woman. "Thank you for asking about the tour."

Tina stepped up close, glanced around, and whispered, "I always ask about everyone – you know – to see if they're still all right."

"Okay, then ..." Alex stepped back to a more comfortable distance. "You have a good afternoon, Tina,"

Walking upstairs she thought, what a strange bird she is. What did she even mean by, 'always asking if people are still all right?'

She said hello to one of the housekeepers she passed in the hallway who looked down at the carpet without smiling. *There are strange people in this place.* Getting to her door, she unlocked it and went inside, relieved to get back to her room.

Sunday night, April 14

Chapter 17

Looking for Murder Clues

GETTING READY FOR THE EVENING, Alex dressed in black slacks and a tailored white blouse with a bright pink sash around her waist for her role as "crime writer" of the game of *Clue*. After the tram tour, she had surprised Mr. Bean with a list of weapons she'd like him to locate and loan to her: a coil of rope, a large wrench, a heavy brass candlestick, a small revolver, a lead pipe, and a thick-bladed knife; explaining that they were for playing the classic board game.

Before cocktail hour, Alex worked out how the game would be played; writing out the players' actions, the clues in rhyme form and, most importantly, what the solution of the "crime" would be.

In the Billiards Room, she had found a beat-up game of *Clue* which she reviewed for rules and cannibalized for parts. However, adapting the board version to live action required thinking "outside the box," literally. With twice as many players as the game called for, Alex thought to divide the thirteen players into teams of two, except for the Pierces who would have three. The teams would then take the names of those in the board game: Mr. Green, Professor Plum, Colonel Mustard, Miss Scarlet, Mrs. White and Miss Peacock.

The object of the game would be to find the hidden weapons, the five "suspect" cards, and the one "murder room" card by searching the public rooms on the first floor with the aid of her clues. When all the secreted objects were found, the players would be able to solve the "crime" by process of elimination, as in the board game. In two of the rooms, the clues would lead to a piece of paper on which was written, "No evidence here of any crime."

In place of dice that moved players from room to room in the board game, each team would draw "room" cards, one at a time. They would then determine which clues applied to that room, and enter to search it for a maximum of ten minutes. If they found the hidden articles, they would write down what they were and leave them in place for the next players to find.

Instead of the board game's black envelope with the solution cards, Alex would store the "suspect" card of the killer, the murder weapon, and the name of the room, in a black felt shoe bag. The first team to come to her with the solution would be the winners and receive a bottle of red wine as a prize.

Alex had decided on the solution of the crime: Mr. Boddy was murdered by Colonel Mustard in the Hall with a wrench. Colonel Mustard had always been her favorite *Clue* game piece; the flat wrench could easily be disguised in the bag; and the Hall was the most unexpected room for the scene of a murder.

Now she had to hurry downstairs to get the weapons from the manager and hide them with the "suspect" cards in all the public rooms. There wouldn't be weapons or "suspects" in the Study or the Lounge; although they would also be searched with their corresponding clues that would lead the players to the cards on which she had written her "no evidence" notes.

Alex read through the clue that would direct people to the dining room:

Don't eat up a lot of time
Searching for me
I'm not hard to find,
If you know where to look
I'm not far from swinging doors
Or far from the cook

I'm not seen from above
But can be seen from below
Three chairs for me!
Now you surely must know.

These verses should direct the players to one of the tables for three that was set up near the kitchen. The revolver and the card of "Mrs. White" would be taped underneath. *Was this too easy?* she wondered. Some of the other clues were harder, like the one that people had to identify as being for the Library that referred to *The Passenger to Frankfurt,* a lesser-known Agatha Christie book.

At the bottom of the stairs, Alex saw Raymond Bean in a serious-looking conversation with Tina Wrenn at the front desk. As always, Tina appeared to be tense and upset, her eyes scanning the room as she continuously picked nervously at a pile of papers on her counter.

Alex walked up behind Raymond, and Tina cried out, "Oh, look! It's Alex!" as though Alex was being talked about and Tina needed to serve notice to Raymond of her presence.

"I'm sorry I interrupted you," Alex said to the distressed clerk. "I just needed to speak with Mr. Bean for a moment."

"Oh, of course! Speak with Mr. Bean!" Tina held up her hands.

"Okay, I will—thanks," Alex responded. "Uh, Mr. Bean," she started uncertainly, aware that the desk clerk was still staring at her. "Were you able to find those — er,'things' I asked you about?"

"I managed to find all of them," the manager replied, easily. "I have them in a box in a supply closet. Come with me and I'll give them to you.

"Oh, by the way, I also have that two-way pager for you I forgot to give you last night. Remember? It's controlled by satellite as we don't have a close cell tower for phones. You can call Virgil Grimm if you need anything after I've gone home in the evenings. His number is programmed into the memory, as I told you. You just hit this button, his number comes up and then you can type in a few words – I think it's up to twenty characters on each of four lines, if you want to. Okay?"

"Yeah, sure. Let me see, here." Alex examined the pager. "I hit this button and then I see his name and press 'enter.' Then I can open it to a little keyboard to put in a message. Got it. That's great. Thanks." She slipped the device in the pocket of her slacks, then followed the manager to get the props for her game.

After a half hour or so, Alex had hidden the five weapons, cards, and notes, and was pleased with the result. *I don't know if even I could find them all again,* she said to herself, walking out of the last room.

Raymond had done a good job finding all the weapons, she thought. The handgun was real, which surprised her. Mr. Bean had assured her there wasn't a bullet in the chamber, so it couldn't be fired. All the rest of the weapons could be lethal, if used with enough force or, in the case of the rope, tightened around one's neck with enough strength to cut off someone's airways. Actual weapons made the game much more authentic and exciting, she thought.

When she entered the bar area for cocktail hour, she noticed Margaret and Chloe were there without Conrad. Walking over to their table, Alex asked them if he would be coming down, fearing he might be out of sorts, or feeling not welcome to spend the evening with the two of them.

"To tell you the truth, I really haven't seen him all day," Margaret said, casually.

It made Alex uneasy she had used the phrase "to tell you the truth," which usually indicated deception. "I'm only asking as I've planned something special for tonight – a live-action game of *Clue,*" Alex explained. "You know, the board game where you have to discover who murdered 'Mr. Boddy' and in what room of the mansion? I suggested it to everyone on the tram tour, and they seemed to think it was a good idea. I've included the three of you as players. I hope you'll join in."

Margaret and Chloe looked at each other, their faces animated. "Of course, we would," Margaret answered, with spirit. "I don't know about Conrad, of course, but Chloe and I will play, won't we, Chloe?" Her daughter nodded, agreeably.

Alex again felt uneasy with Margaret's response, with her lack of interest in the whereabouts of her husband, and in their willingness to play a game without finding out where the man was.

"There aren't many places to *be* here," Alex protested, bringing the subject back to locating Conrad. "Did he take a bicycle? Did he arrange with the hotel for transportation to the pier to go over to St. Anne's? I mean, if you haven't seen him *all day*, don't you think we should make some inquiries?"

"Not really," Margaret said, taking another sip of wine. "All right. I'll tell you what happened. Conrad and Jennifer had an angry confrontation this morning. Chloe and I and David were there, too. It ended badly with Conrad slamming the door saying he didn't want to see Jennifer again, and we haven't seen him since. I think he just wanted to go off on his own for a while and, frankly, I don't particularly want to see *him*, now, either. But I wouldn't worry about him – he can take care of himself."

"Well, I didn't mean to involve myself with your family matters again," Alex apologized, "but I do think we should ask at the front desk, at least, if he arranged for transportation, or was seen leaving the hotel."

"Sure, go ahead," Margaret agreed placidly. "Let me know what you find out," she added, without interest.

Alex feared that the skittish Tina Wrenn wouldn't know anything concerning the whereabouts of Conrad Pierce and would just get upset.

"Mr. Pierce has gone missing?" the perpetually-alarmed clerk exclaimed in response to Alex's inquiries. "I never saw him. Oh, that's terrible! We should look for him. Where could he have gone?"

"We don't know where to look, but his wife doesn't think there's cause for concern. She thinks he wanted to be by himself for a while. I'm inclined to agree at this point, but I don't want you to worry. If he doesn't return later this evening, we'll send out a search party."

By the time they went into the dining room for dinner, Conrad still hadn't made an appearance, which had everyone talking. Edna Butz, overhearing some of the conversation, tossed down menus on a table and huffed, "The chef expected all thirteen of you for dinner; fourteen, with Miss Trotter. He's not going to like that one of you just didn't show up."

"It's still light out for a little while," Amanda said, optimistically. "The last public ferry is just getting back. He might be turning up any time now."

"I just think there've been so many strange things that have happened today," Phyllis said. "You can't say what other weird things might have happened. I mean, I wouldn't have thought I'd go over a cliff, either, but I did."

"An' I was within inches of being creamed by a bunch of wild horses!" Ronette exclaimed. "There's no telling what effect that might have on my mental state!"

Wade sniggered. "You was crazy before. Maybe now you'll be sane," he murmured behind his napkin as Ronette cuffed him on the shoulder.

"I'm getting anxious about Mr. Pierce," Alex said to Jennifer and David. "Margaret confided to me that you had harsh words this morning, so I guess that could explain why he's staying away for now. I can imagine him saying something that he now regrets."

"That's putting it, mildly," Jennifer commented. "He said something he *should* have regretted, anyway."

* * *

AFTER THE CHERRY COBBLER and coffee had been consumed, everyone started leaving, allowing Edna Butz to clear the dirty plates off the tables, and for Virgil Grimm to start mopping the floor.

A few minutes later, everyone reassembled in the hall lounge to play *Clue*. They could all see the front door, which remained unopened.

After waiting for a few minutes to see if Conrad would make an appearance, Alex started explaining how to play the game, reminding them of the rules. "The way we're playing *Clue* is a little different since you won't be making a suggestion to solve the crime in every room, as you won't be exchanging information with the other players. You'll be gathering evidence on your own until you get through all the rooms, and then you'll be able to name all three elements of the murder: the 'Who,' 'What' and 'Where.'" The first ones to finish will be the winners and receive a bottle of fine wine.

"Miss Trotter, this will be so much fun!" Phyllis said, clapping her hands. "I just love it! I've always loved mysteries, anyway, but I've never acted one out like this. Rosemary and I will be the "Miss Peacock" team.

"Okay, fine. You two could be the murderers, you know. In this game everyone is both detective and suspect, just like in the original."

After pairing everyone up and giving them their character names and all the clues, each team drew a card with clues identifying the room they would start searching.

"Remember, leave the weapons and cards undisturbed for the next team," Alex cautioned as they went off to the various public rooms.

"How the hell do we know who the *Passenger to Frankfurt* is?" she heard Ronette ask Wade as they walked away. "Aint that a foreign city? Or is it just a hotdog?"

Yeah, this will be hard enough for some, Alex thought, shaking her head. She had decided to stay in the front Hall Lounge with the "room" cards. Tina was mercifully gone for the day, so it would be quiet there. After everyone had disappeared, she took note of the time – 8:15 – so that she could calculate ten minutes for each of the searches.

When it was 8:25, Alex went down the hallways calling out, "Time's up! Everyone come out from the room you're in and draw another room card!"

Ronette and Wade were the first to return. "Can we go back to the same room again if we dint find nothin'?" Ronette asked.

"Sure, if no one has the solution after they've been in every room," Alex replied. "It's possible – we'll wait and see. Here, pick another room to search."

Ronette closed her eyes as though to improve her chances, and then looked at her drawn card. After reading the clue, her face brightened. "I think it's the Study! Is that right, Miss Trotter?" Alex couldn't help but nod in assent, against the rules. "That's a small room across from the Library, Wade," Ronette explained. "That can't be so hard! Let's go!"

A couple minutes later, when Alex had just given out the last of the room cards and checked her watch, she heard a piercing scream from down the hall, near the Library. Running in that direction, the next sound she heard was Ronette's voice sobbing, "Oh, my God, no! Oh, my God!"

Arriving at the doorway of the Study, Alex could only see teased yellow hair and Ronette bending over behind the sofa.

"What, Ronette! What is it?" Alex cried out. "Why did you scream?"

"It's – it's – it's Conrad Pierce! He's not playing – he's really dead!" Ronette burst out crying for the second time that day. "He's got a big old knife in his chest!"

Alex slumped against a chair as Rosemary and Lawrence appeared in the doorway. "Don't let anybody come in," Alex gasped. "Conrad Pierce has been murdered with a knife in the Study."

Sunday night, late

Chapter 18

A Real Murder with Real Suspects

THE SCREAMS AND COMMOTION that followed the discovery of Conrad Pierce's body brought even Edna Butz and Virgil Grimm out from wherever they were hiding.

"What in tarnation is everybody yellin' about?" Edna demanded as she came stomping down the hallway towards the study, her pencil bobbing up and down behind her ear. Coming up against a wall of people, she stood with her hands on her hips, chewing on her lower lip in frustration, as she was being ignored.

Virgil Grimm, who had loped along behind her, was peeking out from behind her broad back, a mocking smile on his face as he took in the chaotic scene.

In the study, Alex had brought in Margaret Pierce, Chloe Campbell and Jennifer Brown to inform them privately of Conrad Pierce's apparent murder. All three women were shocked at hearing the news, Alex noted, although no one had broken down in tears like Ronette, who was still crying in the corner as Wade sat stiffly by.

After absorbing the report, Margaret stood, demanding to see her husband; but Alex restrained her, explaining that they needed to keep the area from being contaminated until the police had been able to process the crime scene.

"You wouldn't want the police to find your DNA near the body," Alex advised. "In fact, we all need to leave now and seal off this room. "I'll go find see about that radio-phone contraption and summon the police.

"Before I go, I just want to tell all of you how sorry I am for your loss. It was unfortunate that you had bitter words with Mr. Pierce this morning. Who knows how much he may have regretted them, and how he might have redeemed himself." She looked at Jennifer who was blinking to hold back tears, slowly nodding her head in agreement.

"I'll go out first and you all follow me," Alex suggested. "You, too — Ronette and Wade. The last one out, close the door securely behind you."

Alex tried to squeeze through several who were standing outside the door. "Please give us some room. These people have just had a terrible shock and need some privacy. And we need to clear this area. It's now a crime scene. If you'll go back to the main lounge, I'll meet with you after I have a chance to notify the police. In the meantime, absolutely *no one* can enter the Study!"

Spotting Edna Butz behind the others, Alex made her way over to the woman and grabbed hold of her collar.

"Look, Edna, we have an emergency here and we need to contact the police. Where is your so-called 'radio phone,' and who can operate it?" Seeing that Edna didn't move or react, she bawled, "We need to call the police, now!"

Edna's inscrutable expression shifted slightly, her black eyes momentarily losing their hardness until they refocused.

Regaining control, she curled her upper lip and snarled, "So, what's the big emergency? Did somebody lose an earring?"

"Listen, you insensitive clod, a man has been murdered, and his wife and daughters are here, so show a little respect. Now, where is the radio-phone and who operates it? And, you, Mr. Grimm – lock the Study door!"

"Murder! We don't have murders at the Grover Inn," Edna huffed. "You'll be sorry you ever brought this group here – I'll tell you that. Raymond Bean operates the radio at the front desk, usually – or Tina. I would imagine that Mr. Bean is in his cottage now – go out the north end. His is the first one on the left. Lord knows where Tina is."

Alex spun around and headed down the hallway on a dead run as the others looked after her in a state of confusion. Still smiling, Virgil Grimm ambled over to the study door with his key ring, flipping through several keys until he selected one and locked the door.

* * *

ALEX WAS OUT OF BREATH by the time she rang Raymond Bean's bell. The man opened his door, looking startled to find her standing there, panting and holding her side.

"There's been a murder! At the Inn! In the Study! Conrad Pierce!" she got out in bursts. "We need to call the police. Where's the nearest police station?"

"Conrad Pierce was *murdered*?" Raymond Bean repeated, dumbly. "Uh, there are the county police in St. Annes but, of course, they mostly write out parking tickets. There aren't any police right here on the island," he added, unnecessarily.

"Hurry!" she barked at the stupefied manager. "Let's go!"

A few minutes later, Bean had turned on the black box at the front desk to call the police. At his insistence, Alex had to first take him back to the study where he entered to confirm that there *was* a dead body there before he would call. *It did seem hard to believe,* Alex had to admit. Now, apparently, he had made contact and was on the one-way speaker talking to the police desk clerk in St. Annes.

"Yes, I'm sure he's dead," Bean was saying. "No, I don't know when it happened. The body was found a few minutes ago, as I understand it. Okay, that's fine."

After hanging up, he turned to Alex. "They'll be here in about forty minutes."

Oh, brother! Alex thought. *There's a murderer running around loose, probably still on the island, and the police response time is forty minutes.*

Alex walked over to the lounge to meet with the group. The Bertholds, Livermore, Nadine, Phyllis, and Rosemary were already there. Lawrence volunteered that the others had gone upstairs to their rooms.

"When I first got to the study, I thought something terrible had happened to Mrs. Kerley," Lawrence said. "She was hysterical. Of course, earlier in the day the horses had run over her, so she was in a highly emotional state. A little while ago I saw her on her way upstairs, still upset. Her husband was with her, so I didn't interfere."

"We will *all* have to recover from this tragedy," Alex advised. "And beyond that, we'll all be treated as suspects in the investigation. And, let's face it – one of us may actually be a murderer."

Phyllis gasped, "Oh, my!"

"Does anyone know when Mr. Pierce was killed?" Nadine asked. "Because if it was between ten this morning and two-thirty this afternoon, we were all on the tram tour."

"That's right!" agreed Johnny. "I think they can pin down the time of death to within a few hours – at least they can on *CSI* – and that could clear all of us at once. Not that I can imagine anyone here could be a murderer, anyway," he added, apologetically, looking around the circle with a wan smile.

"Besides having an opportunity, which one of us has a motive?" Lawrence asked, rhetorically. "Oftentimes, money is the motive for murder, right? All of us here are strangers to him and couldn't inherit anything, so that should eliminate us, as well."

"There are other motives for murder besides money," Rosemary interjected. "People kill when they're enraged by what someone has done or said, or to stop someone from doing something. We all witnessed how mean and unreasonable Mr. Pierce could be. He rejected his own daughter – that sweet Jennifer Brown."

"People murder for revenge," Phyllis offered. "Which would give Jennifer a motive, although I can't imagine her being capable of such a violent act," she added, noting that the others were giving her shocked looks.

"Or even physically able," Amanda said. "We know that Mr. Pierce was stabbed with a knife. Isn't that a *man's* weapon for murder?"

"Jennifer and David were on the tram tour," Johnny reminded everyone. "Only Margaret Pierce and her daughter Chloe stayed at the Inn with Conrad. Wouldn't they be the last ones who saw him alive? We know the family planned to meet with Jennifer and David this morning, but we don't know what happened."

"Well, I don't think they all murdered him," Lawrence Livermore said, matter-of-factly.

"There might be someone else who wanted revenge," Phyllis teased.

"Who?" the others asked in unison.

Phyllis answered, "I saw Conrad Pierce in a compromising position with Ronette at the other end of the porch last night. I know that Wade was somewhere out in the front yard and could easily have seen them together."

"Phyllis," cautioned Rosemary, "I think we should leave the investigation up to the police, and not speculate further. Pretty soon we're not going to trust anyone here."

"That's true," Alex agreed. "We don't know enough to either exonerate or accuse anybody. It could have been a crime of chance that had nothing to do with Mr. Pierce, personally. He might have come upon an intruder stealing something valuable from the Inn. Anyway, the police will thoroughly investigate.

"In the meantime," she went on. "To protect everyone's interests, I think we should all stay here in the main lounge until the authorities arrive. I'll go upstairs and get the others. It's too bad that all of us will have to come under scrutiny, but that's the reality."

Several minutes later, a visibly shaken Ronette entered the lounge with Wade. Margaret Pierce followed, walking with her head high, tightly holding Chloe's hand. Following them, was Jennifer, dabbing a wadded-up tissue at her reddened eyes, as she held onto David's arm.

As they took seats, sympathies were offered, and expressions were made of how terrible it all was. After that, conversation became guarded. No one wanted to talk about unrelated topics to appear unfeeling; nor did anyone want to discuss details of the murder, that would be seen as being ghoulish or simply crass.

This must be the definitive awkward social situation, Alex mused, *making small talk with people who are suspects in the murder of a man we had dinner with last night. I should have taken that superstition seriously that if thirteen dine together, one will soon die.* Voices from the reception area interrupted her thoughts. Alex said, "It looks like the police have arrived," she said. I'll go check."

Out at the front desk, she found Manager Bean talking to several strangers. As she approached, Bean introduced her as the tour operator who had brought the group to the Grover Inn. *Yeah, like it's all* my *fault,* she thought to herself, defensively.

As Bean introduced her to the others, she had a chance to make an assessment of the team that was there to find out who murdered Conrad Pierce and bring him or her to justice. They didn't look up to the job: Officer Chester Ulmer looked to be about twelve years old – and a little too enthusiastic for her taste; Detective Arlie Tate appeared to be from the "Lieutenant Columbo" school of grooming and wardrobe; though he probably lacked the television character's keen powers of observation; the Medical Examiner, Joseph Bloom, looked the part, with the requisite pale skin and grim countenance of one who worked too many hours under fluorescent lights and looked too often at the face of death.

In considering the two forensic lab employees: Needra Holmes looked efficient and well-prepared, if her close-cropped hair and battered black suitcase were indicators; while Brian Culver had the thick glasses and pocket pen protector one associates with a nerdy scientist.

"Mr. Bean told me that you were on the scene when the body was discovered, is that correct?" Detective Tate asked Alex, breaking into her ruminations.

"Huh? Uh, no, not exactly. I went to the Study when I heard Ronette Kerley scream after *she* discovered the body," Alex corrected, repeating the detective's words, 'the body.' "Her husband, Wade, was in the room, too."

Detective Tate nodded curtly. "All right. I'd like you to go and get Mr. and Mrs. Kerley. They're in the lounge, I presume? Both of them need to come with us when we first view the body. Oh, and you stay close since you were the first one to enter the room after the discovery. I'm sorry about the inconvenience," he added, maybe due to her pained expression.

Inconvenience? Is that what they call it when you have to make a second trip to look at a corpse with a knife stuck in his chest?

Alex left and returned in a minute with the Kerleys and introduced them.

"Right. Mr and Mrs. Kerley, I'd like you to come with us back to the study. Miss Trotter will follow," Detective Tate ordered. "As we enter, just show us how you came upon the deceased, Mrs. Kerley."

"I don't understan' why I gotta go back there. I dint touch the body—it's just where it was when I found it, I'm sure. I don't really wanna see him, agin."

"I realize that, Mrs. Kerley. This will only take a couple of minutes and then you both can go back to the lounge."

Raymond Bean led the group down the hallway, inserted his key in the lock and stepped back, as the door swung open, there was a foul, metallic smell in the air.

"Ugh!" Ronette grunted.

"Is this how the room appeared?" asked the detective without reacting to Ronette or the odor. "Was the light on?"

"No, I had to turn it on," Ronette answered. "No one had searched that room, yet."

"Searched the room?" Tate queried.

"We was playin' a game – you know, *Clue.* Miss Trotter had hidden weapons and cards in all the rooms for us to find, so we could figure out where the murder happened and with what weapon it was done. Oh!" she stopped, putting her hands up to her mouth, and opening her eyes, wide. "That sounds so bad now!"

The detective turned his attention to Alex who stood behind the others. "So, you were in the study earlier and planted the 'clues?'"

"This room didn't have a weapon—well, not one that *I* hid," Alex answered, grimacing. "I only hid a note that read, 'No evidence here of any crime,' which is unfortunately ironic in hindsight, I'll admit. If a player followed the clues, he or she would find the note behind that painting of a sailing ship over there. Let me show you."

"Don't move." Tate snapped. "Dr. Holmes will retrieve it – if it's there."

Miss Holmes walked over to a small oil painting of a schooner on the open sea, and took it down from the wall. Behind the frame was a slip of paper.

"How much did you look around the room before you decided to hide the note behind that picture by the door?" Tate asked in an accusatory tone.

"I didn't look around at all," Alex protested, picking up on the inference. "I had written all of the clues up in my room earlier in the day – they were in rhyme form so it took me a while. Let me think, that one was,

This room is named for what you did in school
Or what you *should* have done.
There's just one card you must obtain –
It's right behind the bounding main.

Tate looked at Alex and blinked once.

"I know it's not Shakespeare," she mumbled, "but it would good enough to lead them to that painting here."

"You remembered *one small painting* in this mansion hotel and where it was?" Tate asked incredulously.

"I had noticed how skillfully the artist had painted the waves. I'm an artist, so I know moving water is difficult to paint. It attracted my attention and appreciation as one who has often struggled representing it."

"And why, with that clue, were you looking over by the sofa, Mrs Kerley?" the detective asked, turning his attention back to Ronette.

"I dint know what the hell a 'bounding main' was. Scuze my French. I just thought, it's a small room so I'll look everywhere."

"All right," Tate said calmly. "We'll get back to your stories when we take everybody's. Just show me how you found the body." He indicated the sofa across the room from where they were standing.

Ronette stood scrunching her forehead in thought.

Wade circled the room and prompted his wife, "You started walkin' around this way, and looked behind everything, Ronette. Remember? I just stood here looking for the words, 'bounding main.'"

Oh, brother, Alex thought, dismally. *We all sound like we're lying. And we're all going to end up in the slammer.*

Ronette started searching the room in the way that Wade had recalled her doing, until she came to the sofa. "I think I sensed something was wrong here – I think I remember maybe a smell or something. Anyway, I just looked over the sofa like this and – Oh, no! It's terrible! He looks even worse!" She jumped back, and turned towards the others. "Then I screamed and Miss Trotter came running in here and that's all I know."

"Okay, thank you," Tate said, crossing over to take a quick look at the corpse. "You all can go back to the lounge. But no one leaves the building for any reason. Mr. Culver will take pictures before we have to disturb the body. Then Dr. Holmes will collect the evidence; and finally, Dr. Bloom will determine the cause of death. I think this one's a no-brainer, Joe," he smirked, looking at the dour Medical Examiner.

Alex, Ronette and Wade gratefully left the study and returned to the lounge, where the others looked up anxiously.

"There's nothing to report," Alex answered the unspoken questions. "They're processing the crime scene and we're to stay where we are. Apparently, Detective Tate wants to speak with all of us, individually."

For the next half hour they sat, nervously flipping through magazines and books, getting up to walk around every few minutes, and staring out in space, lost in their own thoughts. At last, footsteps were heard in the hallway and everyone looked up expectantly as Detective Tate and Officer Ulmer entered the lounge.

Detective Tate cleared his throat. "After an initial inspection of the body, it has been determined that Mr. Conrad Pierce has been dead at least twelve hours. Rigor mortis has already been reversed, leading us to that conclusion.

"Therefore, he was killed before ten o'clock this morning, which means that all of you had the opportunity to commit this crime and should consider yourselves to be 'persons of interest' at this point. I will be interviewing all of you and taking down your accounts of how you spent your day.

"Mrs. Pierce, you're first. I'll talk to you in the front hall. Officer Ulmer will remain here with the rest of you. No one is to leave the room for now. In addition, you're not allowed to talk together about your alibis, before or after your interview; or about any of the events related to this murder.

"Now, Mrs. Pierce, will you come with me?" Chloe turned to stare at her mother with fear in her eyes.

Chapter 19

The First Suspect

AN UNCOMFORTABLE SILENCE followed after the detective left with Margaret during which everyone sneaked a look at Chloe who sat, pale and teary-eyed, wringing her hands.

"My mother didn't do this," she said softly in a monotone, more to herself than to the others.

"Miss Campbell, I wouldn't say anything about the murder if I was you," Officer Ulmer advised.

"I know that my mother didn't do this," Chloe said, again, more emphatically, ignoring the advice.

"Miss Campbell, Detective Tate is talking to your mother first because she was the one who was closest to your stepfather. He'll be talking to everyone to ask them about their whereabouts around the time that Mr. Pierce was killed. No one has assumed that your mother did it."

After several minutes of taking notes on Margaret's movements during the morning, Tate put down his pen and notebook and stared at his subject with narrowed eyes.

"Let's not beat around the bush, Mrs. Pierce," he drawled. "You killed your husband. Why don't you save us all a lot of time and trouble and just confess?"

"Because I *didn't* kill my husband. I'll admit that I *felt* like killing him many times when he drank and acted stupid, but I didn't kill him! I could never have done something like that."

"You just told me there was a heated argument this morning with his daughter whom he fathered out of wedlock – Jennifer Brown. In my experience, a wife who finds out about a husband's bastard child can become enraged and seek revenge."

"That wasn't the way it was. I *wanted* Conrad to have a relationship with Jennifer. She wasn't trying to cause trouble for Conrad, or our family, or ask for money, if that's what you're thinking. She has a professional career and lives with a fine young man. She just wanted to make some connection with her biological parent. *I* was the one who wrote her that we would all be here on this island."

"So, you set your husband up for this confrontation, knowing that he would become furious when he saw his daughter?"

"No, of course not. I had just mentioned it in a note along with other news of the family. It didn't occur to me that she would come here."

"How would you describe your marriage? You said, even just now, that you often felt like killing him."

"I shouldn't have said that – it's just an expression. I didn't mean it, literally. I will admit that we hadn't been getting along for quite a while. He was drinking too much, too often, and he was becoming more disagreeable and angrier. I really didn't know what was wrong with him. I was hoping that this little vacation in a quiet place would calm him down, and put us all back on track."

"When was the last time you saw him?

"I told you that we had the meeting in the study and he left in a huff. That was the last time I saw him. It was about ten o'clock." "Seems to me that he didn't leave," Tate drawled. "Seems as though he was stopped by a knife in his chest," he added, raising one eyebrow, accusingly.

"Not while we were there!" Margaret Pierce exclaimed. "We all saw him leave –Jennifer, David, and Chloe were there, too. You can ask them."

"Don't worry; I will. So, how did you spend the rest of the day? What did you think when you didn't see your husband where you expected to see him? And why didn't you try to find him?"

"After our meeting in the study, Chloe and I picked up lunch boxes in the kitchen to take to the beach. We decided to go on a long walk along the water and we stopped at some point and ate. I think we came back to the Inn at about two o'clock and went directly up to our suite. We were hot and tired, so we just stayed there relaxing and reading until it was time to dress for cocktails and dinner.

"When we came downstairs, Miss Trotter asked me where Conrad was, and that was the first time I heard that he hadn't been seen by anyone all day; but I still wasn't too concerned. He could have gone across to St. Annes, or just gone off by himself on the island. He was very angry with all of us."

"If it wasn't you, who do you think killed your husband?"

"I can't imagine who could have possibly done something so terrible. Conrad had made a big scene in front of everyone when he first saw Jennifer, so I don't think anyone here liked him, particularly. But why would anyone want to kill him? It's ridiculous."

"What about Chloe? What kind of a stepfather was he to your daughter?"

Margaret paled and looked away. She swallowed hard before she answered. "Uh, he wasn't ideal – sometimes he was too strict with her; that kind of thing." Pausing for a moment, she turned back toward the detective. “Why? What are you getting at?” Her smooth forehead had become creased.

“I just asked what kind of stepfather he was,” the detective replied calmly. “It’s a pretty common question in a situation like this, don’t you think? What are you getting so upset about?”

“Well, you’re asking it like Chloe might have had some reason to kill him.”

“Is that how you see it? It's interesting that you jumped to that conclusion. I'll be asking Chloe about her relationship and if she had any reasons to kill him.”

“She didn't have any, and I didn't imply that she did.”

“Let's talk about something else,” Tate said, reasonably. “What about Chloe's own father. Was he involved in her life?”

“Her father and I divorced when Chloe was eight. Richard died four or five years ago from a heart attack. He was a driven man—a business consultant who traveled a lot in his work, so he hadn’t been around much for Chloe as she was growing up.

“She’s turned out to be a beautiful person, in spite of everything, and I’m very proud of her. She’s getting married at the end of summer to a wonderful young man from a good family.”

“Did Conrad approve?”

“He had some reservations—only because she’s so young. But it didn’t matter. It wasn’t up to him. Chloe didn’t need his approval.”

“Were his ‘reservations’ upsetting to Chloe?” Tate asked, evenly.

“No, I’m sure she didn’t take his reaction too much to heart. She had support from me and from her future in-laws. Conrad would have had to go along with what we decided. He had agreed to this family vacation knowing that we would be going over wedding plans. Actually, he was being quite reasonable until Jennifer surprised us all by appearing here on the island, as I said before."

Closing her eyes, she blew out a long breath. "I can't believe somebody actually killed him."

"Okay, Mrs. Pierce. I'm sure it must be quite a shock. Let's leave it at that for now. Don't discuss your answers with your daughter, or anyone else. And, of course, you're not to leave the island at this time."

Margaret walked stiffly back to the lounge, as the detective scribbled notes in his notebook, before he picked up his page to type in a message.

Officer Ulmer answered the buzz and read the message. "Chloe Campbell? Please go to the front hall to speak with Detective Tate."

Chapter 20

The Second Suspect

CHLOE CAMPBELL CAME in hesitantly, looking around for a place to sit. Detective Tate gestured towards the sofa. Once she was settled, he asked her a series of questions concerning general information about her history, taking down her responses without comment and keeping his eyes on his notebook. After he had written a couple of pages, he paused to look up and study her before he spoke. “I understand that you were quite young when your mother married Conrad Pierce, is that right?" He lowered his head, but continuing to look at her as he wrote.

“Yes, I think I was twelve,” Chloe responded, uncertainly, frowning.

“Just becoming a young woman, then,” Detective Tate continued, studying the ceiling for a long moment before he returned his gaze to her.

Chloe's face reddened and her eyes hardened. "You could say that," she responded in clipped tones as her hands gripped the chair seat.

"Was it hard to have a strange man in the house?" he asked, raising his eyebrows.

"Yes, er, no! What do you mean by *strange*?" she sputtered.

"I mean . . . maybe you didn't know him well; or he got between you and your mother; or he acted *strangely,* even *inappropriately;* he might have *abused* you. Am I getting warm?"

"I don't know what you're talking about. 'Inappropriately?'" she queried, in dismay.

"What I'm talking about is that your mother let slip that your stepfather molested you and that you naturally hated him because of it."

"No, that's not true. She wouldn't have said that."

"Yes, she did; or as much as admitted it, after I saw it on her face. She seemed to be shook up about it. Did you just tell her about the abuse since you've been here on the island? If that's so, it must have really set her off."

"No, it didn't. I mean, I didn't. Oh, all right, yes, I told her this morning that Conrad had come into my room late at night a few times when I was younger; only when he had been drinking. He'd stroke my hair and tell me how pretty I was. Maybe try to kiss me on my face. He never raped me, although I hated it when he slobbered all over me like that in a drunken state. I was in constant fear every night when I went to bed that he would come in later. I remember having trouble falling to sleep, and then, having nightmares when I finally did get to sleep.

"I only told my mother because I had blurted out to Jennifer that she had been lucky not to have grown up with him in the same house as I had, and that he had done bad things to me.

"When I explained why I said what I did when we were walking on the beach, she seemed shocked and swore that she hadn't known. How could she *not* have known? I had asked permission to lock my room at night, but she had told me 'no,' that it wouldn't have been 'safe.' Did she think I was afraid of *imaginary* monsters?"
Chloe put down her head and wept softly. Looking up again she said,
"And, yes, she was very angry. But she didn't *kill* him, if that's what you mean."

"How do you know?"

"Because we were together leaving the study, and we spent the rest of the day together. There was no time when she was out of my sight."

"It's pretty convenient, that you're each other's alibis, isn't it?" the detective asked, sarcastically. "You know, when I look at all of you who had opportunity, there aren't many of you who had any *motive*. You and your mother had good reasons to hate the man. Hatred can lead to murder. Jennifer Brown had reason to hate the guy, too, but not as much as you and your mother. Do you see where I'm going here?"

"You're not intimidating me, if that's what you're trying to do, Detective. Yes, I suppose I did hate my stepfather at times. He could be nice, too, but his behavior when I was young had turned me against him. On the other hand, I'm not a killer, and neither is my mother. And that's all you need to know."

"Okay, Miss Campbell. I think we've reached a certain understanding. But don't think I'm through with you—or your mother. I'll be back in touch. You can go, now. That's all for tonight. Tate punched in a number on his pager. "Send back Jennifer Brown" appeared on his screen.

Chapter 21

The Third Suspect

AFTER TAKING DOWN JENNIFER BROWN'S answers to rudimentary questions, Detective Tate wearily studied his subject. “Miss Brown, I can’t for the life of me figure out *why* you came here to the island. You had already shown up on Conrad Pierce's doorstep once and he sent you away. You don’t strike me as being mentally unbalanced, and yet, you decided to do the same thing a second time, expecting a different result. Isn’t that one definition of insanity?

“You see what I’m getting at here? It looks to me like you planned something else besides a verbal confrontation. Something more than you had done before.”

“Now wait a minute, Detective Tate. Yes, I certainly *can* see what you’re getting at. And you’re right about one thing – that I am quite sane, so why would I kill my stepfather after everyone here witnessed his colossal rejection of me? Wouldn’t I realize that I’d be the number one suspect?

"And, if I'm not crazy, at least I'd have to benefit from his death to kill him. I'm certainly not in his will, and I assure you, I'm a successful woman who has a good life. I wouldn't risk all that for some kind of momentary violent act of retribution. I came here on an impulse that I immediately regretted after I first saw my father in the bar lounge when he had a fit. I had thought the setting here on the island would be right for a reconciliation as it's a nice quiet place. I didn't show the best judgment, but I'm not a murderer. I've never even raised a hand to anyone.

"And don't forget that I was with David and others all morning: breakfast first, then our meeting with Conrad, and then on the tram tour around the island. You said my father was murdered sometime in the morning. That would have been before we left on the tour, or shortly afterwards.

"I don't want to point suspicion at anyone else but, in our meeting in the study this morning, Chloe implied my father molested her as a child. David and I then quickly left her and her mother alone, at Margaret's request. We didn't see them again until the cocktail hour. And I never saw my father again.

"To tell you the truth, I was so shocked and disturbed by all that was said in the meeting, I just wanted to get away from *all* of them for a while. And I was glad for the distraction of the tram tour. When David and I came down for cocktails, I hadn't heard that my father had gone missing."

Tate had listened to her recitation leaning back with his arms folded. "I'm of a mind to believe you, Miss Brown—at least until I get the forensic report."

"Thanks—I think," Jennifer retorted uncertainly. "Anyway, I know I have nothing to worry about."

"Yeah, well we'll see about that. Do me a favor. When you get back to the lounge, tell Officer Ulmer I'd like to see Ronette Kerley next."

Chapter 22

The Fourth Suspect

OFFICER CHESTER ULMER called out, “Ronette Kerley!” Hearing her name, Ronette jumped up and stood teetering uncertainly on her high heels for a moment until Wade gave her a push from behind.

“I’m goin', I’m goin', but I don’t know nothin’!” she complained out loud before she wriggled her way out of the room and started down the hallway.

“Mrs. Kerley, sit over here,” Detective Tate directed when she arrived in the front lounge, pointing to a straight-back chair near his.

Sitting down, she crossed her legs at the knees, causing her tight skirt to hike up to mid-thigh.

The policeman proceeded to take down her personal information for the first few minutes, receiving straightforward responses. Furrowing his brow, he paused and steepled his fingers. Looking levelly at his subject, he leaned forward. “Mrs.

Kerley, just why is it that you have been so upset over the death of Mr. Pierce?"

Ronette put a hand over one breast. "I found the body, and I never seen nobody stabbed to death before, that's why."

Tate raised an eyebrow. "I think it might be more personal. How well did you know the deceased? Did you have a relationship with him?"

"You can't call it no relationship. All right—you'll probably hear it from Wade, anyways. Everybody was so critical of Mr. Pierce cuz he didn't admit that Jennifer Brown was his daughter, and I thought, that's none of their business, and ---."

"Your relationship . . ." Tate broke in to bring her back to the subject.

"Well, I jest felt sorry for him, so when he asked me to go out to the porch with him for a ciggie, I went, and I was the only one. I guess the others dint smoke or somethin'. He brought me out a drink, which I thought was real nice, but I think he put somethin' into it, cuz I got all rubbery and couldn't move proper. Before I knew it, he was all over me, and took advantage of me" She sat forward and locked eyes with the detective. "We had sex."

"Did you feel like you were raped? That would have made you very angry," suggested Tate.

Ronette pulled at a loose strand of hair. "I kinda enjoyed it, but it made my husband mad. I dint know it, but he was out there spyin' on me and let me have it later, upstairs. Then when we went on the tram tour, I was almost killed by wild horses what got spooked by somethin' unnatural. I thought I was cursed for what I had done.

Ronette leaned over, getting more into her story."And then, when Mr. Pierce was murdered, I *knew* there was a curse on both of us. The horses meant to kill me, but I was just lucky. Next time, I'm going to get kilt, like Mr. Pierce." Ronette put her head down, sobbing noisily, and wiped her eyes with her hands. The detective nudged her with a box of tissues. "So, you were upset about Mr. Pierce's death because you thought there was some supernatural force at work to seek revenge on both of you for having extramarital sex?"

Ronette looked up, mascara smeared around her eyes giving her a raccoon-like appearance. "That's it. You speak real nice. That's what I thought. Specially since I was the one to find the body. That made it pretty clear to me that it was a message jest for me. Why else was I the one who found him dead? I was the worst player of the game."

"Did you tell your husband that you thought Mr. Pierce had spiked your drink with something that impaired your judgment and, maybe, your ability to resist?"

"If that means that I wasn't thinkin' straight, of course I did. I wasn't gonna take all the blame for myself, was I?"

"What did he say to that? Did he agree that it was Mr. Pierce's fault you had sex?"

"I wouldn't say that. He seemed to blame it all on me. He didn't kill Mr. Pierce, if that's what you're getting' at. I know Wade. He mighta beat him up pretty good if he got the chance, but he wouldna killed him."

Tate nodded slowly, maintaining eye contact. "Okay, Mrs. Kerley, if you say so. That's it for now. Thank you for your responses. Please don't discuss your answers with anyone else, including your husband."

Ronette dabbed at her eyes with a wadded-up tissue as she stood up. Sniffling a couple of times, she jutted out her lower lip before she turned around and started back down the hallway taking small, hobbled steps in her tight skirt.

Chapter 23

The Fifth Suspect

COMING INTO THE LOUNGE, Detective Tate called out, "Wade Kerley!"

"Yessir!" Wade answered, getting up onto his feet.

"Come with me."

After they were both seated in the front hall, Tate propped an elbow on the side table and rested his chin on his fist. "Let's cut to the chase, Mr. Kerley. I know you witnessed your wife and the murder victim having sex on the porch last night. Do you deny it?"

Wade fidgeted a moment."No, I don't deny it. Maybe Ronette would like to, but why would I? I figured that guy for a douche bag right off, and I was right."

"That must have made you mad enough to kill him or *her*," the detective observed, encouragingly.

"Yeah, I went apeshit with Ronette – just enough to make my point. She knows where I come down on that crap. I ain't standin' for no screwing around. She's gettin' another chance cuz she's a good down-ass bitch and ain't usually such a hobag."

"You sound pretty tough. You must have been really mad at Conrad Pierce, then – taking advantage of your woman as he did."

"Ronette tried to finger him for the whole deal, but I wasn't buyin' it. I know how much she likes a good banging. She's got one of those libidos, ya know what I mean? It don't take much to get her goin'.

"Besides, I never seen that Conrad guy again. He weren't on the tram tour that Ronette and I went on to get some culture. Maybe if I'd seen 'im,, I woulda given him what for."

"Where were you between the hours of eight and ten this morning?" Tate asked, changing the subject.

"Ronnie and I went down for breakfast at eight or so. They had cheesy grits and sausages I'm partial to. We wasn't talkin' much. I was still honked off, and she was real quiet for a change. Someone was there talkin' about the wild horses, so I thought that sounded like fun, and told Ronette we was goin'. I mean, little did I know. . ." He shook his head regretably.

"Anyways, we went back up to our room. Ronnie told me she dint wanna go on the tour, that she'd rather go swimmin', but I told her it might be her only chance to see the horses, so she said she'd go on the damn fool tour. I dint want to spend the whole week with us mad at each other. Y'know what I mean? So, we went down and got on the tram. Neither one of us coulda imagined what would happen. I'm jes' glad Ronette made it out alive, with the horses runnin' over her like that."

The detective nodded. "Were you with your wife the whole morning, Mr. Kerley?"

"Yeah, sure. We had breakfast, like I said, then we went upstairs, then down to meet the tram. She can tell you same as me."

Tate flipped his notebook closed "Okay. Thanks for answering my questions. Don't go anywhere and don't discuss your testimony with anyone. That's all.

Wade ambled back down the hallway as Tate's pager buzzed. *They're done processing the crime scene,* was on the screen. Walking out to the lounge, the detective addressed the group, "We are discontinuing the questioning at this time; but all of you are to continue to observe the cautions I gave you earlier, and no one is to leave the island. Right now, you may return to your rooms. It's late, and I'm sure you'd like to get some sleep. I'll be back in the morning," he added, ominously.

Monday, April 15

Chapter 24

The Morning after the Murder

THE NEXT MORNING Alex noted, derisively, that the day was bright and sunny, which totally belied the reality of her world. Not only had someone on her tour been stabbed to death, but she was one of the suspects in the murder investigation.

As she thought about it, she couldn't understand why Detective Tate couldn't just eliminate all those who were on the tram tour and relieve their misery, as Lawrence Livermore had suggested.

No one stabbed Conrad Pierce and then got on the tram for a leisurely drive around the island without blood on their clothes, or even a hair out of place, she argued to herself. She had seen everyone up close, and no one looked like they had recently violently attacked and killed someone. *Of course, Ronette and Phyllis didn't fare too well later on the tour, but that was another story.*

But, if the people on the tour could be crossed off the list, that would leave only Margaret Pierce and Chloe Campbell unaccounted for. Both women are petite, refined and intelligent, and that doesn't match up with the profile of a killer or someone even physically capable of such an act. How could either one of them commit such a vicious crime? What evidence did the lab people find at the scene, and would we learn whatever it was?

All of these thoughts and questions were swirling around in her brain as she descended the stairs for breakfast. Reaching the main floor, she saw the perpetually-hysterical Tina Wrenn at the front desk waving her over. *Oh, great! All I need now is that woman's paranoia. I should ask her why she hadn't checked up on Conrad Pierce more often to see if he was "all right" like she said she always does.*

Aloud she said, "Good morning, Tina. I know you must have heard about the tragedy."

"Oh, I did hear. I did. I can't tell you how terrible I feel. I'm glad I was off last night but, at the same time, I wish I had been here to comfort Mrs. Pierce and her daughter, and Jennifer Brown. The police don't think one of them could have done it, do they?" Her eyes were big as saucers.

"I don't know," Alex answered, truthfully. "I don't think we should speculate about anyone. I just know it wasn't me."

"Oh, I know it couldn't be you," Tina said, with feeling. "I want to tell you something, but . . ." Turning her head, her eyes searched the area, but found no one in sight. Still glancing around nervously, she cupped her hands and whispered to Alex, "You should be careful. Be sure you're never alone."

"Yeah, well, I suppose that's reasonable advice until we know the identity of the killer and what the motive was," Alex said, playing along, but slowly backing away. "Listen, you take care, too. I'll see you later."

Walking towards the dining room, she thought, *that woman is a bundle of nerves or is just plain crazy. Of course, the last couple of times I've seen her, two people have narrowly escaped death in bizarre accidents, and someone else was murdered – but still . . . even Ronette seems more reasonable with her theory of being cursed.*

In the dining room, Alex nodded to Raymond Bean who was having a cup of coffee, and Ronette and Wade, who were eating breakfast. Phyllis motioned her over to take the empty seat at the table she was sharing with Rosemary.

"We've decided to carry on as normal," Phyllis announced after Alex had sat down.

"Well, not *quite*," Rosemary corrected her. "We will cooperate with the police, of course, but we're not going to just sit up in our rooms stewing, either."

"That's right," Phyllis agreed. "Rosemary and the kids are going on a hike when they're cleared to leave the hotel, and I'm meeting with Lawrence to discuss my financial situation. He is so brilliant when he talks about investments, and we all know how handsome and charming he is. He says he wants to *maximize my assets*." She batted her eyes suggestively and struck a pose. "This could mean a lot to my stepchildren, as well," she added, in response to Rosemary's look of chagrin.

Edna Butz rumbled up to the table and held out a menu for Alex, who offered it to the other women to look at first.

"No, go ahead; we've ordered," Rosemary responded to the gesture.

"Okay," Alex murmured in thought. "Let's see. Waffles with fresh blueberries are today's special." Looking up at Edna, she said, "I'd like those with bacon – crisp – and coffee with cream. Thanks." Edna grunted and trudged off.

Alex shrugged. "I think she's upset that I brought a "murderer" to the Inn. I can't worry about that. Right now, I'm just looking forward to homemade waffles. Could be the only bright spot in my day."

As if in response to her prediction, Detective Tate walked into the dining room, his unshaven face further darkened with a scowl. "Miss Trotter, I want to talk to you next," he said, gruffly.

"But she just ordered her breakfast," Phyllis whined.

"Oh, no. Really?!" mocked the detective. "I didn't know that. On the other hand, this must be her lucky day, because I see Raymond Bean over there, whom I need to see first. So, go ahead, ladies, enjoy yourselves. I wouldn't want to deny you having your scrambled eggs just so I could hunt down a murderer."

Alex couldn't help but smile at the sarcasm.

Without further comment, the detective pulled out the vacant chair at the manager's table and sat down. After he dug out a small notebook from his worn leather satchel, he dropped the bag on the floor and picked up a ballpoint pen. "This won't take long, Mr. Bean. I just need some information about the hotel. Like who owns the place, for openers."

"The owner? Well, the owner is Barrington Hall the Third, from Palm Beach. Er, is it necessary for you to contact Mr. Hall? He's given me the full responsibility of running the hotel so that he only needs to visit once or twice a year. I'm sure he wouldn't want any adverse publicity from this unfortunate episode."

"Yeah, well it does seem to be inconvenient for many people," the detective deadpanned, glancing over at the women's table. "It's such a bother. But, yes, I'd like his contact information. Also, if it wouldn't be too much trouble, I'd like the names of all the employees, their positions, and dates of employment. Are there any new hires, or have you had any special problems with anyone on your staff?"

"Oh, no. Everyone has been here for several years, and there have never been any real problems – just the occasional tardiness or a rare inattention to duty. I guess Tina Wrenn, at the front desk, is the newest employee, but she's been here for over two years. No, once somebody gets a job here, they don't leave. It's a very special place to work."

"I can see that," murmured Detective Tate, watching Edna Butz lumber by with a tray of food resting on her hip

“Well, all right, we'll let that go. Since I have to wait until everyone has had their leisurely breakfast, why don’t I go with you to look at the employee records so I can get that done with. I’ll want to talk to all of them, by the way. I understand that everyone lives right here on the property – in those cottages I’ve seen on the grounds.”

* * *

AN HOUR LATER, Alex found herself facing a stony Detective Tate in the front hall, his preferred “interrogation room.” Instinctively, she straightened up in her chair, assuming both a serious posture and attitude.

“So, you didn’t know any of these people before you arranged this trip? You didn’t know that Jennifer Brown was Conrad Pierce’s illegitimate daughter?” the detective asked, incredulously.

“No, of course not. They all responded to my advertising independently. The surnames are different – there was no way to know of the relationship.”

“But you saw right away that Conrad Pierce was going to create problems and probably ruin your group’s stay at the Inn, isn’t that right?”

“Detective, there’s always someone in a tour group who is controversial or disruptive. This is the first time that one of them was murdered.”

“Are you being glib, Miss Trotter?”

“What? No, I’m sorry. I’m truly shocked that anyone I knew, much less someone in one of my travel groups, was murdered. If I had any helpful insights, I’d tell you. I’d like to say that no one who was on the tram tour that left the Inn at ten o’clock had blood on them, or was disheveled. Couldn’t all those people be eliminated as suspects?”

“And that group conveniently includes you, right? Maybe you’ve heard of murderers who disposed of clothing, or criminals who wore gloves in committing a crime. Why don't you just tell me what your movements were yesterday morning."

Alex looked off in space for a moment. "Let's see, I ate breakfast at eight-thirty with several others from the group. Then I had only enough time to go upstairs to grab a couple things for the tram. I went downstairs and met with Mr. Bean who was driving us. He left to get the lunches for everyone, and I stayed with the group to make sure they all boarded.

"After we came back, at about two o'clock, I went to the Billiards room and found the "Clue" game box and went upstairs to make up rhymes for people to find the weapons and the other cards that you know about. I went down to hide them about an hour before cocktails, and after I was finished I joined the others in the bar lounge. You know the rest."

"Yeah, I know that you were in the room with the dead body with a knife in his chest and you didn't notice. Good thing *you're* not a detective."

She ignored the insult. "We've been over that. Why ever would I kill Conrad Pierce?"

"How about because he had become a 'problem'?"

Alex pulled back her shoulders. "How about asking someone who's a 'problem' to leave, rather than murdering them?" she countered.

"Had you asked him to leave?"

"No. I told him that he'd have to improve his behavior, but that I wanted him to stay. He agreed and offered a sort of apology to the group for his outburst."

"So, you never noticed that anyone outside of the family had a grudge against him?"

"I didn't see much of him after that. But I can't believe that a stranger would have strong feelings about him on the basis of his being loud and rude during the cocktail hour. Of course, I can't believe that any one of the family members could have committed this murder, either."

"Like I said before," Tate said with a sly smile, "It's a good thing you're not the detective – because *somebody* did it. And as far as I'm concerned, *anyone* here could have done it, and that includes you."

Chapter 25

Interrogating the Rest

AT THREE O'CLOCK IN THE AFTERNOON, an exhausted Arlie Tate leaned heavily back against his chair in the front hall as he waited for his next subject to report for an interview. So far that day, he had questioned Alex Trotter, Amanda and Johnny Berthold, David Albright, Nadine Rodgers, Rosemary Davis and Phyllis Hanover. Reluctantly, he was starting to think that Alex Trotter might be right; that none of these people was even capable of stabbing someone to death. And the fact that Conrad Pierce was a stranger made it all the more unlikely. Thinking back over his interviews, he had decided that this was about the most woefully inadequate bunch of suspects he had ever come across.

If he wasn't mistaken, the last one, Phyllis Hanover, had actually *flirted* with him. Asking him if he was married? That he looked like he needed to go out and have a little fun? What kind of a suspect acts like that with a detective interviewing her as a suspect in a murder investigation?

And the others weren't much better. Rosemary Davis was about as upstanding a potential murderer as you could find: a college biology professor who studied turtles. She had never even spoken directly to the victim. And he believed her when she said she considered Pierce's conflicts involved only his family members and didn't concern her.

Nadine Rodgers was a refined, soft-spoken widow in her sixties who wore gold jewelry and had manicured hands that had nary a broken nail. While she appeared to be fit with a trim figure, he thought she was more concerned with her figure than being physically strong.

The Bertholds were young and athletic, but were almost absurdly open and transparent as to be above suspicion. Amanda Berthold practically bent over backwards to implicate herself by saying how much she disliked the late Conrad Pierce for making sexual overtures to her; and for being loud and vulgar, in general.

Johnny Berthold volunteered that Conrad Pierce's lewd remarks to his wife had made him angry, and that he had to control himself from attacking the man right then and there. Either Johnny was conning him by appearing to be naïvely truthful; or he actually was. Tate thought, regrettably, that it was the latter.

His best hope in this group had been David Albright, whose girlfriend Jennifer Brown had been cruelly rejected by the victim who, in all likelihood, was her father. David, at least, had a good reason to hate the deceased. But, unfortunately, the man appeared to be annoyingly reasonable and honest. He said he had accompanied Jennifer to the island against his better judgment, fearing that her surprise appearance might provoke Conrad Pierce to become violent towards her, as the man had already slammed his door in her face, making it clear he wanted nothing to do with her.

According to David, he was there solely for protection and hadn't interfered in any way with Jennifer's interactions with her father. He hadn't even directly spoken to Conrad Pierce, he said; and there had been no testimony to the contrary.

Things looked pretty bleak. So far, only Margaret Pierce and Chloe Campbell looked good for the murder, and then only because they had motive and opportunity. Neither one seemed physically able to shove a knife into a resisting middle-aged man who outweighed each of them by at least fifty pounds. Maybe they had done it together, but that was statistically unlikely.

He had one more tour group member to interview before he questioned the employees. While he sat thinking about that, Lawrence Livermore came around the corner.

"Oh, fine, Livermore. Take a seat over there," Tate directed, coming out of his reverie as he pointed to his interrogation chair.

"I have your name and address, sir. Just tell me, what was your purpose in coming on this trip to Bedford Island? You're traveling alone, right?"

"I *am* traveling alone, but I had joined the tour group by way of an invitation from Mrs. Nadine Rodgers, whom I was acquainted with through correspondence."

"And how is it that you were 'acquainted with Mrs. Rodgers through correspondence?' the detective repeated, with exaggerated diction.

Ignoring the snide tone, Livermore answered easily, "Good friends of hers have invested in my hedge fund and recommended me to her as a financial advisor. I'm sure she felt more comfortable meeting me in person before she could decide to invest, herself. As I live in Charleston, it was convenient for me to accept. Also, I needed a vacation and was intrigued by the remoteness and natural beauty of the island, as she described it."

"That all sounds very proper, Livermore. "I would think that all wealthy widows like, say, Phyllis Hanover, would be ripe pickings for you. Am I right?"

"I don't believe I like the insinuation Detective, that somehow I prey on widows of means. It's a simple fact that a certain percentage of qualified investors are women who have survived their successful spouses."

"I'm sure that's true, Livermore; and any woman would find you a very attractive, well-mannered person of means. You're in the general age group of widows and you look like you'd make an ideal suitor. What's the percentage of investors in your group who are widows?"

"I can't say, Detective Tate, but I'm sure it's in the same range as for every other hedge fund manager. Is my fund the subject of your inquiry, Detective?"

"No, not really; although certain things jump out in the course of an investigation. But, let me ask you, what were your movements yesterday morning?"

"I went down for breakfast, early, about eight o'clock or so, and sat with Mrs. Rodgers, the Bertholds, Rosemary Davis and Phyllis Hanover. After breakfast –"

"Had you spent the night with Mrs. Rodgers?" Detective Tate interrupted.

"I'm sorry, Detective, but I'm more discreet than that. I don't 'kiss and tell.'"

"Well, I'm sorry, Livermore, but I'm not discreet. Did you spend the night with Nadine Rodgers?"

"No, Detective, I did *not* spend the night with Mrs. Rodgers."

A glint came into Arlie Tate's eye. "One second, Livermore. Did you spend the night with Phyllis Hanover?"

"Er, yes, as it turned out. We had spent the evening talking together on the front porch, and then we both decided to go upstairs at the same time. I asked the lady into my chamber for a nightcap, and we simply fell asleep from the sedating properties in the liquor. Mrs. Hanover returned to her room early in the morning, and came down to breakfast with her friends."

Lawrence Livermore leaned forward in his chair and spoke in low tones. “I trust this won’t be repeated in any other circles. Mrs. Hanover is a genteel southern lady whose reputation is of great value to her.”

“Oh, I know firsthand what value she places on her reputation, Livermore. Don’t give it another thought. So, after breakfast, you did – what?”

“After breakfast, well, I went upstairs with Mrs. Rodgers, as we had talked about taking the tram tour together. I had just enough time to pick up a few things, and –”

“You went with Nadine Rodgers to her room?”

“Well, yes. Her room is near mine, but faces the front.”

“So, there was about a half hour before you had to be down for the tram. Did you and Mrs. Rodgers have sexual relations, or did you use the time to go downstairs, and maybe meet up with Conrad Pierce? Perhaps you got in an argument –”

“I find this manner and line of questioning to be very objectionable, Detective. I’m forced to besmirch someone else in order to defend myself. Yes, Mrs. Rodgers and I had a brief dalliance before we went downstairs for the tram. Again, I say this as one gentleman to another, in complete confidence.”

“Of course, Livermore. I’d say we’re about equals, as gentlemen go. I think that’ll be all, for now. Thank you for your cooperation.”

Chapter 26

Interviewing the Staff

"UH, EXCUSE ME, DETECTIVE," Raymond Bean apologized timidly, coming into the front hall just far enough to see Arlie Tate. "Are you ready for me? You said for me to be here at three-thirty. I've been waiting around the corner since I was a little early. When I saw Mr. Livermore come out, I thought maybe I could come in."

"Yeah, Bean, that's fine. I'm as ready as I'll ever be. Have a seat."

The detective picked up his notebook and flipped through it. After moving his finger down a page, he looked up. "So, we talked earlier about your employees and went over their records. I can't believe how many years everyone has worked here, and yet the salaries seem to be no higher, or even as high, as you'd see elsewhere for the same positions. You must be a damn good manager, Bean."

Raymond Bean grinned sheepishly, relaxing his face. "Thanks, but I think you'd have to ask the employees if that's the case. As you know, it's a lovely old building and our guests are very appreciative of the amenities we offer, so the work is very rewarding. Of course, I'm an employee, too, so I can speak for myself about that."

Tate stroked his chin. "Yeah, that's all well and good, but I'm thinking that some of your guests aren't all that agreeable and easy to please. From what I hear, Conrad Pierce caused quite a stir in the bar lounge when his long-lost daughter surprised him by showing up. Were you there? In the bar?"

"Yes, I was there but, of course, I don't involve myself in the guests' personal relationships."

Tate raised an eyebrow. "Of course you don't, Bean. I understand that. But it must have been very upsetting to have a guest create a scene like that; since your job depends on everyone having a good time in your hotel."

The manager's face tightened; his mouth became a thin straight line. "Mr. Pierce made an apology to the group for his outburst. I believe that he over-reacted due to the shock of seeing his daughter, who's a stranger to him, and whom he couldn't have expected to see."

Tate nodded and looked down at his notebook. "Okay, that may have been the case. I wasn't there. But, let's move on. Why don't you tell me about your movements yesterday morning at the time when we know Mr. Pierce was murdered?"

The manager leaned forward and placed his hands on his knees. Striking a conversational tone, he began, "Well, as usual, I arrived early at the Inn —about eight o'clock. I went to the dining room for a little breakfast before I left to check on the tram in the garage. I drove over to the pier to put some gas in it and, later, brought it around to the front a little before ten.

"Miss Trotter told me that not everyone was there and asked if we could wait a couple of minutes. I told her that I would go get the lunches and she should get people to board while I was gone. By the time that I got back, everyone was on the tram except for the Pierce family. Jennifer Brown said that she didn't think they would be coming, so we took off."

Detective Tate rubbed his chin. "And there were a couple of freakish accidents during the tram tour that could have turned out very badly, as I understand."

Bean shifted in his chair. "Yes, that's true, but those were both very unusual situations."

"Have there been other such 'unusual situations' that nearly cost the lives of Grover guests?"

"Detective Tate, Bedford Island is a natural habitat for a great number of wildlife, so it's to be expected that there would be the occasional encounters with an animal or reptile where someone could be injured. Nothing has occurred that could be called a tragedy, of course."

"Oh, really? There have been other injuries? I'd like to look into those. After these 'accidents' that occurred yesterday, what happened?"

"Miss Trotter and the others agreed to end the tour early and return to the Inn. We got back about two o'clock. Before I went to my cottage for a rest, Miss Trotter asked me to find some items for the group to play a game in the evening."

"The weapons for the *Clue* game," Tate acknowledged. Raymond nodded. "Where did you find the knife?" Detective Tate followed-up.

"I got it from Chef Kasmarek. I told him why I needed to borrow it for just that evening. I saw the knife that was in the deceased, and it's not the same knife."

"Are the kitchen knives accessible to anyone?"

"They're not locked up, if that's what you mean. But everyone knows you have to ask permission to remove any equipment from the kitchen. The chef is in charge."

"Someone probably wouldn't ask to borrow a knife to stab a guy to death," the detective flatly intoned.

Raymond Bean's round cheeks reddened. "No, sir." He paused. "But I just can't imagine any of my employees being responsible for such a violent act. They're all good people."

"So you say, so you say. But I didn't see much personal history on any of your people in their files."

"Old records have probably been lost over time," Raymond Bean responded, turning up his palms and shrugging.

"Okay, okay," the detective said, resignedly. "Let's call it a day, for now. Thank you for your cooperation. Please keep your responses to yourself. Could you locate Virgil Grimm and send him in?"

Ten minutes later a bent, shadowy figure shuffled into the front hall. "Virgil Grimm, right?" asked the detective, uncertainly.

"That's right, but you got nothin' on me."

"Well, we'll see about that, Grimm. Take a seat. Yeah, that chair. I have just a few questions for you. Do yourself a favor and lose the attitude. I can always find a reason to take somebody in. Know what I mean?" The detective had a cruel smile on his face as he squinted at his subject.

"Now, tell me, Grimm, I've got your personnel file here, with very little information." He held up a thin manila folder as proof. "You've been here nine years—where were you before that?"

"I, uh, worked for the state. I always done janitorial work. It suits me. I can work on my own at night and I don't have to mingle with nobody."

"I take it you don't like people much. You must have been around in the evening when Conrad Pierce and the others were in the downstairs rooms that you clean. What did you think of Mr. Pierce? I understand he wasn't a very likable guy. Is that what you thought?"

"I dint give him much thought one way or the other. I don't pay much attention to the guests. I just pick up their trash. They don't bother me, and I don't bother them. I can tell you, though, Pierce was a big mouth. I wasn't surprised when I heard he'd been knocked off. It's no big loss."

"Did you expect him to be murdered?"

"I'm not sayin' I was *expectin'* him to be killed—just that he insulted most everybody. I wouldn't blame his wife if she did it. He was hittin' on every other woman, even the tour leader, and then he yells at the wife for his daughter showing up."

"I heard about that. What else did you overhear?"

"At dinner, he tole Mr. Livermore that he would investigate his finances, and tole his daughter to shut up about him being her father. After dinner he went outside with the blonde in the red dress."

"You don't seem to have missed much for not 'bothering' with people. Did Livermore seem upset when Pierce told him he'd look into his hedge fund?"

"I dint notice – the two women who are hot for Livermore were talking over each other to make a play for him."

"You're a regular fount of information, Grimm. You don't miss a thing. One more thing. Tell me – where were you yesterday morning between eight and ten o'clock?"

"I was in my room in the basement, sleepin', like I always am at that time. I don't usually get up till noon. I told you, I'm working most of the night. And I'm not squealing on anyone in particular. I'm tellin' you what I saw and let the chips fall where they may."

"Yes, well, I'm sure they will. Thank you for your responses. As I tell everybody, don't share them with anyone else.

"You know where Edna Butz is?" the detective asked. Virgil Grimm nodded. "Good. Let her know I'd like to talk to her now."

A couple of minutes later the waitress came steaming around the corner, her mouth clenched defiantly as each foot landed heavily on the wood floor.

"Miss Butz, please take a seat."

"I don't have too much time, Detective," she snarled.

"Of course. Excuse me for interrupting your break. Now that we've covered the niceties, let's get down to business. Tell me, how do you spend your time when you're not serving meals in the dining room?"

"I have an agreement with the boss that, unless I'm needed to wait tables, my time is my own. As it is, I have to be around here from eight in the morning until about eight o'clock at night."

"I understand, Miss Butz, that you have a long day, but you seem to disappear between meals. Where do you go?"

"I share one of the cottages with a housekeeper – Mrs. McCool. I go back to my room, there, or to the worker's lounge in the basement. Why? What difference does it make where I go?"

"Well, I understand that you were on the scene when the body was discovered. How is it that you were right there when he was found?"

"Now, wait a minute. It's not my fault that those silly women started caterwauling so that a person couldn't have any peace. I just wanted to see what the hell the commotion was all about. I don't know why those people can't behave themselves but, obviously, one of those morons murdered the guy." Edna folded her beefy arms across her distended stomach and stuck out her lower lip defiantly.

"That may be, Miss Butz, that may be. But, where were you after breakfast, for instance? Did you run into Conrad Pierce who was maybe rude or insulted you? Something like that? I know that he was one mean son-of-a bitch. What did he say to you?"

"Oh, no, you don't. Don't try to pin this on me! I dint see that jerk after breakfast. And I wouldna go to prison for messing with some no-goodnik like him. I keep my nose clean and don't put it in nobody else's business. I could tell he was a bad egg, but I hardly seen the man. I think he was there for one dinner and one breakfast."

Tate set down his notebook and sighed. "Okay, fine. Let's just call it a day, Miss Butz. Thank you for answering my questions. Just don't talk about your interview with anyone else, and ask Ms. Wrenn to come into the hall."

Moments later, Tina Wrenn seemed to hop into the room. "Did you want to see me? Is it me you want to see?" she asked, nervously.

"Yeah, Miss Wrenn, just relax. I'm not going to bite you, y'know." The detective checked back in his notebook and scanned a page. "Now, I understand you started working here just over two years ago. Are you happy here?"

"Oh, I'm not thinking of leaving. You didn't hear anything about me wanting to leave, did you? Because, I never said anything about leaving."

"No, Miss Wrenn. I didn't mean to imply that you wanted to leave. I'm aware that every employee here has been in their jobs for quite some time. I expect that you'll follow that pattern. I've heard this is a nice place to work, that your guests are usually appreciative. Isn't that so?"

"Oh, yes, they are. It's terrible if any of them get hurt. I want everyone to stay well while they're here."

"Well, of course you do. Are you saying that many guests get hurt?"

"Oh, no. I didn't say that. I wouldn't say that. I only said that I hope no one gets hurt. That's what I meant, of course. Wasn't it terrible that poor Mr. Pierce was killed?"

"Yes, and that's why I'm here, Miss Wrenn. That's what this is all about. Do you know anything about his murder? Where were you yesterday morning when we know that Mr. Pierce was stabbed to death?"

"I was at the front desk, of course. Where else would I be? I mean, I saw Mr. Pierce and his wife and stepdaughter come downstairs early. Later, they walked in the direction of the library and study. I heard that they were going to meet with Jennifer Brown and David Albright. I always see everybody when they come downstairs because the front desk is right there."

"Did you see Mr. Pierce come out of the study?"

"I did. I saw him go outside onto the porch and then I lost track of him. My attention was diverted when Mr. Bean asked me for the list of people who had signed up for the tram tour and the itinerary that Ms. Trotter had requested. I never saw Mr. Pierce again." Tina bit her lower lip and teared up.

"All right, Miss Wrenn. I really don't want to upset you any further. If you have anything else to tell me, I'll be around, okay?"

"O-k-kay," Tina managed, choking back more tears.

Oh, shit, thought Detective Tate. *Now I'm apologizing to my murder suspects. This place could make anyone go bonkers.*

The rest of the afternoon was taken up with interviewing Chef Kasmarek and the kitchen staff, as well as the housekeepers; all of whom produced no more useful information. No one had seen anything. No one knew anything.

Maybe tomorrow he'd get some more lab results to help him narrow his investigation, Tate thought. At this point, the only ones who looked good for the crime were Margaret Pierce and Chloe Campbell, who both fulfilled the classic criteria, but he wasn't satisfied with either of them. And he certainly wasn't prepared to make an arrest and turn the case over to the District Attorney.

9

Monday night, April 15

Chapter 27

Sharper Than a Serpent's Tooth

A GLUM-FACED GROUP GATHERED in the bar lounge that evening for cocktails. Everyone had come down right at five-thirty, perhaps to be sure they didn't miss anything; or perhaps, so they wouldn't be singled out as being a suspect. Since being interviewed by Detective Tate, the group seemed to have banded together, finding themselves under attack by the legal authorities. As each person entered the room, the others managed a wan smile and nodded in tacit recognition of their shared plight.

As though in blatant disregard to appear innocent, Ronette Kerley was again wearing the tight, low-cut red dress that had attracted the attention of Conrad Pierce, which had led to their later sexual escapade.

"I think Detective Tate has a lot of nerve thinkin' one of us did it," Ronette said with fervor, slamming down her beer on the bar. "Why don't he just lift a fingerprint off the knife and arrest the guy who done it? Probably was one of those campers who was makin' off with a big ole Chinese vases or somethin', and Mr. Pierce caught 'im."

"While I appreciate your sentiments, Mrs. Kerley," Lawrence Livermore responded. "I can't imagine how or why a camper would want to carry a three-foot vase along with his survival supplies. And, as for fingerprints, the police need to match them against others for identification. You can be assured that, if they lifted prints, we'll all have our fingers dipped in ink and rolled onto white cards. Unless they've gone digital and use glass slides."

Before anyone could react to Livermore's knowledge of current forensics, Raymond Bean came in, carrying a large plate of cut-up vegetables and dip. "Here are some crudités to have with your cocktails, everyone; compliments of the chef. By the way, tonight's specials are grilled swordfish with squash, skewered beef with sliced carrots, and battered chicken with smashed potatoes."

After he had left the area, Amanda Berthold frowned in puzzlement. "Is it just me, or has all this talk about murder made even *food* sound violent?' Swordfish?' 'Skewered?' 'Battered?' 'Smashed? ''Sliced?' Seems like murder is on the chef's mind, too. I mean, he couldn't have put something peaceful-sounding on the menu like *cured* ham and *sweet* potatoes? Personally, I can't wait for things get back to normal. Oh, I'm sorry, Mrs. Pierce, Chloe—I didn't mean to sound unsympathetic. I'm not. It's just . . ."

"I understand what you're saying, Amanda," her aunt cut in. "And you're right – it's all any of us can think about; and that won't change until the case is solved, I'm afraid. I wonder how long they can keep us here. Right now, we don't want to leave, anyway, but what happens at the end of our week if they haven't yet made an arrest?"

"I don't believe that they can hold us here without showing good cause," Alex opined with more confidence than her scant legal knowledge justified. "At the worst, they might say we can't leave the country, so that we could be available, if necessary. If they get the lab work back soon, the evidence should certainly exclude us."

"Well, this isn't much of a cocktail party," Phyllis Hanover chimed in, holding up her glass of wine. "Let's lighten up a little. I can't believe that any one of us is guilty, either, so let's not worry about that. We should try to relax and enjoy the few days that we have left in this lovely old hotel on this beautiful island."

Putting her hand on Livermore's arm in a proprietary manner, she said, "Speaking for myself, I had a wonderful afternoon talking to this delightful man about financial strategies that would give me peace of mind so I could live comfortably for the rest of my life. The plan would heal my relationship with my stepchildren, as well. Those of you who are in a position to invest a substantial amount should talk to him about what he can do for you."

Nadine Rodgers came around to the financier's other side. "I've already done that," she said in a tight voice, putting her hand firmly on his other arm. "In fact, Lawrence and I have talked about a lot of things over the last several months, haven't we, Lawrence?" She smiled up at the man who seemed flushed under his tan.

Alex weighed her options on how to diplomatically diffuse the situation. *What happened to that warm and fuzzy feeling of being fellow murder suspects?* she wondered.

Noticing that Raymond Bean had come back with Virgil Grimm, she held back from saying anything. Virgil started picking up discarded cocktail napkins, as the manager walked over to remove the relishes platter that held only a few diced vegetables appearing to have drowned in water that remained after the ice melted.

"If you're finished with this tray, I'll take it out of your way," Bean announced to the group in a rhyming couplet.

After he left for the kitchen, Alex tried to rekindle the group's camaraderie. "Uh, before we go in for dinner, I want to thank all of you for being so resilient in carrying on and making the best of things in the face of the tragedy that's affected all of us to some degree. I agree with Phyllis and Ronette. It's unimaginable that one of us is guilty of this treacherous act, and I commend all of you for cooperating with Detective Tate to help him find out who is responsible."

She gestured toward the dining room. "They should be ready for us for dinner. Sit at any table you like. You're free to do whatever you want after dinner. I think most of us have lost our interest in island history for the time being; but if anyone would like to know about previous inhabitants and events on the island, I'll be in the library after dinner."

* * *

THE CANDLELIT MEAL was consumed without much interest or conversation, with most leaving right afterwards and going off in different directions.

Lawrence and Nadine, who had sat by themselves, had a second cup of coffee before they leisurely made their way over to the staircase. As they started up the steps, Lawrence pulled Nadine close and murmured, "And, now for some dessert, my dear." In response, Nadine nuzzled against him, putting her arm around him.

Upstairs, they passed a housekeeper in the hallway coming out of Nadine's room after she had turned down the bed. As the couple arrived at the door, Lawrence bent over and gave Nadine a kiss on the forehead. "I'm sorry I won't be able to stay with you, you know – after," he murmured. "A couple of the others asked to meet me outside and give them a broad overview of what I can do for them. Phyllis said she has a couple of questions, too."

"Oh, Lawrence, I'm so disappointed," Nadine said, as she closed the door behind them.

Some time later, Lawrence emerged from Nadine's room, pausing for a moment after he closed the door, smiled to himself and drew in a deep breath. Making his way down the hallway, he brushed off his clothing, smoothed back his hair and squirted breath freshener in his mouth as he retraced his steps back to the staircase.

Downstairs, he strode purposefully out to the front porch and looked around. Spotting Phyllis in her bright floral caftan sitting alone on one of the wicker sofas, he went over to join her.

With his arm tightly around the delighted woman, he kissed her deeply for several seconds, probing in her mouth with his tongue. Releasing her, Phyllis was all smiles as she purred, "Oh, Lawrence, I knew that you'd be here as soon as you could and not let me down. You're such a fine Southern gentleman to insist on being company for Nadine and helping her out with her finances, too."

Lawrence looked down modestly. "Oh, it's what anyone would do in the same circumstances. Of course, it's just business, but it does take time. As I've explained to you, Nadine asked me to join her on this trip, so I need to be attentive to her. I'm glad you understand, my dear. You're the beautiful, sexy lady who has won my heart." He kissed her again on the mouth, and then on her neck.

"Uh, Lawrence, I think we'd better go upstairs with this, don't you?" Phyllis gasped.

"Let's just walk around a little, first," he cooed. "The moon is bright enough tonight to see our way along the paths. I hope that's all right with you. I've just been sitting for too long."

An hour later, he and Phyllis were walking up the steps of the Inn to the porch. Giving her a little squeeze, he asked, "Are you ready to go upstairs, now, my dear?"

"If I can make it. I'm just about out of breath with all the walking, Lawrence. I may have to go right to sleep," she said, coyly.

"I don't think you'll be able to go to sleep," Lawrence teased, taking her arm and opening the front door for her.

Walking up the flight of stairs up to the second floor, they headed down to his room. Once inside, he turned on a lamp and scanned the room, a puzzled look on his face. "That's strange. The housekeeper didn't turn down the bed. I suppose that means we don't have any chocolates, either," he teased, clucking Phyllis under her chin. "Why don't you just pull down the covers, and maybe pull down something else to get comfortable, while I take out these cufflinks and get out of this starched shirt. We'll get by without the chocolates." He raised his eyebrows, suggestively.

As he busied himself at the dresser, Phyllis stepped out of her dress and laid it carefully over a chair. Going over to the bed, she pulled back the covers and prepared to slide in onto the cool sheets when she stopped and stood frozen; unable to move or react. As her eyes widened in comprehension, her mouth flew open to emit a high, ear-piercing scream. Dropping the bedspread, she ran to a corner of the room.

At her scream, Lawrence had jumped, causing his cufflinks to go flying. Spinning around, his eyes went first to the bed, but seeing nothing there, he looked over at Phyllis, cowering on the floor, stabbing her finger toward the bed.

"My God, woman. What's the matter?"

"A snake! A huge snake! There, on the sheets! I just pulled back the cover and its head came out. Go look. But be careful – he's coiled, ready to strike with huge fangs. Go look. You'll see what I'm talking about."

There was a loud banging at the door and people were heard out in the hallway. "What's going on in there? What's the problem?

"Open the door! Do you need help?"

Wild-eyed, Lawrence stared first at the door, then at Phyllis, then back at the door, seemingly unable to decide what to do.

Phyllis, shaking in fear, looked pleadingly at him. "Let them in! For the love of God, let them in!"

Lawrence went to the door and opened it a crack, just far enough to recognize Alex and Rosemary in their bathrobes, looking anxious.

"There's some kind of viper in the bed," he explained to the startled pair. "Call the maintenance man, Miss Trotter."

Alex quickly patted her pockets to confirm what she already knew; that she didn't have the pager. "Oh, darn," she grumbled as she took off down the hallway. Getting to the open stairway, she cupped her hands over her mouth and yelled, "Mr. Grimm! Mr. Grimm!"

Just as she started down the steps to try to find him, he magically appeared at the bottom of the staircase, looking up at her. "Whaddya want? You know what time it is?"

"It's an emergency! We need you upstairs, now. There's a snake in Mr. Livermore's bed."

Grimm responded by climbing the stairs at a rate of speed previously thought impossible for him. Within seconds, he had arrived at the top.

"Follow me!" was all Alex said, as she started back down the south end of the corridor with the janitor trailing behind, sweeping the walls. Arriving at the last room, Rosemary remained in the hallway.

As Rosemary stood back, Grimm pushed the door open for the three of them to enter en masse. Across the room, a whimpering Phyllis Hanover was backed into a corner with her arms wrapped around herself in a futile effort to cover her revealing lingerie; while Lawrence Livermore stood near the bed holding a desk chair out in front of himself like a lion-tamer.

Exposed on the bed sheet lay a coiled, six-foot long snake with red, yellow, and black bandings. The creature's jaws were stretched open wide, displaying curved fangs that were dripping venom onto the pillow.

"That's an Eastern coral," Grimm said, matter-of-factly. "See the yellow stripes? Like they say, 'Red and yellow, kill a fellow. Red and black, friend of Jack,' so you know it from a scarlet king snake. This here one's deadly," he added, unnecessarily.

"Oh, my God!" Lawrence uttered, in disgust. "Just get him out of here. Can you do that?"

"What's going on here?" It was a woman's voice coming from outside the room. Without anyone responding, the door swung open to reveal Nadine Rodgers who, without invitation, charged in, her chenille bathrobe flapping open with her long strides. Once inside, she stopped and gaped at the scene in apparent confusion. After a moment, she gasped, "Oh, my God!" her face clearing with understanding.

She turned and slowly retreated from the room, as Lawrence called after her, "Nadine, wait –" but he didn't finish his statement or follow her. Looking defeated, he sat down on his desk chair and put his head in his hands.

Tuesday morning, April 16

Chapter 28

Another Mystery

THE NEXT MORNING, Alex sat up in bed in a cold sweat, feeling panicky. Had she been awakened by a noise? Had some other terrible thing happened? Coming to her senses, she thought she was probably just reliving the drama of last night.

What else can go wrong? I'm almost afraid to go downstairs, but I have to make sure that Lawrence Livermore reports the incident to Detective Tate. That snake didn't slither there on its own. The word "slither" made her shudder. *Who would put a snake in the man's bed?* The answer seemed obvious – *a 'snake in the bed?' C'mon! It would have been the perfect revenge for Nadine Rodgers. But Nadine had seemed as shocked as anyone else to see the snake. If Nadine had left it there, she couldn't have been so genuinely taken aback and repulsed by what she saw. Unless, it was only the sight of Phyllis in her slip that had surprised her.*

Dressing, Alex kept mulling over the possibilities of who could have tried to harm Lawrence Livermore. This second murderous act seemed to contradict the theory that Conrad Pierce had come upon a thief who had stabbed him. Alex had to accept the likelihood that someone in her group was a psychopath who was responsible for both incidents. And since she was responsible for everyone's welfare, she thought she'd better do a little sleuthing herself to help out Arlie Tate; not that he was incapable. She had to admit that he had impressed her with his intelligence and savvy. But he couldn't be everywhere. She had many more opportunities to observe her own people; and she couldn't overlook the staff, either. They certainly were an odd bunch, at the very least, and one of them could be a killer.

* * *

LATER, WHEN SHE WENT DOWN for breakfast, she noted that the tour members were sitting as far apart as the table locations and room size allowed. Apparently, the unity they seemed to feel the night before had deteriorated, or even changed into suspicion of one another. Most likely, they had heard about the attempt made on Lawrence Livermore's life.

Alex observed that the latest victim of malfeasance was sitting alone. Perhaps the others now feared associating with him. Phyllis, looking pale, was sitting with Rosemary. Margaret and Chloe were sharing a distant table, as were Jennifer and David. The Kerleys were sitting across the room at a table for four. Nadine and the Bertholds hadn't come down yet.

Alex took advantage of the opportunity to talk privately with Lawrence, and make a statement that she was accepting the man, despite the fact that someone else had wanted to see him dead.

After ordering, Alex leaned in close to her tablemate to speak softly. "Mr. Livermore, I really don't want to get involved with your personal affairs." She reddened at her unintentional double entendre. “But you *must* tell Detective Tate that someone hid a poisonous snake in your bed. You could have been *killed* if you had been bitten badly enough. Whoever left that coral snake there is guilty of attempted murder,” she asserted, feeling no compunction about making legal pronouncements without any knowledge of the subject.

Before responding, the financier touched his napkin to his lips and cleared his throat. “I’m sure that’s good advice, Miss Trotter. To be honest, I’d like to forget the whole business as it’s embarrassing, to say the least. Also, I don’t want to implicate someone who might have felt justified to seek retribution for, uh, certain indiscretions on my part.”

“I know that you're talking about Nadine,” Alex said, “and she's the other reason I wanted to talk to you. I don’t think Nadine had anything to do with this. I was there when she walked into your room last night and, believe me, that woman was really shocked—and not just to see Phyllis there in her underwear. I think she was shocked to see the snake. In fact, if she were the responsible party, she wouldn’t have been at all surprised to see Phyllis *or* the snake.”

He let out a deep sigh. “I hope you’re right about that. Nadine’s a fine woman. I hate to think that I could have caused her do something vicious like that. If you're confident that Nadine had nothing to do with this, I will talk to the detective. Whoever brought in the snake might be the same scoundrel who stabbed poor old Pierce – and that certainly wasn’t Nadine.”

To Alex’s mind, the appellation, ‘poor old Pierce’ seemed as inaccurate as it was insincere. The memory of the odious man must have become radically revised due to his violent end to explain the softened description.

Just then Detective Tate appeared, and the already subdued group became silent as everyone put down their silverware and coffee cups and looked expectantly at the man.

Pausing to look around, the casually-dressed policeman sauntered over to the most distant corner table. “Mrs. Pierce,

Miss Campbell, I'd like you to come with me, please," he intoned loudly enough for everyone to hear.

The two women looked blankly at each other, until Margaret, turning back to the detective asked, tremulously, "Does Chloe have to come, too?"

"Yes, ma'am. That's why I said, 'Miss Campbell,'" he responded dryly.

Only after the three of them had left the room did anyone resume talking; and then, it was in whispers as speculations ran wild regarding what had just happened.

* * *

MINUTES LATER, out in the front hall, Margaret and Chloe were sitting close together on the sofa, holding hands, as they nervously eyed the detective, waiting for him to speak. They didn't have to wait long.

"I'll come right to the point," Detective Tate said without preamble. "I'll need hair samples from each of you to match against hairs found on the clothes of the vic – uh, Mr. Pierce."

Margaret uttered a breathy "Oh," and squeezed her daughter's hand.

"Now before you get all bent out of shape," the detective drawled. "It wouldn't be incriminating if one or both of you would have transferred a strand of hair onto his clothing. In fact, think of it as excluding you, if we can match your hair to our samples. You've already admitted that you were with the deceased in the morning.

"I'm actually hoping that you *aren't* a match so we can get somewhere with this investigation. I will tell you that both strands on the clothes appeared to be blond, however."

"What about fingerprints?" Margaret asked hopefully.

"Unfortunately, there were no prints. No surprise. That's like the one thing every perp makes sure not to leave behind.

"Needra Holmes from the lab is waiting for you in the study, so you can go back now. It'll take just a couple of minutes and then you're free to go about your business. I don't have anything else right now."

With that dismissal, mother and daughter stood up and started down the hallway as instructed. After they had disappeared from view, Lawrence Livermore came around the corner.

"Detective Tate?"

"Livermore. What's on your mind?" the detective asked, neutrally.

"I thought you should know that someone came into my room last night when I wasn't there, and left a poisonous snake, a coral snake; as I understand it, in my bed linens. If I hadn't seen it before I got into bed, I could have been fatally bitten."

"You, or someone who was with you," drawled Arlie Tate. "I presume you weren't alone last night, were you, Livermore?"

"I don't appreciate your characterization that I'm some kind of Lothario, Detective, but yes, Mrs. Hanover happened to be there. But she wasn't the intended victim. No one could have known that Phyllis would have been there with me."

"No one except your alternate bed mate," deadpanned the policeman.

"It wasn't Nadine Rodgers, if that's what you're implying. Miss Trotter was there and can tell you —"

"Miss Trotter was there, too?" the detective interrupted, his eyebrows raised.

Lawrence sighed loudly in frustration. "She and Rosemary Davis responded to Phyllis' screams," he explained with exaggerated patience in his voice. "Miss Trotter told me this morning that Nadine was completely shocked when she arrived on the scene. Besides, Nadine is a refined woman who would never resort to such a crude scheme, nor could she have been able to find and transport a poisonous snake, for heaven's sake."

"That's the first thing you've said I can agree with, Livermore. Not by herself, anyway. So, who has a key to your room? Or was it broken into?"

"No, there was no apparent damage to the lock and door," Lawrence responded. "As for access – the cleaning staff, management, security – I don't know who all. I can tell you that either the chambermaid left the snake, or it was left after she had been there, because the bedding wasn't turned down as it should have been with a chocolate left on the pillow. I had seen her on her rounds at nine o'clock, but I didn't I enter my room until after ten thirty."

Tate made a jotting in his notebook before looking up. "Have you honked off someone besides Mrs. Rodgers while you've been here?"

"I don't 'honk people off,' Detective. I've made every effort to be congenial with the others. I never even had words with Conrad Pierce, like most of the others had," Livermore sniffed. "My thought was that the attempt to kill me may be the work of the same person who murdered Pierce; some fiend among us who's just plain evil."

"Yeah, well, that may make for a good movie plot," Tate said with a smirk, "but I'm still partial to things like motive and opportunity, not to mention evidence. Unless I see someone sticking pins into a stuffed doll, I'll continue with my usual investigation, which right now includes Nadine Rodgers, who you seem to think is a paragon of virtue. Take my word for it; no one is."

Out in the reception area, Tina Wrenn watched intently as Nadine was coming down the stairs with Alex.

"Mrs. Rodgers!" the receptionist called out excitedly as they neared her desk. "I have a letter here for you," Tina waved a long white business envelope in the air as proof.

Nadine's eyes widened as she read the return address, while Alex stood by. Turning away, Nadine ripped open the envelope and pulled out a single folded sheet of paper. Moving over to sit on a bench against the wall, she quickly scanned the paragraphs, her face creased in concentration. Hearing footsteps, she refolded the paper on her lap and looked up to see Detective Tate peering down at her.

"Mrs. Rodgers? Would you come with me? I have a few questions for you."

Nadine appeared to lose her usual composure as she scrunched the letter into the pocket of her slacks and shakily stood up. "O-o-kay, Detective. Sure. Of course," she added with more certainty, squaring her shoulders and taking a deep breath.

After they had disappeared down the hallway, Tina looked over at Alex who had been making a show of flipping through some travel brochures in the hanging rack by the reception desk.

"Psst! Miss Trotter. That letter for Mrs. Rodgers? It was from the Federal Bureau of Investigation. That's the FBI. I can't believe that nice, respectable Mrs. Rodgers is being investigated as a spy or a terrorist or whatever."

"Watch what you're saying, Tina," Alex cautioned, looking around to see if they were being overheard. Then, lowering her voice she said, "First of all, spies would most likely be investigated by the *CIA* – and people being investigated by either agency would hardly receive a letter to notify them. But it is very curious that the FBI would contact her, especially sending it to a vacation address. I noticed it hadn't been forwarded. Whatever it was about, couldn't it have waited?

"Let's just keep this to ourselves, Tina. We don't know anything about the contents of the letter. There could be a perfectly innocent explanation – like someone in Mrs. Rodgers' family has been missing and the Bureau just learned something important about that person's whereabouts.

"Besides, there are other *known* crimes we have to worry about, like who killed Conrad Pierce, and who put a poisonous snake in Mr. Livermore's bed?"

Tina reeled backwards until she fell against the desk. "A snake?"

"Yes, Tina; an Eastern coral snake, according to Virgil Grimm." Alex made a show of rolling her eyes. "Anyway, last night, Mr. Livermore walked into his room and found it under the bedspread, coiled and ready to strike. Evidently, someone got a key to his room, snuck in and left it there to bite him, which might have killed the man. Do you know who could have done such a thing? It could be someone who works here."

Tina looked stricken as she slowly shook her head. "N-n-o! Of course not. Why would someone who works here do such a terrible thing?"

"I don't know. I was hoping *you* could tell *me*," Alex countered. "You've worked with these people for years. Anything like this ever happen before?"

"Like this? A poisonous snake left in a guest's bed? Another guest stabbed to death? No, of course not. How could you even think that?"

"All right, Tina, calm down. Somebody here did these things, so I think we can all forego being shocked about violence at the Inn from this point on; nor should anyone take offense at being questioned about attacks on the guests."

Just then Nadine came back into view as she scurried along the hallway from the front room, breathing hard; her face showing an excited flush.

"Tina!" Nadine called out as she approached. "I need transportation right away to get to the dock to catch the next public ferry to town!" She held up her watch as if in confirmation of the nearness to departure time. "Can someone drive me, or can I rent a bicycle or car or something? I need to get over to St. Annes as soon as possible!"

Chapter 29

Tina on the Hot Seat

"GEE, I WONDER what *that* was all about?" Tina asked Alex as they watched Nadine hurry off to meet Raymond Bean for a ride to the main dock.

Alex pursed her lips, "Well, gee, if I had to guess, I'd say it had something to do with the letter from the FBI. I don't think people need to catch the next ferry for emergency souvenir shopping."

Tina ignored the sarcasm, lost in thought. "If she hadn't been so insistent, I would have told her that Mr. Bean was planning on taking everyone on the tram tomorrow morning to the ferry, if they'd like to go to St. Annes, or on a tour of the south end of the island to visit some ruins and the wetlands."

"I think I'll take a pass on the ruins and wildlife in the wetlands. I've seen enough of the dead and the deadly," Alex said, dryly. "Shopping could be a mood lifter, though. Does Detective Tate know that people will be leaving the island?"

"I know he asked Manager Bean about the schedule of activities and he didn't say they couldn't," Tina answered. "I mean, he can't expect people to just sit around waiting to be arrested," she said, defensively.

"No, not everyone, but *one* person should be getting ready," Alex countered. "Listen, Tina, I'd like some information from you. I've been thinking that, since I'm the one who brought this group here, I need to do what I can to help Arlie Tate. And I think you know something that you're not telling – something that could be helpful in getting to the bottom of these attacks."

Tina shrank back and looked down at the floor. "I don't know what you're talking about," she murmured.

"Don't worry. I don't think that *you* had anything to do with these terrible acts, but ever since I got here you've acted jittery – as though you're afraid of someone. Are you?"

"What could there be to fear in a lovely old inn like this?" Tina challenged.

"That's not an answer. That's another question. I'm talking about some of the employees who seem a little odd. Virgil Grimm, for instance. Why is he always sneaking around in the background and suddenly appearing when something bad happens? He was right there when Conrad Pierce's body was found. And he was at the bottom of the stairs when the snake was found in Lawrence Livermore's bed and knew just what kind of snake it was. You know, he never can be found when you need him. What do you know about him? Where did he come from?"

"I know that he worked for the state," Tina replied.

"Yeah – so does the governor. Can you be any more specific?"

"You'd have to ask *him*. I have my own job to worry about. I can tell you that he has a room down in the basement – near the furnace." She paused before continuing to speak in a whisper. "He's not there much after two o'clock." She looked up at the ceiling. "I'm just saying ..."

"I think it's what you're *not* saying that's *most* interesting," Alex said under her breath. "Okay, Tina, I'll check out Virgil Grimm, if I can. What about Edna Butz? Why does she have such a chip on her shoulder? She seems to hate her job and yet she's been here for umpteen years. Do you know what's keeping her here?"

"Jobs aren't that easy to come by for everyone," Tina replied, tersely.

"I can appreciate that. But she's a *waitress,* not a steel factory worker," for Pete's sake. Tina looked blank. "Oh, never mind," Alex huffed. "I just mean that waitress jobs are plentiful and easy to come by, I would think. Where did she last work?"

"I'm not sure," Tina said, vaguely. "I think she knew Mrs. McCool before she came here – she's the housekeeper she shares a cottage with. Her name was Edna Mae Henderson back then."

"She changed her name from Henderson to Butz?"

"Back to Butz. Butz is her maiden name. That's all I know."

"That's very strange," Alex mused. "And I suppose that Virgil Grimm used to be Virgil Smiley."

"I don't think so," Tina said, soberly.

"It's a wonder that Raymond Bean can put up with this crew," Alex said, shaking her head. "What's *his* story, by the way? Why do you think he's been here for so long? Surely, he could find another job in hotel management. He must be a genius to hold everything together here with so many difficult personalities."

"His mother is in a nursing home in St. Annes called Whispering Pines. It faces the ocean just north of town."

"Sounds pretty nice. So, he's here because his mother is nearby? Why couldn't he just move his mother, if he found work elsewhere?"

"Mrs. Bean is in a very special home," Tina answered. "It's beautiful. You should go see it when you're in St. Annes, tomorrow. You can easily walk there from town. His mother's name is Lucie."

"Well, I don't think I want to spend my time in town visiting an old people's home," Alex said, dismissively.

"No, really, *you should go and see Lucie*," Tina said, sharply. "She would love to have another visitor besides her son; although he's there at least twice a week.

"You'll have to excuse me now, Alex," Tina said, suddenly, picking up a sheaf of papers she always seemed to have on hand to rifle through. "I need to get back to work. I think I've given you enough information to check out. Don't forget everything that I told you – except that you never heard it from me," Tina added, slowly, with emphasis.

"Of course not. I'm not sure what you *did* tell me, but I'll do my best with what I have. I'm going to start checking out the basement, right?" Alex asked in an exaggerated burlesque style.

"Yeah. And you could take this with you," Tina mimicked the dramatic delivery as she pressed a small hard piece of metal in the tour director's hand. Alex uncurled her fingers and looked down at the snaggle-toothed bronze pass key glimmering in her palm.

Tuesday afternoon, April 16

Chapter 30

Virgil Grimm

BY THREE O'CLOCK that afternoon, Alex had made her way down the back stairs to the basement and was standing just outside the employees' break room.

Seeing a light inside the lounge, she had flattened herself against a wall and was inching along until she could peer through the crack of the half-open door, taking care that she wouldn't be seen. At the opposite corner of the room, she recognized one of the young housekeepers who was curled up in a large easy chair reading a book. Judging by the girl's concentration, the story was holding her attention; but was she alone in the room?

Alex stood still and waited, holding her breath to listen. There was no sound, except when the girl slipped her finger under a page and turned it, pressing it in place. After a couple page- turnings, Alex decided that she could risk walking past the open doorway on the other side of the hallway. Stepping across, she counted to herself – *one, two, three* – before tiptoeing past the room, without turning her head to look in. Once she got well past the doorway, she leaned back against the wall to take a moment to calm herself.

What was she doing creeping around the basement? What if she were to be seen by someone? Why hadn't she worked out a cover story if that happened? Getting hold of herself, she thought, calmly, there shouldn't be anyone else down there. Upstairs, she had observed Virgil Grimm slouching his way toward the kitchen before she headed down. Obviously, he was on his way to get his lunch, which would occupy him for at least half an hour; and after that it was his custom to stay upstairs, according to Tina.

At any rate, Alex was committed, and now she had to complete her mission. *And what was that?* she asked herself. She couldn't be definitive, but she felt that once she got into Virgil's room she could discover more about the man who was so mysterious. Maybe she would find some actual *evidence* that he had been involved with the criminal acts, like a canvas pouch that naturalists use to transport snakes. Not that that would prove anything, she had to admit. But, whatever, there must be something there that would either add to her suspicions about him, or would calm her fears. Detective Tate had no apparent cause to enter Virgil's room legally, so she could be helpful to him by acting as a spy; or so she had convinced herself, to justify her trespassing.

Just clarifying her mission to herself gave her courage to keep moving, despite the deepening gloom of the space. Making it around the next corner, she came into an open storage area. It was a low-ceiling room only lit with dull yellow light from a few bare bulbs in the ceiling. *What was their wattage, anyway – fifteen?* Squinting, she could just make out the stacks of dusty boxes she'd have to walk around as she looked for some kind of pathway through the area.

Stopping to blink to improve her vision, the sudden knocking of a pipe made her jump backwards and her heart leap into her throat. She had a flashback to – what? Oh, yes -- every horror film she had ever seen. In particular, the scene where the foolish young woman goes down into the dark basement while everyone in the theater waits breathlessly for the maniac to jump out to slash her with a knife. Alex thought she must be playing both roles; the savvy audience that knew enough to be scared, and the naive girl who shouldn't have been tempting fate. At least, unlike the typical movie victim, she wasn't half-naked and barefooted, she thought, wryly.

She had to hold onto a rough wooden ladder so she wouldn't fall over, realizing that the scary noise had made her legs go rubbery and her mouth become dry. Weren't these bodily signals that she should choose the option of flight? But, as she looked ahead, she was heartened to see just a few feet away the rectangular shape of a doorway. *That must be Virgil Grimm's room,* she thought.

As she crept towards the door, she could make out a hand painted sign on it that read: FURNACE ROOM. *Okay. That was all right.* She had to be close, according to Tina Wrenn, (who wasn't exactly a reliable source, was she?) *Stop it.* She had asked the nervous desk clerk to reveal confidential secrets about the other members of the staff. Alex had to trust her now.

Sidling past the furnace room, she found herself in another hallway with only one ceiling light. *Where were the windows in this place?* Maybe that's why Virgil was always brushing against walls – he was used to walking through near-darkness all the time.

Taking a few more cautious steps, Alex came to a warped, peeling door. Standing there holding her breath, she was suddenly too scared to try the knob. Arguing with herself about the insanity of sneaking into some stranger's room, and then reminding herself of why she was there, she put her hand on the handle; but it didn't turn. Raising a trembling fist, she knocked twice. No response. Of course – no one was there. She knew that.

Okay. It's now or never, she told herself. She reached into her pocket and pulled out the key, stabbing it at the lock, but the key just jumped around in her fingers without finding an entrance. *Calm down!* she reminded herself. Gently, now, she rested the tip of the key into the old-fashioned lock and inserted it straight in. Feeling it grab, she turned it first to the right – no – and then to the left – yes. The flimsy door swung inwards, beckoning her into the darkness of the world of Virgil Grimm.

Now her mouth was full of cotton. She couldn't even make enough saliva to swallow. Didn't matter. She needed to find a light switch, or a lamp, to turn on, to see whatever was there. Then she could make a hasty retreat back to the safety of the first floor. *Why hadn't she brought a flashlight with her?* Shaking her head in disgust, she decided that she must be the worst spy in the history of the world.

Stumbling in the darkness, she walked into a pole – no, not just a pole. Her hands felt it and found something else -- stretched fabric over a wire shape. *A lampshade*. It was a floor lamp. Hallelujah! Feeling further up the shaft, she found the small knob of the switch and turned it to the right.

Looking around in the pool of light, she was able to see most of the room. No surprise that it appeared to be very bleak, lacking in both color and personal effects. Not that she had expected stylish décor. She smiled to herself imagining Virgil with something real cheerful, like white-washed Country French furniture with yellow and blue cushions.

Instead, this space looked like a sepia-toned photograph. Everything was brownish – an old sofa, a scarred coffee table and, across from those, a book case and a cabinet that held a vintage TV and VCR player. At one end of the room was a lumpy-looking unmade single bed, and at the other end of the room were an old school desk and a file cabinet.

The latter was where Alex decided to begin her search, as there appeared to be nothing else of interest in the room. Checking her watch, she saw that it was almost 3:30. She had to hurry – just in case Virgil decided to come down after his lunch.

Opening the top drawer of the file cabinet, she read the tabs off a few manila folders in the hanging files – ADDRESSES, MANUALS, MEDICAL BILLS, UTILITIES." Nothing there.

She pulled open the second drawer and found that it didn't have any hanging files; only piles of 8" by 10" photographs. Dozens of them. All black and white, it appeared. Grabbing a handful, she carried them over to the floor lamp to look at them. Holding a few up to the light she gasped in shock and staggered backwards, collapsing on the sofa.

Tears stung her eyes as she shook her head in denial. Forcing herself to look again, she sat there with her mouth open staring at pornographic photos of children; both girls and boys, from preschool through the teenaged years. Some were pictured by themselves in suggestive poses, while others were in pairs or more, engaged in make-believe sexual acts with each other and with adults.

Alex felt the bile rise in her throat as she flipped through a few more of them to convince herself of the scope of depravity of the collection. After glancing at a couple of dozen, she couldn't bear to look at any more. Grabbing a few out of the pile, she tucked them down her front, inside her blouse. She had to get out of that room and get some air.

Standing on shaky legs, she glanced again at the VCR machine which had, by then, taken on a malevolent look. She knew better than to think that it was used for playing rented box-office hits. No, this was a vehicle for a perverted pedophile to bring his subjects to life.

Lurching over to the small book case, she dropped down on her knees to inspect what she had at first assumed to be paperbacks. She saw now that they were all videotape cases. Picking up a couple of them, she saw crudely-printed titles on the covers: *Lolita Bares All, Babes in Boyland,* and '*Little' Debbie Does Dallas.*

Slipping the *Babes* tape in her shirt behind the photos, she replaced the others back in the bookcase. Then, making her way over to the file cabinet, she put back the photos in the second file drawer where she had found them. As she quickly shuffled through them, she couldn't discern that they were kept in any order; no grouping by ages or sexual positions, *God help me that I'm looking for categories in kiddie porn,* she thought.

As soon as she could compose herself, she slowly backed up to check for any evidence of her visit. Startled by seeing the pass key that she had left sitting on the coffee table, she grabbed it up and nervously looked around again, before she turned off the floor lamp.

Recalling the direction and steps to the doorway, she managed to feel her way back in the darkness with more confidence than when she came in. Getting to the door, she grasped the handle and turned it. Stumbling outside into the hallway, she pivoted and expertly reinserted the key in the lock, turning it to the right. *Click.* She had made it.

Moving back down the hallway, her legs now carried her seemingly without effort. Thinking through her escape, she recalled her route to reverse it: Turn at the furnace room, walk through the storage room past all the boxes to get to another hallway, and then to the right till you come to the stairs and take them to *freedom*.

She couldn't consider the importance of what she found in Virgil Grimm's room now. She had to stay focused on making a clean getaway. In only seconds she had glided by the furnace room, and then made it to the ladder where she had previously stopped. Making her way past a pile of cartons, she could see the light streaming in from the second hallway that was only thirty feet away. As she stared at the beacon offering her safe passage, a stooped figure crossed in front of the light and came shuffling towards her. She caught a glimpse of a grey uniform, lit from behind. She stopped dead, clutching her chest.

Tuesday afternoon, April 16

Chapter 31

Comparing Notes

"WAS YOU LOOKIN' FER ME, LADY?" the shadowed person asked. Alex turned cold as she recognized the low monotone voice of Virgil Grimm.

"What? Oh, Mr. Grimm. Sorry, but you startled me," Alex squeaked, keeping her arms crossed in front of her. "Uh, yes, I *was* looking for you, as a matter of fact," she repeated his words, stalling to give herself time to think. "Tina, at the front desk, told me that your room was down here in the basement near the furnace room."

"Well, whadidya want?" the handyman sneered, stepping close enough for Alex to smell his sour breath and see a bubble of spittle in the corner of his mouth.

"What did I want?" she asked, dumbly. "I, er, wanted to tell you that my shower had very low water pressure this morning and I wondered if you could do something about it." She smiled weakly hoping that her improvisation would fly.

"Do you know how *old* this here building is?" Virgil Grimm snarled, apparently accepting her complaint as being truthful. "It's over a hundred years old. That's how old some of the pipes are, too," he added. "What did you expect?"

"Yes, well, I see your point," Alex nodded, backing away. "Never mind. I must have been showering when someone else was, anyway. I'll just go back upstairs now." She hunched her shoulders, turned, and started walking away.

"That was the only reason you came down here to my room?" Grimm asked after her, suspiciously.

The hair stood up on the back of her neck. *Was that an accusation? Does he know that I smuggled out some of his porn?* Alex swallowed hard, pulling at her blouse to loosen it before she turned around, again.

"Yes, of course," she responded with more confidence than she felt. "Just my shower. I didn't have anything special to do so I thought I'd pop down here to mention it to you." *Good. Casual and nonchalant.*

"I don' like people coming down to my room. I'll come upstairs when I'm needed. You just have to page me."

"Absolutely," Alex agreed, with more enthusiasm than was warranted. "I'm sorry you feel that I invaded your private space. I won't do that again." Without waiting for another response, she turned on her heel, grabbing at her front to support her contraband, and walked ahead to the hallway where she took the corner and headed for the stairs.

Speeding past the employee's lounge, she didn't even glance inside. Once she got to the stairs, she took them two at a time, energized by adrenaline. Only when she had closed the basement door behind her did she stop and take a breath.

Rounding the first corner, she was relieved to see that Tina Wrenn was sitting at the front desk. When Alex got up to the counter, she leaned over and asked in a breathy voice, "Tina, have you seen Detective Tate?"

"I have, as a matter of fact," the clerk replied, smiling smugly. "I think he's ready to make an arrest."

"No!" Alex cried out, reflexively. "Why do you think that?"

"A few minutes ago he walked by, whistling, and I asked him how things were going. He said, 'Fine. I shouldn't be around here too much longer.'"

"Which way did he go? I need to see him. There's no time to waste."

"He was on his way back to the study to see the lab people. Why did you need to see him in such an all-fired hurry?"

"Don't say anything," Alex cautioned, looking around, "but I just came from Virgil Grimm's room."

"Oh, you went inside?" Tina's eyes had opened wide in surprise.

"Of course I did, as you very well know. Don't play dumb," Alex answered, annoyed. "That man is a pervert who collects child pornography. Were you aware of that?" Tina looked away. "Oh, forget it. I just have to tell Arlie Tate. He needs to arrest that guy."

Just then, footsteps were heard down the hallway, and both women looked up to see the detective coming towards them.

"Detective Tate, I need to talk to you," Alex called out as he approached.

Tate stopped and smirked. "Oh, do you have another observation that will eliminate you and your group as suspects, Miss Trotter?"

Alex screwed up her mouth in frustration. "That's not fair, Detective. I'm just trying to be helpful. As it happens, I *do* have some information that implicates someone who is not on my tour," she added, raising her chin, assertively.

"I must be clairvoyant," Tate said with a smarmy smile. "But, okay, I've got a minute. Let's go over to the reception area. This should be good."

Once there, Alex sat forward on the edge of the sofa, fixing the detective with an intent stare. "I came across some damning evidence," she intoned, solemnly. "Concerning Virgil Grimm. The night maintenance man."

"Oh? Like, that he has served time for lewd and indecent acts with a minor?" Arlie Tate asked, matter-of-factly.

"What? He's an actual child molester? He's an ex-con? You knew?" Alex expelled, in a rush.

"Yes, to all the above. As I told you before, *I'm* the detective and you're the one who didn't notice a dead guy with a knife in his chest in the same room."

"Well, I've made big strides since then, thank you," Alex crowed, trying to recover her composure. Earnestly, she continued,

"How did you know all that about Virgil Grimm? Is he a suspect, then?"

"No, not really. I thought the guy was a little off, and there wasn't much in his file, so I ran his name through 'NCIC,' uh, the National Crime Information Center, and – bingo! – there he was; a former resident of the Graybar Hotel. His employment record included his eight years in the can as being a 'state employee.' He cleaned toilets in the slammer, so he could add that work experience to his resume, I guess."

"What did the guy do to be sent to prison?" Alex asked. "And what's he doing working here?" she added, indignantly.

"He was fingered as a 'chomo,' a child molester, when he worked as a custodian in the public school system – which must have been a 'toy store' for him. He was arrested after he flashed a couple of teenagers with his 'meat thermometer,' and the girls went running to their teacher. Apparently, when the police investigated, they dug up other allegations of 'inappropriate touching' and discovered his collection of kiddie porn, too, so they put him away. He's been working here since he got sprung a few years back.

"Raymond Bean finally admitted that he knew the guy came here outta prison. Bean explained that there are very few children who come to the island, as there's so little for them to do, so he thought there wouldn't be a problem. I have to say that I agree with him. Someone should give the little perv a break. Better than having him on welfare, courtesy of the taxpayers."

"Well, he still possesses child porn and that's a crime," Alex asserted, triumphantly.

"Yeah, it's a crime, but I've got bigger fish to fry right now, and I don't even want to *know* how you came to find out about his collection," Tate said, as a warning. "By the way, I never noticed how 'flat-chested' you are," he smirked, looking pointedly at the boxy shape in her shirt front.

"Fine. We'll leave it at that," Alex responded, crossing both arms in front of herself, causing the photos to make a crinkling sound. "I just hope that you checked out Edna Mae Henderson while you were at it," she added, not willing to give up too much ground. "Who?" Tate frowned in confusion.

"Edna Mae Henderson is the real name of Edna Butz – you know, the 'Storm Trooper of the Dining Room.' She might have served time too – for trying to impersonate a human being."

"I did run Edna Butz," Detective Tate mused, not reacting to Alex's wisecrack. "Henderson is her name? That *is* odd. Yeah, I think I'll do that. Maybe we have our own prison rehab facility here."

"By the way, Detective, what did Tina mean by saying that she thought you were close to an arrest?"

"Oh, I suppose she thought that because I *said* that, more or less. The only DNA evidence on the body of Conrad Pierce was his wife's. I'll admit I'm not sold on her as the perp, but that's what I've got."

"Margaret Pierce didn't kill her husband any more than *I* did," Alex complained.

“Yeah? Well, you’re not cleared yet, either, sister; so I wouldn’t be so generous handing out the ‘get-out-of-jail-free’ cards if I were you.”

Tuesday evening, April 16

Chapter 32

An Accusation

UPSTAIRS, ALEX GRIMACED as she extracted the stolen pornography from under her shirt. Being careful to not even glimpse the tape and photos, she held them upside down as she pulled open a dresser drawer and stuffed them under some clothes. *It's not safe to throw them away here,* she reasoned. She had almost been caught with them twice now – once by Virgil Grimm and once by Detective Tate.

She shuddered when she thought back to her encounter with the janitor in the basement. Her lame excuse for prowling around in the darkness – *'My water pressure is low'* – came back to her, making her groan. *Good thing for me the guy isn't too bright. That's what they say about criminals. They usually get caught because they're not smart.*

Flopping down on the bed, she stretched out to think about where things stood in her efforts to assist Arlie Tate, not that he appreciated her efforts. The detective didn't see Virgil Grimm as being a likely suspect, even with his criminal past. If

Virgil didn't stab Conrad Pierce, and she had to admit there was no apparent motive, then who did? The only people with a *possible* motive still were Margaret Pierce, Chloe Campbell, and Jennifer Brown. Alex couldn't believe it was any one of them; or any woman, for that matter. It struck her as being a man's mode of killing, requiring a man's strength.

And it had to be somebody who was staying or working at the Grover Inn. Okay. That narrowed it down to just a few. She had been right that there was something wrong with Virgil Grimm. She thought back to her conversation with Tina and the other "clues" the desk clerk had given her. She'd just have to visit Lucie Bean in the nursing home tomorrow. There must be some reason Tina wanted her to meet the woman.

* * *

WHEN SHE GOT OFF the bed to go downstairs for cocktails, she decided she would just go as she was. The wrinkles would fall out. Or not. At any rate, there was no need to dress up. She was better off in her slacks and low-heeled shoes, anyway, in case she needed to make a quick get-away. Thinking of the hotel's rules for "dressing for dinner," she thought of how the phrase had taken on a new meaning lately. *By the end of the week I'll probably be wearing a bullet-proof vest and running shoes,* she thought to herself.

Catching her image in the dresser mirror, she noted that her hair had frizzed up more than usual; probably from the damp basement. Pushing it behind her ears as a quick-fix, she shrugged at the minimal improvement.

At five-thirty, she warily made her way downstairs to the bar area, checking behind her and to the left and right for anything suspicious. She was almost disappointed to realize there was no one around.

Walking into the lounge, she waved at the Bertholds and Rosemary who were talking at one of the tables. *Where was Phyllis?* she wondered.

Ronette and Wade Kerley were standing at the bar when Alex walked up to place her order with Tim Williams. "Not tonight, Ronette," she heard Wade say to his wife as Alex waited to get Tim's attention. "I feel the same way you do – I just wanna get it over with. I don't look forward to it any mor'n you do."

Alex turned aside, not wanting to appear to be listening, but not moving away so that she still could hear what was being said. *What were they talking about? Sex? I thought they were such a lustful pair.* Ronette was again wearing her tight red dress, and Wade had on his saggy plaid sport coat. *These two sure didn't bring many clothes with them.* A tap on her shoulder made her jump. She spun around to find Margaret and Chloe standing there.

"Sorry if I startled you," Margaret apologized. "I just wanted to say hello and let you know that we were here. You seemed to be lost in thought."

"Everyone seems to be uncomfortable around us nowadays," Chloe lamented.

"Oh, no, I'm just a little jumpy right now," Alex said, waving off Chloe's valid observation. "How are you both? Did you go to the beach today, or what?" Alex asked, trying to avoid the unspoken subject of the two women being suspected of murder.

"We *did* go to the beach," Margaret readily answered. "It was a nice way to get away from everything and relax for a while. So quiet and peaceful. While we were there, it seemed hard to believe that Conrad had been murdered, and that Chloe and I are still under suspicion. Why can't Detective Tate come up with another suspect? We certainly didn't do it – and I'd like to be able to put my husband's remains to rest."

"The usual chardonnay for you ladies?" Tim Williams asked, startling them all. The three women looked confused for a moment before nodding in assent.

"And we'd like two margaritas after you take care of the ladies," a male voice called out. David Albright and Jennifer Brown had come up behind them.

Jennifer wrapped her arms around Margaret and Chloe. "I heard what you just said, Margaret. It makes me so mad that you aren't shown any sympathy for your loss. Just because you were the closest to the murder victim, you're the chief suspects instead of being treated with consideration as the bereft."

Alex looked past the group in time to see Lawrence and Phyllis entering the lounge area. Phyllis' hands were fluttering, making her gold charm bracelet jangle, as she kept up a steady stream of conversation. As the pair approached the bar, they walked past Alex's group. Lawrence leaned over the bar to place their order with Tim.

Hmm, Alex wondered, *where's Nadine?* The last time she had seen her, the woman she had been in a big hurry to get to town.

Tim set down the glasses of chardonnay and the iced margarita glasses on the copper bar and turned back to take care of Lawrence. Alex cradled her chilled glass as the others picked up their drinks and started walking away, saying they were going to find a place to sit down, and that she should come along.

"Thanks. You go ahead. Maybe I'll join you, later," Alex said, distractedly.

Left alone, Alex took a sip of the chilled wine and surveyed the room. Wade and Ronette were seated together in one booth, scowling at each other, but keeping their voices down. *Still in conflict about what would or would not happen that evening?* The Bertholds were laughing at something Rosemary had said. Margaret, Chloe, David and Jennifer had taken places at another table.

Alex took another sip of wine; breathed in slowly and exhaled deeply, enjoying the calm of the moment. *Before the storm?* She looked down the bar at Lawrence and Phyllis, who were touching their glasses together in an apparent toast that Phyllis was making.

As she watched them, Nadine strode past her and stopped in front of the couple, who looked up in surprise. "Lawrence, I'd like to speak to you," Nadine said in icy tones. "And I think you'd like it to be in private." Her back was to Alex but it wasn't hard to imagine the fury on the woman's face, judging by her rigid posture and her hands on her hips.

"Nadine, I wondered where you were!" Livermore ventured, with forced cheerfulness, his lips drawn back into a tight smile. "Sure, I'd love to have a chat. I haven't seen you all day."

"You can drop the debonair act, Mr. Gilbert," Nadine ordered.

'Gilbert?' Alex blinked in surprise. *What's going on here? He's changed his name, too? First, it was Edna Butz who's really Edna Henderson, and now Lawrence Livermore is really Lawrence Gilbert?*

"Gilbert?" Phyllis cried out, turning towards Lawrence for confirmation or denial.

"Uh, yes." Lawrence said, slowly, responding to Phyllis, but looking at Nadine. "You're right, Nadine. We should find a place for a *private* conversation."

"Why'd you change your name, Lawrence?" Phyllis persisted. "I'd like to hear about that. Gilbert is such a nice name. It's much nicer than Livermore."

"Gilbert isn't such a nice name if it attaches you to your criminal past," Nadine countered.

"Criminal past? What's this all about?" Phyllis demanded, turning again to Lawrence who had just taken a gulp of his vodka drink and was looking off into space.

"I guess I'm the one who'll answer that," Nadine responded, not waiting for him to speak. "You seem to have moved in as his girlfriend-de-jour," she said, acidly. "You're probably an investor, as well. Actually, the two things go hand-in-hand with Lawrence Livermore, or I should say, *Gilbert.*

"You're just jealous that Lawrence and I are together. He's been nice to you only because you invited him here." Phyllis' face cleared with recognition as a thought struck her. "You're the one who left the snake in his bed because he was with me."

Alex moved closer to the two women, ready to intervene if the hostility came to blows.

But Nadine remained cool. "I would hardly pick up a poisonous snake for any reason," she stated with clarity. "When I heard the commotion last night and walked down the hallway to see what had happened, I was shocked to see the snake; but even more surprised to see *you* there with Lawrence. You should know that he had been with *me* earlier in the evening. And he wasn't just being 'nice to me.' In fact, our lovemaking exhausted me so much that I fell right to sleep, only to be awakened when you started screaming your head off."

"Lawrence, is that true?" Phyllis asked, hotly. "Did you make love to Nadine, too, last night? Is that why you had to 'rest' after you came downstairs and we had to walk around for an hour before you wanted to go upstairs?"

"Phyllis, you know that I'm very fond of you," Lawrence pleaded, as she turned away, her face ashen.

"From what I've learned about Lawrence," Nadine broke in, "he's very fond of all wealthy widows. No offense," she shrugged, regarding Phyllis. "I found him to be quite charming too, I have to admit. And he seemed like some kind of financial wizard. But, fortunately, as a precaution, I paid a visit to the Securities and Exchange Commission back in Chicago before this trip. This morning I got a report from the FBI.

"The FBI?" Phyllis asked, alarmed.

"*Nadine, please*," Lawrence urged. "This isn't necessary. We can talk about this in private, like you suggested." Turning to Phyllis he said, "There was a little misunderstanding of what 'were' and 'were not' proper procedures in a complicated financial scheme, and I paid the price for it. But that was in the past," he said, darkly eyeing Nadine.

"He was in *prison* in the past. What's in the present is that he's been using an assumed name since the Dodd-Frank law required hedge fund managers register with the SEC," Nadine snapped. "So he needed a new name, and not just *any* name. That's what I learned in town today at the Internet café. Seems that 'Livermore' was the name of a successful stock speculator in the '20s and '30s. *Lauriston* Livermore made and lost several fortunes by playing smart hunches and quickly cutting his losses. He's thought of as the original hedge fund manager.

Alex noticed Virgil Grimm nearby picking up discarded napkins, a sly smile on his face. *Like you should be feeling so high and mighty,* she thought. *Child molesters are much worse than inside traders. In prison, child molesters are despised by murderers. Oh, this is getting too weird.*

"Unfortunately," Nadine continued her narrative, "after his last bankruptcy, he shot and killed himself – alone in a Manhattan hotel cloakroom. Perhaps the strangest part of the story is that, at the time, he was married to a woman whose *previous four husbands* had all committed suicide.

Turning to glare at Lawrence she said, "Why you would take the name of such an ill-fated man, I can't imagine."

"Lauriston Livermore was the most brilliant Wall Street strategist of all time," Lawrence shot back, drawing himself up and sticking out his chin. "He was worth $100 million after the crash of 1929 by selling short. He was a genius."

"Lawrence, tell me, is *that* why you go by that man's name?" Phyllis asked, grabbing hold of his coat lapels. "Or is it like Nadine said, that you're trying to hide your identity because you're a criminal. Who are you?" she demanded, thrumming her fists on his chest.

"Phyllis, I'm no criminal," He took hold of her hands to stop her assault. "Not by intent, anyway. I'm a capable investor and a good man. You can trust me."

"You'd better check with his ex-wives, first," Nadine cautioned. "According to the FBI, he's been married to three wealthy women, all of whom divorced him. The last wife left him when he insisted she sell all her jewelry and property to pay back clients who were coming after him. The SEC is still checking out his current investment practices.

"Wait a minute," Nadine wheeled on Lawrence. "I just thought of something. Conrad Pierce said at dinner last Saturday night that he was going to look into your investments. He was stabbed to death the next morning. Did he find out about your past or your present dealings and threatened you with exposure?"

Phyllis audibly gasped. "That's right!" she exclaimed, breathlessly. "Conrad did say something about investigating you." She looked stricken, her eyes widening in dismay. "Did you stab him?!"

"Phyllis. Nadine. Listen, both of you. This is insane. Conrad never investigated my investments that I know of and, if he had, he would only have been impressed with my success. There is nothing in my past that he could have used to threaten me with 'exposure' for being some kind of a fraud. Besides, ask yourselves, how would he have been able to find out anything in this isolated place without phones and the Internet? We couldn't get the damn police here for an hour after the man had been found stabbed to death, for God's sake.

"For the record, I never saw the man after that dinner," he said more calmly. "And you, Nadine, are my alibi. I hope you haven't forgotten our time together after dinner or our brief tryst after breakfast the next day. We know that Pierce was murdered sometime before noon. I was on the tram tour sitting with you, Nadine. Did I ever get off the tram?

"Look, I've tried to be a gentleman with you ladies. I can't help that I've been attracted to you both, and that I wanted to spend time with both of you. I certainly didn't mean to hurt either of you. At the very least, please don't think of me as some kind of monster who's capable of stabbing someone to death.

"I'm the same man you thought I was. Just with another name. He flashed a broad smile, looking from one woman to the other. "Give me a chance to exonerate myself. I can help you both in so many ways." He raised his eyebrows, seductively.

"Anyway, I see that it's dinner time. May I have the pleasure of accompanying you ladies into the dining room? I believe that there's a lovely veal dish on the menu. We shouldn't keep the chef waiting.

Nadine rolled her eyes, shaking her head. "No, Lawrence," she said. "Not this time. I think I'd like a little space and time away from you." She turned on her heel and walked away.

Phyllis stood there, looking stunned. "Lawrence Livermore, or whatever your name is, you have brass balls, I'll give you that. You need to take a good hard look at yourself, and decide who in the hell you are. In the meantime, I'm joining my *friends* for dinner."

After both women had left, Lawrence noticed Alex at the bar a few feet away. "I guess you heard all that."

"Yeah, it looks like everyone did," Alex said, inclining her head towards the lounge area where the others sat staring back at them. "Sorry. I imagine that you would have liked to have kept your personal history to yourself. But don't feel bad. You're not the only one here with secrets from your past. In fact, I think you're in good company.

"And for the record, I don't think you murdered Conrad Pierce. You may be a womanizer and a scam artist, but you're not a murderer."

"Thanks – I think. And you're a most attractive young woman, in a very natural, relaxed sort of way," he smirked, briefly eyeing her up and down, taking in her unruly hair and rumpled clothes.

Touché! Alex thought, her lips curling up in response to his stinging left-handed compliment. *Well played.*

Moving over close to her, Livermore offered his arm and gave her a knowing look. “Shall we go in to dinner? I believe the special is veal, done up as osso buco.”

Wednesday, April 17

Chapter 33

Meeting Lucie Bean

THE NEXT MORNING Alex had to force herself to get out of bed. It didn't help that she had a dull headache from drinking too much wine the night before. And who could blame her? She had been the last one standing to assume the role of Lawrence Livermore's companion and sympathizer for dinner and the rest of the evening. Through it all, she had decided that the man wasn't really evil; maybe a little promiscuous. He had made her head spin with an explanation of machinations in the world of wheeler-dealer finances to prove to her that he didn't cheat, intentionally.

Still lying in bed, she hoped that the day wouldn't bring more angry confrontations among the guests at the Grover Inn; or more revelations of criminal pasts. Two ex-cons in a group of thirteen people must already be above average.

Back to thinking about the murder, she held out little hope that Detective Tate was close to a solution that would remove the dark cloud of suspicion over everyone, including herself; although he still seemed inclined to put the blame on Margaret Pierce.

As for her own efforts to solve the crime, she wasn't looking forward to following up on Tina's tip that she should interview Raymond Bean's mother in the nursing home. Even if the woman knew something significant, Lucie Bean would hardly want to open up to a stranger; particularly about anything having to do with murder.

It was almost comical to imagine how that interview would go. There she'd be, startling the woman by barging into her room, after which she'd introduce herself as a guest at the Grover Inn; and, by the way, there had been a certain unpleasantness – well, a murder – and did she know who did it? Perhaps her son knew something and had told her.

Wait a minute – that was it. *Tina Wrenn thought that Raymond had some knowledge or suspicion about who was responsible, and she thought that he would tell his mother*. The old lady had nothing much going on in her life. It would have been something interesting to talk about.

Alex had to admit that it could be a good lead, after all, but she still had to get over the hurdle of convincing a stranger to share a confidence. Well, she wasn't without her charms, was she? Besides, old people who sit alone all day must be thrilled to have visitors and would want to talk their ears off.

Looking over her wardrobe, she selected a cotton print skirt and a crisp white blouse to wear that would convey respectability and innocence. She might be able to carry this off, after all. And wouldn't Detective Tate be impressed if she came back with the name of the murderer whom he could just go and arrest! She would no longer be the object of his put-downs, telling her that she had been oblivious to a "dead guy with a knife in his chest in the same room."

Looking out the window, she was surprised to see several wild horses calmly grazing in the front grounds of the Grover. She hadn't seen any since the day a herd had stampeded over

Ronette Kerley – the same day that Conrad Pierce had been murdered. Their peaceful reappearance might be a signal that things were getting back on the right track.

***

AT TEN O'CLOCK, Alex was at the head of the line of the Grover guests who were waiting to board the tram. She noted that Lawrence Livermore was missing, which didn't surprise her. Either he had continued imbibing after he got to his room last night and was sleeping in, or he wanted to avoid running into the two women who had warned him to keep his distance. Both reasons were understandable to explain his absence. Except, Phyllis was missing, too, she now realized. *Hmmm.*

As Raymond Bean started to get out of the driver's seat to exit the tram, he stumbled and fell to his knees on the floorboards. Grabbing onto the dashboard, he pulled himself up onto his feet and smiled to cover his embarrassment and show he wasn't hurt. As further proof, he bounded down the tram stairs and stood aside to let the others board.

As Alex was about to mount the two steps, she caught sight of a shiny object that looked like a piece of jewelry on the floor. Taking the first stair, she reached out and picked it up and put it in her pocket, thinking it might be a charm from Phyllis Hanover's bracelet.

After the others got on and were seated, Raymond Bean boarded and resumed his seat. Turning around, he asked, "Who wants to be taken to the Inn's ferry, and who wants to go on another tour of the island?"

"The ferry!" everyone shouted in unison.

Amanda Berthold laughed out loud. "I guess we all want to get off the island. We need a change of scene, and some of us want to do some shopping. I can't understand why Phyllis didn't want to come."

"She decided to take what she thought was a better offer," Rosemary answered, sounding dubious. "What can I say? She's a grown woman who can make her own choices," she added, resignedly. "Nadine, why don't you sit with me? It'd be nice if you joined us. We're going to shop, lunch and tour a couple historical homes, if that would appeal to you."

"Oh my God, Look!" Ronette shrieked as the tram started up. "Those horses! I haven't seen any since – that day!"

"Don't worry about them," Rosemary advised. "They won't bother us in the least. What happened to you was totally out of the norm."

As the tram moved forward, a mare and colt sauntered across the drive ahead, the mare glancing up as she took her time to lead her offspring to the other side. "See, she's not showing any fear," Chloe remarked.

Driving by other members of the herd, the animals continued to calmly graze, ignoring the vehicle, although it passed within a few feet of them. A little further along, on the other side of a hill, Raymond Bean had to sharply apply the brakes as they came up on a large black stallion standing in the middle of the road. The great horse simply tossed its mane and held its ground as Raymond had to steer around him.

Ronette squirmed in her seat, but managed to stay quiet as they drove by the last of the horses. "Maybe I'm not cursed anymore," she said under her breath.

* * *

ARRIVING AT THE ST. ANNES' dock after the crossing, the group broke up, moving off in different directions. Alex hurried away from everyone, lest she be invited to tag along, and would have to think up a good excuse not to. She didn't imagine that it would sound reasonable to say, "No thanks. I'm just going to visit a nursing home."

Stepping inside the first store she came to, a swimwear shop, she looked around for someone to ask for directions.

"Are you looking for a one-piece or a bikini?" asked an attractive young woman, who was just coming out of the backroom at the sound of the bell.

"No, I just want directions to a nursing home," Alex replied, wincing. "I'm visiting someone for the first time who's at the Whispering Pines. Do you know it?" Noting the clerk's puzzled look, Alex held up a bikini and eyed it appreciatively, as though she might consider making a purchase. "But these are nice," she said, to earn sympathy and a shred of self-respect.

"Yeah, sure," the clerk answered, uncertainly. "The Whispering Pines is right up Water Street – just keep walking for about six blocks. Can't miss it – it's right on, well, the water," she smiled, abashedly. "It's a beautiful place. Not like most nursing homes," she added. "You can try that on if you'd like. It would look real good on you, I think."

Leaving the shop, Alex headed north, as she had been directed. After walking beyond the commercial area, she came to a neighborhood of large, southern-style homes, one after another.

The parkways had been planted with live oak trees that arched over the street creating an attractive tracery of shadows on the street. Individual yards were made colorful with profusions of violet and pink azaleas in carved-out circles, backed by deep green evergreens that were set against the buildings' foundations.

Just past a lovely lowland style frame home with a deep front porch, Alex came to a crushed gravel drive that disappeared beyond a stand of pines. At the street, a black metal sign with gold letters read: "Whispering Pines." Alex gulped, reflexively. She was there. *Might as well go in, I've come this far,* she thought, to bolster her courage.

Following the curve of the drive a hundred feet, a sprawling white gabled building came into view. *This was a nursing home?* Taking the walk from the driveway, she came to broad stone steps that led up to a colonnaded porch. A tall arched door was set into a deep framing.

Again, Alex needed to swallow hard. This imposing place wasn't making her feel any more comfortable about her mission. As it was, she would be looked at suspiciously visiting an elderly woman whom she had never met. And then, she sought information about the patient's private conversations with her son concerning a murder. Even if she were at one of those 'active retirement communities,' where they welcome strangers, this task would be tricky, she thought.

Standing in front of the door, before she had realized it she had lifted and dropped the heavy brass knocker. Within moments, a woman's voice with a southern accent came over an intercom.

"Ye-as, kin ah help ya'll?"

"Uh, yes. I'm Alex Trotter, a friend of Raymond Bean's, from the Grover Inn? I'm just stopping by to visit his mother, Lucie Bean, if it's convenient." Silence. "If she's resting, or indisposed, I could come back another time." Silence. "All right, then, I'll just be on my way."

"No, that's fine, Miss Trotter. You just took me by surprise. Lucie doesn't get many visitors. Only Pastor Dale and her son, Raymond. I'm sure she'd be delighted to have a lady caller."

A buzzer prompted Alex to pull down on the curved handle to open the thick door. Stepping inside, she found herself in a bright, but windowless, oak paneled anteroom that was lit by an overhead domed skylight. The room's solid walls and thick carpet created a hushed entry to the home that, apparently, was reached through a second doorway.

Alex walked through it and was met by a patrician-looking woman in a high-necked dress whose silver hair was pulled back into an old-fashioned chignon. "Miss Trotter?" she asked, extending her be-ringed hand which Alex numbly shook. "Welcome to Whispering Pines. I'm Annabel Adams. One of our aides, Mindy Briggs, will be here directly to take you back to Mrs. Bean. As you know, she's in the Memory wing, so there's no open access to her suite."

"The Memory Wing?" Alex asked.

"Yes, didn't Mr. Bean tell you? His mother has Alzheimer's disease. She doesn't even know him, although he's here at least twice a week. He just worships her. She is very sweet and cooperative, although she's in her own world. She'll probably think you're Eleanor Roosevelt. She calls anyone who's not a nurse, 'Mrs. Roosevelt.' Mrs. Bean would have been a young woman when Eleanor Roosevelt died, but, apparently was quite taken with her life."

A young, dark-haired woman approached, wearing an old-fashioned stiff white uniform. "I'll take you back to Lucie Bean. She's so excited to have a visitor I had to help her change into good clothes. She'll probably ask you what she can do to help the soldiers who are just coming back from the Pacific. It's best if you just play along as she has no comprehension of reality."

Alex followed Mindy Briggs down a long-carpeted hallway, past a plant-filled lounge where a couple of white-haired ladies worked on jig-saw puzzles and a foursome of three women and a single man played cards.

When Mindy Briggs and Alex arrived at another locked door, the nurse opened it with a key from a large key ring. Walking down a hallway, they passed two closed doors until they came to a third door with a small gold nameplate that read, "Lucinda Bean." Mindy knocked softly, and then called out, "Mrs. Bean?"

"Is it Mrs. Roosevelt?" a small high voice asked. Mindy looked questioningly at Alex who shrugged a "why not?" response.

"Yes, it is, and she's anxious to meet you," Mindy answered, cracking the door open.

"Come in! Come in! Oh, my goodness, to what do I owe this honor?" Entering the spacious room, Alex saw a pink-faced sprite of a woman wearing a fine-knit suit and pearls, sitting on a pale green loveseat.

"I've been rolling bandages, but I'd be happy to be put to work doing anything else," the elegant Mrs. Bean advised her visitor.

Alex turned towards Mindy who raised her eyebrows to question whether Alex could handle the situation on her own. Alex nodded and turned back to address Lucie.

"You're doing a wonderful job, Mrs. Bean. I'm glad to see you looking so well. How do you like it here? I should tell you that I know your son, Raymond."

"I love it here. This is the nicest place I've ever lived, but I don't have a son. Why, I'm not even married! I was, once, but he disappeared."

Alex looked around at the well-furnished sitting room. There were custom-made draperies at the windows, polished tables with lamps and skirted upholstery made cozier with pillows and soft woven throws. Beyond, she could see doorways to a bedroom and a bath. *This is a nursing home?* It was more like a fine New York hotel suite. This place had to cost a bundle. How did Raymond Bean afford this place? Or was his mother a wealthy widow?

Alex spent the next several minutes in the make-believe world of Mrs. Bean, playing the wife of the war-time president from the middle of the last century, but knew it was hopeless to ask any questions about the murder at the Grover Inn.

As Alex took her leave from Lucie Bean, she promised to visit again, knowing that she would be instantly forgotten, and the next woman who walked in would take her place as Eleanor Roosevelt.

Stopping to thank Annabel Adams on her way out, Alex absent-mindedly picked up one of the facility's brochures and tucked it into her purse. Walking away from the nursing home she was totally perplexed: *What was Tina Wrenn thinking? If she knew the state of mind of Lucie Bean, why would she advise her to come here to see the woman? Was she missing something?*

Chapter 34

Confronting Tina

AT THREE-THIRTY, RAYMOND BEAN was waiting at the dock to take everyone back on the tram. Alex felt a shock go through her when she saw the man and it dawned on her – she had used her *real name* at Whispering Pines. What was she thinking? Annabel Adams had told her that Raymond Bean visited his mother at least twice a week. Someone would probably mention her visit to him the next time he was there. Hopefully, that would be after Saturday morning when she would be on her way home.

Taking her usual seat behind the driver, she tried to calm herself. *I didn't sign in at the nursing home. Maybe they won't remember my name. It isn't as common a name as Jane Smith. Why didn't I say my name is Jane Smith?*

"Miss Trotter, did you hear me?" It was Chloe. "I asked you what you did in town. We lost track of you right after we arrived. We tried finding you in the boutiques later to have you join us for lunch, but you didn't seem to be anywhere around."

"What? Oh, yeah. I was shopping for swimsuits. You know how many you have to try on to find one that looks half-way decent. I must have spent a couple of hours in dressing rooms. And then I didn't even buy one." *Lame, but it was the best she could come up with. Besides, she* had *tried on* one *swimsuit to placate the clerk, and then had to make up an excuse not to buy it, saying that it didn't "suit her."*

Was it her imagination, or was Raymond Bean giving her the "stink eye" in the rearview mirror? He couldn't have already heard from Annabel Adams at Whispering Pines because he had stayed on Bedford Island. She had to calm down. Even if he did hear that she had paid a visit, she could just say that Tina Wrenn had mentioned the name of his mother's nursing home and, while walking around town, she happened on the place. So, on a whim, she stopped in, saw his mother for two minutes, and left. She hadn't told him because it sounded kind of weird, when she thought about it. *That's not too bad.*

Nevertheless, when Raymond pulled the tram up to the front door of the Grover Inn, she was the first to get out and hurriedly make her way into the hotel to avoid any conversation about her day. She only hoped that Tina hadn't left yet. Coming into the Inn, she was relieved to see the receptionist fussing with something on the counter. Did the woman ever stop moving?

"Tina, I just came back from St. Annes," Alex huffed. "I saw Lucie Bean."

Tina didn't look at her. "Hi, Mrs. Pierce, Miss Campbell, Mr. and Mrs. Berthold," she called out. "Did you all have a good time in town? I see you were quite successful with your shopping."

Alex stepped back and glowered at Tina. The woman looked at what everyone had bought, and asked them where they had lunch, and what all they had done in St. Annes. Alex was losing patience as Tina appeared to be stalling for time before she had to explain to her why she had been sent on a wild goose chase.

After several minutes, the small talk had been exhausted, and the last of the hotel guests had started up the stairs to their rooms.

Watching them disappear, Alex glanced around to see if anyone else was nearby before leaning over the counter to lock eyes with Tina. "So?"

"So, what?" Tina responded, innocently.

"You know what I'm asking. Why did you send me to St. Annes to visit an old lady who's so out of it that she thought I was Eleanor Roosevelt, and that we're about to battle the Japanese at Okinawa?"

Tina tried unsuccessfully to hide her amusement. "I didn't know she was *that* delusional. You don't look much like Eleanor Roosevelt," she grinned. "But what did you think about Whispering Pines? That's what I wanted you to see – and Mrs. Bean's suite of rooms."

"It's very fancy and Lucie has an unusually nice apartment. So what? What does that have to do with solving the murder of Conrad Pierce, I'd like to know."

Tina shrugged. "I'm only trying to steer you in helpful directions. The investigation is up to you."

"Tina, for God's sake, stop playing games with me. Virgil almost caught me rummaging through his room. Then I had to talk my way into a high-toned nursing home where I had no business being, and for what? I could still get in trouble for that little maneuver since I gave my real name. That was my own stupidity, I know, but I'm not getting any closer to finding out who murdered Conrad Pierce. Be honest with me – *do you know who did it?*"

"No, I don't. Really. But you're in a better position to nose around to find answers for the weird things that have gone on around here that must be connected to his death. Would it help you to know that Mrs. Bean is not a wealthy widow?"

"She doesn't have money? But how can she afford – or Raymond Bean – afford to pay for a place like that? Wait a minute, I picked up a brochure from Whispering Pines. Let me see what it costs to keep her there."

Alex fished in her purse and pulled out the glossy booklet. Flipping through pages of colored photographs, including a chandelier-lit dining room, the inviting lounge she had seen, and a couple of well-appointed private living spaces, she looked at the back page where the rates were discreetly listed in a smaller italicized font. She ran her finger across several lines describing care, person(s) and costs. "Here it is. A single person rate for an apartment in the 'Memory wing' costs $15,000 a month, not including nursing care or salon treatments."

Frowning up at Tina, she said, "Raymond Bean doesn't make that kind of money. Something smells here, but I don't see how Conrad Pierce fits into the picture. The man had money, but he wasn't robbed; he was killed."

"I can't be seen talking to you for so long, Alex," Tina said, picking up papers. "Mr. Bean wouldn't approve of that and *I need this job*."

Heavy steps were heard coming towards them. Both women turned to see Detective Arlie Tate. "Ah, Miss Trotter. Just the person I wanted to see." He looked tired and overwrought, with his shirt coming out of his waistband, and his face shadowed by dark stubble.

Alex flushed, pushing her hair behind her ears. "Moi?" she asked, feeling uncomfortable about what was coming next.

"Let's go up to the front room," the detective advised, without expression.

Once there, she sat down primly on a straight-backed chair and waited for the policeman to speak first.

Detective Tate stroked his chin as he leafed through a pile of papers on his lap before glancing up at her. "I just thought you'd like to know you were right – Edna Butz served time — as Edna Henderson, her married name. Not for 'trying to impersonate a human being,' as you suggested." His lips curled up a little. "Seems that she shot *Mister* Henderson when she found him in bed with another woman. It was ruled a case of voluntary manslaughter since she was acting in a 'heightened state of emotion' and wasn't rational at the time; nor had she planned to kill her husband, according to the verdict," he read from the top sheet.

He glanced up at Alex. "Apparently she's capable of taking a life when provoked. What I'd like to know is whether you're aware of any trouble between Conrad Pierce and Edna Butz. Did he ever insult her? Make fun of her? Anything like that?"

Alex frowned trying to remember any time she had even seen the two people in the same room. "The only time Edna Butz was anywhere around Conrad Pierce was when she served dinner Saturday night; and then, she was only in the background. They didn't have any words with each other that I know of. As I recall, Margaret Pierce gave her husband a good poke when he started arguing with people at the table, and he didn't say much after that."

"Edna wasn't in the lounge when Conrad Pierce was so loud and obnoxious during cocktail hour?"

"No, I'm sure of it. We never saw her before we went in to dinner."

"So, we're back to the fact that the only people who Conrad Pierce offended were those in your group," Arlie Tate said, drumming with a pen.

"There were others present who could have *taken* offense," Alex said. "Employees of the hotel. Let's see— there was the bartender, Tim Williams, and Raymond Bean, and Virgil Grimm.

"And one of those employees is a felon," Alex reminded him. "Of course, you don't seem to think that a guy who's a pedophile can make a career move to murderer. Now, we know that there are *at least* two employees who are felons. Why is it that Raymond Bean hires people who have been in prison for violent crimes?"

"I've wondered that myself," Arlie said, nodding.

Stretching his legs and folding his arms, he leaned back against his chair. "Since you seem to be my new partner, you should know that I phoned the owner of the Grover – Barrington Hall, *the Third*, if you please. Anyway, this guy Barrington said that he inherited the place from a favorite aunt and only holds onto it for sentimental reasons. Years ago he made Raymond Bean totally responsible for the day-to-day operations so he doesn't have to bother with it. He complained that the place is a money pit that has never turned a profit since he's owned it.

"I asked him if he knew that Raymond Bean has felons working here, and he said he did. Bean had explained he was providing a social service to rehabilitate people whom no one else would take on. Even so, Hall says that he pays these people top rates for these jobs. I didn't think so when I saw the payroll sheets.

"Hall's happy with the way Bean runs the place, except that he has to pay so much to keep it going."

Alex had been frowning and shaking her head during the detective's recital of his phone conversation with the Grover's owner.

"What is it?" Arlie asked, finally.

"Well, since you confided in me, I'll tell you. Tina Wrenn told me to visit Raymond Bean's mother in a high-class nursing home in town. I went to see Lucie Bean today. She's in la-la land, living in the lap of luxury, but she didn't inherit money to pay for it.

How do you think Raymond Bean pays for it?"

Arlie raised his eyebrows. "You're saying he's ripping off this Barrington Hall? Okay, maybe, but what does that have to do with the murder?"

"I don't know, yet, but everything I hear about how this place is managed by Raymond Bean smells to high heaven. This latest information really tears it. This place should be making a profit. Do you know what it costs to stay here?"

"A hundred or so a night, I suppose," he shrugged.

"Try two to three hundred, depending on the room size. And the place is booked months in advance. It's the only hotel on the island – you may have noticed."

"Well, you check out the bookkeeping if you want," Arlie said, sounding unconvinced. "I'm gonna talk to Edna Butz, again. You find out anything else, you let me know. Just don't break into anybody else's room." He gave her a warning look.

Alex flushed. "Yeah, of course. Uh, look at the time," she joked, holding up her watch. "I have to show up for cocktails in less than an hour. That's when all hell breaks loose. I'll stay in touch."

She jumped up, turning away to cut off any further conversation – especially about breaking into people's rooms.

Wednesday evening, April 17

Chapter 35

Confronting Raymond Bean

AS ALEX HOPED, she was the last one to arrive in the lounge area that evening. If everyone was socializing by the time she got there, she'd be free to get Raymond Bean alone and get him to talk about himself; his interests, his history, maybe his *mother*. Not that it would be easy. Thinking back, she couldn't recall one single thing the man had ever revealed about himself. All that he ever talked about was the Grover Inn. Now she knew better. She knew that he was devoted to his mother; maybe to the point of becoming a thief to be able to take care of her. She wondered how many people even knew about his mother. He apparently had told Tina Wrenn. But why keep it a secret from the others?

Alex had debated with herself about whether she dare bring up the subject of his mother to him. Maybe she should dive right in and roll out her story about how she had "happened by" the nursing home and stopped in on a whim. That would cover her if he had heard from Annabel Lee. But, if he didn't buy into her visit as being coincidental and innocent, it would be the end of the conversation, at the very least. It could make him suspicious about what she was up to.

No, she had better stay on safe topics, she decided. After all, her only objective was to get a sense of what kind of person he was; to rule him in or out as a murder suspect. The picture that had emerged so far was a contradictory one -- either he was a benevolent man who offered redemption to ex-cons, or he was an unscrupulous embezzler who was cooking the books big time. Either way, he could be involved in the murder: he could be shielding a guilty felon, or he could be capable of taking a life, himself.

But how could she get the man to reveal much about himself without him suspecting her motives? If he saw through her, and he was the ruthless killer of Conrad Pierce, she could become his next target. She wished she could have worked out some dialogue in advance but, without knowing anything about the man, how could she predict what he might be willing to talk about? She'd have to play it by ear. She'd sound more natural if she was unrehearsed, anyway. At least, by attempting this little deception during cocktail hour she could have a glass of wine to settle her nerves. Maybe two.

Walking into the lounge, she saw that Bean was seated alone at the bar, his balding head glowing orange under the pendant light. She was in luck. But now that she had the opportunity, she wasn't so sure she wanted it.

As she approached, Tim Williams jerked up his chin in greeting, causing Raymond to turn around to see who was coming. Alex suddenly felt weak in the knees. *Was Raymond Bean looking at her accusingly? She never remembered him to have such a probing stare.*

"Oh, hi, Mr. Bean – Raymond." She waved at Tim. "Looks like I'm the last one down this evening. Would you mind if I joined you for a drink?"

"You're welcome to sit here, but I don't drink," Raymond Bean answered. *Was there a tone of disapproval?* Alex wondered. "I was just keeping an eye on things," the manager went on. "Making sure there's not any trouble. There's been a lot of dissention in your group – as you know." He grimaced. *Again, with the disapproval.* "Looks like the Kerleys are arguing about something, but you can expect that with married couples."

Alex glanced over at the pair, wondering if they were still having the *same* argument. She was surprised to see Ronette dressed casually in slacks and a polo shirt. Certainly, a far cry from the red cocktail dress she always wore in the evenings.

"Tim, could I have chardonnay, please? Sorry to interrupt, Raymond. As you were saying, married couples have little spats from time to time. By the way, were you ever married? I don't think I've ever heard you mention your family." *Nice serve, Alex,* she thought to herself. *Your volley, Mr. Bean.*

"I was never married. I had other obligations."

Alex thought, *You're not getting off that easily.* "To your own family, you mean?" *Return that one.*

"Well, er yes. My mom needed me to stay close over the years."

"Oh, yes, that reminds me," Alex said. "Tina Wrenn mentioned that your mom is in a lovely nursing home in St. Annes. That must work out well for you; to have her nearby. *Had she really said that? It was a truthful statement, and didn't sound very provocative,* she thought.

"It has been my privilege to be able to take care of my mother." The manager sounded defensive. "She's a wonderful person who has known a lot of grief. Life isn't fair, you know. The best people often have to struggle while evil people prosper."

Where did that *come from?* she wondered. *Were they still talking about his mother? Alzheimer's was a serious disease, but the woman appeared to be in pretty good shape, well cared for, and content in her delusional world.* "True enough. Some people even get away with murder." Alex ventured, holding her breath. *This one might be a bridge too far.*

Bean appeared not to have heard her as he stared off into space or, if he did, he was imagining Alex suffering the same fate as Conrad Pierce. Finally, he said, "Of course, that's true. But I can't right all the wrongs in the world. My only objective is to protect my mother from as much misery as I can, to make up for what she's been through. Even so, I can't protect her from everything."

Instinctively, Alex sensed this wasn't the time to disclose her snooping, even though she could let Raymond Bean know that she was aware of all that he had done for his mother. "You sound like a wonderful son. Your mother is lucky to have you to watch out for her best interests." Alex took a long swallow of her wine. *Now what?*

"Your staff here seems to do a good job for you. Hopefully, they make your life a little easier," she suggested, changing to another subject she wanted him to comment on.

"They help out in many ways," Raymond agreed. "They've haven't always been perfect, but they've redeemed themselves; just as 'Moses took the redemption money from those who were above those redeemed by the Levites.'"

"What?" Alex asked, incredulous at the detour in the conversation.

"What did I say?" Raymond Bean responded, sounding shocked, himself. "Oh, that's from a verse in the Old Testament that just came to mind – I don't know why. I guess because I used the word 'redeemed.' Don't pay any attention. Well, it seems to be time for dinner, doesn't it?" Bean made a show of checking his watch.

Alex thought back to her doing the same thing as cover an hour ago when Detective Tate had implied that he knew about her breaking into Virgil Grimm's room. But what had she caught Raymond Bean doing? He just quoted some Biblical reference to Moses that made no sense to her. Maybe there wasn't anything to it.

Walking into the dining room, she caught up with Phyllis and Lawrence Livermore. "Phyllis, seeing you reminded me. I picked up a decorative little silver tube on the floor of the tram. I thought it might be one of your charms. It has a ring on one end."

"Well, I'm wearing my silver bracelet, and I'm not missing anything," Phyllis said, holding out her arm to give it a closer look. No, I don't have a charm anything like that, anyway, but thanks for trying to be of help."

Alex nodded and stood back to let them by, lost in thought. *I seem to be striking out tonight. I thought I could come up with some useful information from Raymond Bean, but all I made him admit is that he's a loving son, a fair-minded boss, and a devout reader of the Bible. I have absolutely nothing to tell Detective Tate.*

Seeing Ronette and Wade come by, she flashed a quick smile in greeting. "Hey, would you two mind if I joined you for dinner?" she asked, impulsively.

"No – that's fine," Ronette replied haltingly, sounding as though it wasn't fine at all. "We might have to get up before you're done, though."

"Not a problem. You just leave whenever you want. I'll be okay." *They've argued about doing 'whatever' for two days and now they can't wait until after dinner?* Alex thought.

Later Wednesday night

Chapter 36

Two New Suspects?

ONCE SEATED, Alex picked up on the tension in her dinner companions. The normally chatty Ronette sat staring a hole in the table, while Wade, who never showed any emotion, appeared ready to explode as he violently twisted his napkin into a wad and crushed packets of crackers with his thumbs.

Alex decided she'd try out some conversation with Ronette who looked less likely to bite her head off. "I see you dressed casually this evening, Ronette. I've kinda given up on so-called formal dress, myself. I prefer being comfortable, don't you?"

Ronette squinted at her. Leaning closer she said, "You know you got your top on inside out and backwards?"

"What?" Alex pulled at the brown jersey to get a better look at it. Feeling at the neck she got hold of the label that faced out. "I can't believe I put it on backwards. Thanks for telling me. I wonder how many people noticed and didn't say anything?" She thought back to how Raymond Bean had seemed to look at her strangely. *No wonder. And I thought he knew something incriminating about me. I am a lousy detective, just like Arlie Tate says.*

Alex mined what humor she could out of her careless dressing. Ronette went back to sulking, and Wade tied knots in the straws while they were waiting for their meals. Alex found herself looking forward to the ill-tempered Edna Butz coming out of the kitchen, just to have someone to talk to.

Edna finally banged through the kitchen door with a platter of plates on her hip and sauntered over to their table. "You had the barbequed chicken," she said to Alex, as though it was an accusation.

"Yeah, that was me," Alex answered.

"Well, we ran out of the sauce, so it's just baked." Edna set down the plate without apology. *What kitchen runs out of barbeque sauce?* Alex thought. *It's just ketchup and vinegar with seasoning. I think that woman still holds me responsible for bringing a 'murderer' to the Grover Inn. She has a lot of nerve, considering* she's *the one who 'slaughtered her man,' literally, and went to prison.*

Ronette, Wade and Alex commenced eating in silence. After several minutes, Wade announced that they'd better get going, "just in case."

Alex hastened to say that she didn't mind their leaving before she had finished her meal. *Good-by and good riddance,* was her internal thought.

As the couple walked away from the table, Alex overheard Ronette grumbling to Wade, "This is the dumbest scheme you ever had and that's sayin' somethin'."

Edna Butz came around with a coffee pot, overfilling Alex's cup leaving a puddle in her saucer. Alex sighed as she sopped up the coffee before taking a sip. *Something's not right,* she thought. *I've always wondered what those two were doing here, anyway. They live less than two hours away – they could visit anytime without staying on the island. And they hardly look like people who stay in expensive resorts. Then there's the fact that Wade saw Conrad having sex with Ronette. He could be his murderer. Why haven't I explored that more?*

I can't just sit here while Ronette and Wade are getting into trouble. Besides, I need something to tell Detective Tate

Having made a decision, she got out of her chair, folded her napkin and laid it next to her dirty dinner plate that Edna hadn't taken away when she slopped coffee all over the place. *Yikes, what an operation.*

Quietly slipping out of the dining room, she looked around the corner before tiptoeing down the hallway to the lobby. Seeing no one around, she stopped to listen. Silence. Spotting a wing chair that faced the back wall, she went over and sat in it, scrunching down to wait -- for what, she didn't know.

Just as she was feeling a crick in her neck, she heard voices coming her way. She slunk down even lower.

"You don't know when he'll be there?" It was Ronette. "How the fuck did you think you could meet 'im without settin' a time?"

"When the sun went down. That's what he said," Wade responded meekly.

"Oh, yeah? Well, it takes a while for the sun to go down, and then it's down for a long time. We have clocks, y'know. Well, let's get the hell outta here; and I hope for your sake that he's there."

Hearing the door open and close, Alex jumped up to look out the front window. What she saw made her blink in disbelief. Wade and Ronette were leaving with their suitcases. So that's why they were all nervous and upset – they were about to make a get-away. And not for any legitimate reason, either, or some emergency, or they would have said something at dinner. No, they obviously were up to no good and she had to find out what it was.

Having made up her mind to follow them, she thought she'd better contact Arlie Tate first. She might be getting in over her head. Hopefully, she could figure out how to operate the radiophone at the front desk, since she didn't trust Raymond Bean to make the call. She thought she remembered how he had used the black box on the night of the murder. The police station number must still be around. If not, she'd call 9-1-1.

Ronette and Wade had now disappeared from sight, so she had to hurry. Running over to the reception desk, she picked up the phone on the back counter and flipped a switch. It lit up. *Good, so far*. Opening a nearby drawer, she was relieved to find the number for the county police. Picking up the microphone, she dialed the number and pressed the PTT (push to talk) button. After a couple of rings, a woman answered, "Sheriff's Office. How can I help you?"

"Hello? This is Alex Trotter at the Grover Inn calling Arlie Tate. Is he there? It's an emergency."

The scratchy voice advised that Detective Tate wasn't there, but she could get a message to him. She'd have to settle for that. "Tell him that Ronette and Wade Kerley have just snuck out of the Inn with their suitcases to meet someone. I'm going to try to follow them, but he should get here ASAP!"

Assured by the dispatcher that the detective would get her message, Alex put down the phone box, and took off for the front lobby. Flying through the front door, she was alarmed to discover that the sun had now set completely. Recalling Wade's words that they were meeting someone "when the sun set," she panicked that she might have missed them. Or, if not, the darkness would make any effort to follow them more difficult, if not impossible.

Where would they be likely to meet someone? There was only the road or the water. She didn't see any headlights or tail lights on the road. Assuming she hadn't missed a car that picked them up, she would go around the back of the Inn to the dock. She suddenly remembered something Ronette had said at that first dinner, that Wade had a friend with a boat who might come around. *That must be it. But Ronette had made it sound like it would be for a ride – 'a spin.' That's what she had said.*

Alex had walked down to the closed pier once before, but not in the dark. There were several paths around the grounds; some went to the cottages, some to gardens and one led down to the pier. Hopefully, she'd find the right one.

Looking at the ground so that she didn't stumble, she followed one gravel walkway that seemed to be going in the right general direction. When she next looked up, she saw that it was leading to a lighted building – one of the cottages! She couldn't take the time to go back; she'd have to make her way around the little house, through the weeds and brambles, as best she could.

As she made her way, stickers clung to her clothes and scratched her arms. Continuing on, the ground became wetter and spongier until she found herself slogging through mud. Her footsteps made sucking sounds as she pulled each sunken shoe out of the ooze. Progress was slow, but after several minutes she saw a reflection of light on the channel water; but she couldn't yet make out the boathouse that was located at the pier.

Going on intuition, she turned to her left, walking in the marshy land along the water's edge. Making her way in the darkness, she didn't see the metal construction horse that had been set up to keep people away until she was on top of it. Tripping over a leg, she tumbled forward and landed face-down in the mire. *Ooh! The hell with this!* she cursed, swiping at her muddy face with muddier hands. *I should just let Detective Tate handle this on his own. Too bad if he arrests the wrong person! Oh, what am I saying?*

Sitting up, she was surprised and encouraged to see a small light coming through the darkness. Was it a boat piloted by Kerleys' friend, or was it Detective Tate? The light disappeared; then reappeared. She must be close to the boathouse, and the watercraft was shifting to the left and right as it moved towards it.

Getting to her feet, Alex trudged along, and within a couple of minutes she saw the silhouette of the building. Urging herself on, at last she came to it and leaned against a side wall to catch her breath.

"Donde estan?" a man's voice called out from the water. '*Where are you?*' she translated to herself. *The Kerleys were meeting someone who spoke Spanish?*

"You must be talkin' to us!" Ronette yelled back. "We're right here! C'mon, toss me a rope and I'll tie you up."

Alex heard some thumping noises, and then the boatman's voice again, crying out, plaintively, "Ayudame a dios!" *Help me, God!*

Alex thought things must not be going so well. Should she reveal herself now? No, she still hoped that Detective Tate would appear to take charge of the situation. She had to keep herself concealed as long as possible.

"Here ya go! We gotcha now," Wade said over the sound of footsteps on the boards. "Hey, you're not Jose! Where's Jose? You got the order?"

"Si, si, Meester Wade. Me llama Manuel, amigo de Jose. Totalidad esta aqui." *I'm Manuel, Jose's friend. It's all here.*

"Talk English, for Chrissakes!" Ronette demanded. "Wade! Did he say he got all the shit? What's Spanish for 'shit'?"

"I think he said it's all here."

"Well, it looks like it's more than we got room for, anyway. Let's start packing it up, Wade."

No one spoke for several seconds. Then Ronette asked, "Why you holding your hand out? The deal is that you *hombres* get paid the rest after Wade sells them, although I dunno why you agreed to somethin' that stupid.

"Oh, don't hush me, Wade. He don't understand English."

"Por gasoline por el barco! Cien dolores!" *A hundred dollars for gas for the boat.*

"You have one finger up an' I don' think you mean *one dollar* for gas," Ronette said. You mean *one hundred* dollars? You want *one hundred dollars*?"

"Keep your voice, down, Ronette. You wanna bring everyone down here to get into our business? A hundred dollars is probably fair for the distance from his last stop. We'll still make out. I got some cash – maybe enough. Yeah, here you go, but that's all I've got. Sorry about the singles with it."

"Gracias, senor. Llevan las cajas." *Take the boxes.*

Alex did not move from her spot as she waited out whatever transaction was taking place. She could hear cargo being moved off the boat, which apparently the Kerleys were packing in their suitcases. *What was going on? And where was Arlie Tate?*

"Ronette, can you take another couple? Yeah? Good. That should do it, then. Now we gotta get back to our room without bein' seen."

"Adios, amigo!" Wade called out as the boat motor started.

"Yeah, grassy-ass, Speedy Gonzalez!" Ronette shouted, derisively.

Alex moved cautiously back around the corner of the building to stay out of sight. Within a couple of minutes, Ronette and Wade emerged from the other side of the boathouse pulling their suitcases behind them. At the end of the pier, they carried the luggage over to a path that went back to the Inn when Alex lost sight of them in the darkness.

She sat still for several minutes waiting for Arlie Tate, until she thought she should get back up to the Inn herself, not to lose track of Ronette and Wade. But, as Alex stood up to leave, she heard the sound of a distant motor. Walking around to the front of the boathouse, she saw a light coming towards the dock. Was the Latino guy coming back? As the boat got closer, she could make out the blue letters on the white power boat: POLICE.

Within a minute or two, Detective Tate had docked the craft, having slipped a line over a pylon. Stepping onto the pier, he stared at Alex and shook his head. “What happened to *you*? You look like you've been mud wrestling. Sorry I missed it,” he grinned. “You're the loser, right?”

Alex ignored the sarcasm. “I couldn’t let the Kerleys out of my sight when I thought they were escaping. I missed a path and then fell over a construction horse. But that’s not important. I just witnessed Wade and Ronette smuggling something illegal from a Spanish-speaking guy in a boat. Must be drugs. I overheard them saying they were going back to the Inn about ten minutes ago, and that they had to get back to their room without being seen, so you know it’s totally illegal. You can just go up and arrest them. Conrad Pierce must have known what they were up to, so they had to kill him.”

“Slow down. Is this the ‘*emergency*’ that you called me out here for? Do you know how many people you want me to arrest for doing something illegal, or for murdering Conrad Pierce? I'm losing count.”

“I caught these people red-handed!” Alex protested. “What else do you need?”

“Well, for starters, did you see *what* they were ‘smuggling’? No. So how do you know it was illegal? But I’ll check into it. Taking delivery of anything by boat after dark is suspicious. Could be contraband, could be avoiding custom duties. Not my area, but I’ll investigate what they were up to, and turn them over to the Coast Guard, if need be. It’s still quite a leap from smuggling to committing a murder.

He placed his hand on her back. “C’mon, Nancy Drew, let’s go up to the Inn. You look like a mess – probably have some chiggers on you. Leave the interrogating to me. I have a feeling that Ronette and Wade will crack pretty easy.”

They started walking up the same path the Kerleys had taken several minutes before.

"So, Alex, what other criminal activity have you uncovered since I last saw you – what's it been? Four hours? I hate for you to limit yourself to just one couple. Did you come up with anything during your cocktail time, or did you restrain yourself until dinner?"

She made a little growling sound. "Funny. I did get to talk to Raymond Bean alone, but he didn't give up much. He says his mother's a saint and she doesn't deserve to be sick. No information about how he pays for her nursing home, and I don't see how I can get a look at his bookkeeping.

"He's a weird guy, though, I can tell you," she continued. "I said something about how loyal his employees are and he quoted a verse from the Old Testament about Moses taking redemption money. Oh! I missed that! Redemption money!" she exclaimed, elbowing Arlie.

"That's a big clue?" Arlie asked. "Calm yourself, Alex. I'll ask Bean to see the books, but if he doesn't let me, I can't see getting a warrant for probable cause. And you know, the owner isn't going to bring any charges.

"Okay, we're here. I'll go up and talk to the Kerleys. *You* go up to you room and take a nice hot shower. Don't worry – I'll keep you in the loop. I'll see you tomorrow, okay?" He made a show of scraping some mud off her face and shaking it off his finger. By the way, your shirt is on inside out. You're too pretty to be running around looking like such a mess – you know that?"

Thursday, April 18

Chapter 37

The Last Suspect

THE NEXT MORNING ALEX WOKE up early with pressing questions on her mind to ask Arlie Tate: *Had he arrested the Kerleys for smuggling? Had he arrested Wade or Ronette or both, for murder? Had he been able to inspect Raymond Bean's bookkeeping?*

The detective might still be in the Inn with the Kerleys. If he wasn't, she'd take the ferry over to St. Annes to maybe find him at the police station. There was no point in following more leads to solve the murder until she knew what Arlie Tate had learned from last night's suspects.

Sitting up in bed, she was reminded of her latest adventure as her eyes lighted on her crumpled brown slacks and jersey that she had stripped off the previous night and left where she was standing, unwilling to deal with the sloppy mess at the time. Hopefully, they were dry now so that she could clean them up enough to be able to repack them.

Getting out of bed, she picked up the pants and shirt and carried them into the bathroom. As she shook off some loose dirt over the sink, something fell out of one of the pants pockets that clunked against the counter and started rolling away.

Grabbing it before it fell on the floor, she saw that it was the fancy silver doodad that she had thought was Phyllis Hanover's charm when she found it on the floor of the tram yesterday. Last night she had shown it to Phyllis, but she had never seen it before.

Holding the object, Alex turned it over in her hand, fingering it. It was basically a tube with an opening at each end. Was it a whistle? Made sense, but it was so small and slender. Washing it off under the faucet, she blew into one end to try it out. Apparently, it was broken, or it wasn't a whistle, because it didn't make any noise, other than a breathy sound. So, what was it? And whose was it? And, did it matter?

She thought back to when she found it. It was after Raymond Bean had fallen trying to get off the tram to let the others on. She was the first one to board and had picked it up where he had fallen. Probably it was his. She'd take it down with her to breakfast and show it to him.

While she was putting on her makeup, and tamping down her unruly hair, she felt uneasy. There was something in the back of her mind about the kind of whistles that don't make a noise – no, not that don't make a *noise;* it's that the noise they make isn't in the *range that people can hear*. That's it. It was a *dog* whistle that has a pitch above human frequency. But, why would Raymond Bean have a dog whistle? He certainly didn't have a dog. Dogs weren't allowed anywhere on the island.

Hmmm. There was definitely something suspicious about Raymond Bean having a dog whistle, and she didn't intend to give it back to him until she had figured out what it was.

In fact, she'd better keep it her little secret. It could be another clue about Raymond Bean's activities that she should investigate; which meant that she shouldn't mention it to Arlie

Tate, either. He didn't seem to appreciate all that she had discovered so far in her sleuthing – like turning up a bunch of ex-cons. She thought back to when her roommate Beth and she had joked about the place being another Devil's Island – because of the wild animals, not the wild people. Wait till she told her about what had happened this week.

Hurriedly dressing in a knit top and the same black slacks she had on the night of the murder, she was ready. Maybe wearing the same slacks was symbolic of coming full circle – from the crime to the solution.

Before she left her room, she glanced out the window to see what the day looked like. There were several wild horses on the front grounds again, like the day before. Were they the same ones? Probably. She seemed to remember hearing that herds of wild horses roamed in a certain range. Watching them peacefully grazing brought her mind back to the horses that had stampeded over Ronette on that ill-fated tram excursion last Sunday. The horses that day had looked calm too, at first. Then, the lead stallion had reared up and the others had bolted, as though they were frightened to death. Strangest thing she had ever seen.

Thinking about that reminded her that she'd better get down to breakfast to try and locate Detective Tate to see what happened with the Kerleys last night.

Walking into the dining room, she saw that only Amanda and Johnny had made it down for breakfast. Alex gave them a little wave "hello" in passing, but Amanda excitedly motioned for her to come over to their table.

"Alex, wait till you hear this!" Amanda's eyes were as big as saucers. "When Johnny and I came down about a half-hour ago, two Coast Guard officers were in the lobby with Arlie Tate, arresting Wade and Ronette Kerley. I don't know what the charges were, but you should have heard Ronette. She was raising a ruckus, yelling at the officers, and I quote, 'It can't be illegal to be married to a moron, so why are you arresting *me*?

He's the one you want!' Not exactly the loyal wife, but she may have had a point.

"What do you think they could have done? I mean, they've been with us all the time. Do you think it was about the murder? But why, then, would the Coast Guard be involved?"

"Well, I'm afraid that *I* had something to do with this," Alex said, wincing. "I don't know if I'm allowed to tell you, but it'll most likely get out, anyway." Alex leaned forward, lowering her voice. "Before anyone else was finished with dinner last night, I saw Wade and Ronette leaving the Inn with their suitcases. Since they hadn't advised me of an early departure, I decided to follow them. They walked down to the Inn's pier where a boat pulled up – I thought to take them away. I stayed hidden to see what would happen next, when a man in the boat called out to them in Spanish."

"In Spanish?" Amanda asked, like she hadn't heard right. "I mean, I wouldn't have thought the Kerleys were bi-lingual."

"Well, they aren't, as far as I know, but there didn't seem to be much need for conversation as the meeting had obviously been pre-arranged for a simple drop-off. Turned out that the boat was loaded with some kind of cargo that I couldn't see. It must have been illegal, though, since they had snuck off in the dark and everything. Anyway, the Kerleys transferred whatever it was to their suitcases. The boat took off and the Kerleys went back to their room.

"I met up with Arlie Tate and told him what I had seen and heard. By the way, is he still here in the hotel, do you know?"

"No – I didn't see him after the Kerleys were arrested, anyway," Amanda replied. "But, oh my God! The Kerleys are smugglers? Who would have thought? Do you think it was drugs or guns?"

"Maybe it was diamonds," Johnny interjected. "Isn't that something smuggled into the country by boat?"

"Not from *Mexico*," Amanda remarked, as though stating the obvious.

"We're on the wrong ocean for the boat to have come from Mexico," Alex reminded them. "Anyway, I'm sure we'll hear what it was all about, soon. My real concern is that we find out who murdered Conrad Pierce, and I'm not so sure that the fact the Kerleys are smugglers sheds any light on that. What worries me is that Detective Tate still hasn't come up with evidence pointing to anyone other than Margaret Pierce who had left some hairs at the scene, which can be easily explained. I can't believe that Margaret could possibly do such a thing – or Chloe, and they're the only ones with any motive at all."

Alex turned her attention to the doorway. "Oh, swait. There's Detective Tate now. Will you excuse me?" Without waiting for a reply, she took off after him.

"Were you looking for me?" Alex asked, catching up with the detective who had walked away after glancing in the dining room.

"Not at the moment, but since you're here, I do have something to tell you. Take a seat." He indicated a bench.

Alex sat and looked up excitedly. "The Bertholds told me that Ronette and Wade were arrested this morning by the Coast Guard, so it must have been smuggling. Was it guns or drugs?"

"Whoa. Simmer down. They took delivery of a hundred and fifty boxes of Cuban cigars. Not the brightest plan since they'd be hard to fence to anyone legitimate who could sell them for enough to make it worthwhile. Ronette claims she had nothing to do with the scheme. Maybe not, but it's not my case. At any rate, I don't think this has anything to do with the Pierce murder. They obviously came here to avoid legal ports of entry like Miami and Jacksonville that are regulated by Customs."

"I guess that's what *I* am for Bedford Island," Alex offered.

"Yeah, you're 'Miss Homeland Security.' Well, anyway, that seems to wrap things up for the 'Case of the Cuban Cigars." The Coasties weren't really interested and turned the matter over to the Sheriff's office. They'll get involved if our investigation leads to anything. But I should thank you on behalf of the Coast Guard and Customs for sniffing out Wade's little scheme, in case he's involved with some major smugglers."

"So, you're saying I'm a good detective, and I've been helpful to law enforcement," Alex goaded him.

"I'd say you've been more lucky than good, but you can take credit for it anyway. Oh, by the way, I've been checking out some of the other employees here, and the trend continues. Seems that Chef Kasmarek has overstayed his visa, Tina Wrenn has a sheet for drug arrests and minor thefts, and Tim Williams had hit and killed someone while driving drunk, having already lost his license for DUIs."

Alex blinked and stared hard at him.

Arlie continued. "I still can't find a connection between any of the employees and Conrad Pierce, so Margaret's still the only one who looks good for the murder. I'll be talking to her some more. I'm not convinced she's told me everything she knows."

Alex nodded emphatically. "I'm not done checking everyone out, Arlie. And my success last night gives me just the encouragement I need."

Arlie put a firm hand on her knee. "Yes, you *are* done, Alex. You've done a good job, but a lot of these people have records, and some of them for violent crimes. I can't let you nose around anymore. This isn't a game like your *Clue,* you know. I'm serious, Alex. Alex, do you understand?"

She had stared off into space, lost in her thoughts, while fingering the dog whistle in her pocket. *A whistle that humans can't hear, but a dog can. A dog, or a cat, or some other animal ... like a horse. That was it. It was a high-pitched whistle that horses can hear that would frighten them, but can't be heard by humans!*

"Alex, I asked if you understood me."

"Yes. In fact, I understand more than you know, Arlie. I've gotta run now. I'll see you later."

“Alex!” he called after her retreating figure. “No more snooping! I’m serious! I don’t want you to get hurt!”

Chapter 38

Playing the Horses

ALEX TOOK THE HALLWAY that led to the back door and basement stairs. Once outside, she made her way to the south side of the Inn, having to grope through a thicket of vegetation until she could find a peephole to give her a view of the front grounds. Over by the pond was what she was hoping to see: the herd of wild horses. The large black stallion stood protectively by as a couple of mares and a colt bent down to take a drink in the clear water.

She was struck again by how peaceful the scene was. The sun had risen high enough to dry off the morning dew and warm the air, creating a perfect springtime day. Standing in her sheltered spot, all she could hear was her own breathing as she remained still, watching the shaggy-coated animals.

After a minute or two, she pulled the whistle out of her shirt pocket and, with shaking hands, put it up to her lips. Looking around, she satisfied herself that no one else was in the area, but took a few moments to review her plan and check out her position for escape. She was well back from the horses, was totally hidden, and had a short route back to the Inn. She was ready.

With a soft breath, she blew into the whistle for a second. The stallion stretched out his powerful neck and tilted one ear forward. Then, turning his head, he moved his ears back and forth several times in an effort to pick up any sounds around him. The two mares and the colt by the pond nervously stepped back away from the water. Several others in the herd became skittish and started walking in circles.

Alex blew one burst of air through the whistle. The stallion pawed the ground and snorted, his ears pinned back against his head. The rest of the herd started crowding behind him and whinnied; just as the horses had done the previous Sunday.

She put down the whistle and stayed still. The big black horse again tilted his ears back and forth, one at a time. He was still on alert, but he hadn't picked up on an imminent threat from which to run. Choosing a lesser course of action, he turned and loped across the grounds in the opposite direction, leaving the herd to follow him.

She had seen enough. There could be no doubt: this dog whistle had been used last Sunday to panic the horses into stampeding over Ronette. Alex had blown the whistle for only a couple of seconds today, which had been enough to cause a fearful reaction in the herd. She felt sure that if she had continued to blow on it, she could have incited he horses to stampede.

Now that she knew how the horses had been intentionally frightened, she had to prove who had done it, and for what reason. She was sure, also, that Phyllis hadn't accidentally fallen off the cliff, but had been pushed. Both incidents must have been brought about by the same hand. It seemed most likely that Raymond Bean was the culprit, but she had no proof. She had to find the evidence that would put that whistle into the manager's hands and worry about his motivations, later. Nothing made sense right now.

Back in the hotel, she went straight over to the reception desk where Tina Wrenn was mechanically stamping papers.

"Psst! Tina!" Alex whispered loudly enough to get her attention. "I need your help. Do you know where Raymond Bean is right now?"

"No, not right this minute," Tina answered, dubiously. "But you need to know where he's going to be this afternoon. I was just about to look for you to tell you -- he's going into St. Annes to visit his mother."

"What?" Alex couldn't help but cry out. "Oh, my God. This can't happen, especially now. He'll find out that I was there to visit Lucie. How do you think he's going to take *that* news?"

"Not well," Tina answered the rhetorical question. "I'm supposed to ask everyone if they'd like to go with him in the van to catch the ferry to town, but maybe you'd better not," she advised.

"No kidding. Well, I guess now I'll have to move up my plans, and you're going to have to help me. You've already given me clues to uncover a few secrets about this place – like, when you sent me down to Virgil Grimm's room so I'd find his child pornography. I think you did that because you thought he was the murderer."

"I thought you should know about his criminal past; that you'd tell the detective who would take another look at Virgil."

"Well, I did, but Arlie Tate doesn't believe that Virgil killed Conrad because he didn't have a motive. But, because of you, Tate has discovered that everyone who works here has a criminal record-– including you."

Tina turned ashen. "I've been clean for two years," she protested, her eyes filling with tears.

"That's great, Tina. I didn't tell you that to upset you; just to let you know how thorough he's being. I don't hold your past against you. You know I've considered you a confidant. I'm pretty sure that Raymond Bean is the one responsible for at least some of the trouble we've had this week; and maybe even the murder. At this point, I'm almost sure I can connect him to a dog whistle I found that was used to make the horses stampede over Ronette Kerley. If so, he must have pushed Phyllis off the cliff, too, and probably even left the snake in Lawrence Livermore's bed. But I don't have any proof. Do you know if this is his whistle?" Alex held up the silver tube for Tina to get a good look.

"I don't know," Tina whimpered, "but you're right that Raymond Bean's a bad person. I think he tells the owner, Mr. Hall, that we make more than we do, and then he takes a percentage to pay for his mother's nursing home. I know that we make less than other people in the same jobs at other hotels. But what can we do? Who else would hire us?

Tina put her hands over her face for a moment, then shook her head. "I hoped that you would expose him for stealing our money. I don't think the owner knows anything about it. That's why I wanted you to go see Lucie Bean. How can he afford to pay for that on his salary? But you can't confront him – it's too dangerous. Just tell Detective Tate what you suspect."

"Tina, I have to act now. Bean's going to know that I'm on to him when he visits his mother and they tell him that I was there. He's not stupid. There's no *good* reason for me to have gone to see his mother. I have to get proof of whatever he's guilty of while he's gone, and you're going to help me get it. I need one of those 'magic' keys to get into Bean's cottage."

"No," Tina objected. "You'll be found out. And if you are, you could end up like Conrad Pierce!"

"Let's not get too dramatic. Just give me the key, Tina, and I'll worry about covering my tracks. The only way to get the goods on the man is to go through his house. The bookkeeping must be there and anything else that can point to his guilt that we can't get to legally."

Tina frowned, pursing her lips, thinking it over, but didn't make a move. Alex leaned towards her and put out her palm. "Give me the key, Tina. You don't have to be an indentured servant anymore if you just give - me - the - key."

Tina swallowed hard, blinking back tears. "You can't even call for help if you get in trouble!" she squeaked.

"Give me the key," Alex said again, calmly. "I can be in and out within an hour. He'll be gone for at least four hours. There's nothing to worry about. Raymond Bean is the one who should be worried."

Tina turned around, opened a drawer and turned back. "There," she said, pressing the skeleton key in Alex's hand.

"Thanks, Tina. You won't regret this. You're doing everyone here a favor. The next time I see you, Raymond Bean should be in custody, charged with whatever crimes he's committed, and you'll be free from his tyranny forever."

"Do you really think so?" Tina's asked, her voice quavering.

"I've known things weren't right here for a long time. I'm always waiting for the next bad thing to happen."

"So—there have been other suspicious 'accidents'?"

"Yes, but nothing that couldn't be explained away – a fall, a missing piece of jewelry, a sudden illness. Enough to make me worry about all the guests, though. You know what I mean? After a while, it just seemed to me that there couldn't be so many 'accidents.' It made me a nervous wreck to think that someone else could get hurt – or worse, and then it happened."

"Yeah, I see what you mean. I just wish I knew if Raymond Bean or Virgil Grimm was the murderer. I'm still not writing off Virgil as he's a known felon, but right now I have to investigate Raymond Bean and see what I come up with. "

Thursday afternoon

Chapter 39

Breaking and Entering

ALL THE GUESTS signed up with Tina for the tram ride to the ferry that afternoon. Alex wondered if they were eager to get off the island, or just wanted to keep an eye on one another. In the wake of the arrest of Wade and Ronette Kerley, the level of suspicion in the group had risen once again.

Raymond Bean, noting that Alex wasn't on the list, caught up with her as she was getting her lunch and asked if she wouldn't like to come, too. She had answered that she couldn't as she had some "exploring to do," managing to keep a straight face.

At one o'clock, Alex and Tina stood by a front window and watched as Bean and his ten passengers drove off in the van.

"I'll wait for another five minutes," Alex said, "just to make sure that they don't come back for something one of them forgot. Then I'll walk down to Bean's cottage. The housekeepers will be cleaning rooms for a while, so they won't be around to see me go in."

"Why don't I go with you?" Tina suggested. "I could be the lookout."

"No, if any of the staff sees that you're not here, they could sense that something's wrong and start checking things out. Besides, the more people involved with breaking into Bean's house, the more possibilities that he'll find out."

"Ooh, that sounds so bad – breaking into his house," Tina said, dismally.

"Tina. I know it isn't totally legal." She made a face. "Okay — it's not legal at all. But there's no other way. Just make sure you don't give me away. Remember, we're in this together. You need to stay at your desk and do your job, and *act normal*. If I'm caught, I could be in big trouble."

Alex thought of Detective Tate's warning to *her* that she was disregarding, and hoped that Tina wouldn't disregard hers.

"Anyway, the van's been gone for several minutes – long enough that they would have returned by now for a forgotten item. I'd better go over to Bean's cottage and get this over with. Besides, I don't want to have to hurry going through the place, especially since I have no idea what I'm looking for, other than the financial records."

"I'll come after you if you're not back in two hours." Tina said, still not comfortable with the plan.

"No, you just stay at the front desk. I'll get back to you when I'm finished."

Walking out the side entrance, Alex had a feeling of deja vu. She was again scanning the area to make sure no one else was around as she was about to pull off another dangerous mission. Thinking back to when she had snuck into Virgil Grimm's room, she comforted herself that this wasn't as risky as that had been and she had gotten away cleanly that time – although it had been close, she reminded herself.

Starting down the path that led to the manager's cottage, she thought back to when she took this same route on the evening of the murder to tell Raymond Bean to call the police. Recalling that night, she remembered that he had only opened the door a crack when he answered the doorbell.

Was there something inside he didn't want her to see? Or, was it a normal response when a near-stranger is outside your door late at night screaming that someone has been murdered? That *was* another possible explanation.

Once she got to the door of the white frame cottage, she knocked and waited; just in case. Relieved that there was no answer, it suddenly occurred to her that there could have been a cleaning person there, or one could be stopping by, later. On second thought, it was a small house that the manager could easily take care of himself. The man was only in his late forties.

Nevertheless, she should have considered all possible interruptions. At that moment, the only other potential visitor she could think of was a repairman like Virgil Grimm. Wouldn't that be ironic? He hadn't caught her searching *his* room but could walk in on her in Raymond Bean's house. That was unlikely. Raymond Bean would probably arrange to be at home if there was a needed repair.

No more excuses—it was now or never. Stiffening her spine, literally and figuratively, she tried the key in the door. The lock gave way and the door swung open. Quickly closing it behind her, she slowly raised her eyes to survey the room, afraid of what she might see. Looking around, she stood there with her mouth open, staring in amazement.

The room gave the unmistakable impression that an old woman still lived there, even down to the sharp aroma of talcum powder in the air that tickled her nose. *Of course, Lucie Bean must have lived here before she went into the nursing home,* she reasoned. Bean had told her that he hadn't married so that he could take care of his mother. *But he hasn't redecorated since she had been moved into Whispering Pines?* Given the extent of the woman's senility, she must have been there for at least a couple of years.

She couldn't imagine a man feeling at home here. The walls were painted a soft rose color, trimmed in ivory. Across the room was a floral chintz-covered sofa on which nested several ruffled throw pillows in pastel colors. A light green crocheted throw was draped over one arm.

In front of the sofa was a mahogany drop-leaf table on which lay what appeared to be a couple of old-style photograph albums and a large bible covered in bumpy-grained black leather.

On each side of the sofa were needlepoint-covered chairs. On the floor next to one of them was a basket that made her gape in astonishment. It was filled with skeins of pink yarn, along with a pair of plastic knitting needles with several inches of knitting on them in the same color. Had she walked onto a movie set -- *Psycho,* maybe? She couldn't imagine that Raymond Bean was knitting something, but why would he keep his mother's needlework where she had left it?

Tearing herself away from the knitting paraphernalia, she looked at the wall across from the sofa where there were low cabinets containing books that had a tube television set on top. *The man certainly doesn't spend much money on himself, even if he is a thief,* she mused.

Turning to her right, she saw a red brick fireplace at the end of the room. Next to it was an easy chair with a lamp table. A nondescript landscape painting hung over the mantel, while the only decorations on the mantelpiece were several framed photographs.

Turning to her left, she saw a large kneehole desk with a file drawer at the other end of the room. On the desk top were several matching accessories: leather pad, letter tray, pencil cup, letter opener, and a clock. Alex noted that the time was 1:25. She had been in the house for at least fifteen minutes. She still had plenty of time, but she'd better resist the temptation to go through the desk and the albums before she had seen the whole cottage.

To the right of the desk was a doorway. She crossed the room and went through it, finding herself in a small kitchen in which cabinets, a two burner cook top and a refrigerator, were installed on one wall. Against the opposite wall were a table and two chairs. At the near end of the room was a pantry closet, and at the far end was the door to the outside.

Back in the living room, she turned towards the back of the home and entered a short hallway that had three doors. The left door opened up to a bathroom furnished with a pedestal sink, a toilet, and tub. She noticed light was coming through the plastic shower curtain that had been pulled across the tub.

Opening the center door in the hallway, she saw only sheets and towels and other household supplies. Nothing of interest. But several flat boxes showed more promise. She'd have to come back to them.

Through the third hallway door was the bedroom, which was also decorated in the feminine taste of a bygone era: floral printed wallpaper, lace curtains, and a Martha Washington bedspread on the queen-sized bed. Alex recognized the spread by its distinctive terry looped geometric pattern. It was similar to one that her grandmother had owned.

Raymond must have let his mother have the bedroom when she lived here and he slept on the sofa. I guess he really has been a loving son. But how could he sleep in such a feminine room now?

Alex turned her attention to the six-drawer maple dresser opposite the bed. A piece of glass had been fitted over the top on which were placed several perfume bottles and half a dozen framed photographs. Above the dresser hung a scalloped-edge mirror that had become cloudy with loss of its silver backing.

A matching man's chest of drawers stood against another wall. Its surface also held several framed photographs, as well as a man's hair brush and a leather box.

Alex went back into the living room to double check if there were openings to more rooms that she might have missed. There were none. She had seen the whole cottage.

Glancing at the desk clock, she saw it was now 1:50. She'd better get busy. She should leave by two-thirty to be sure to avoid any of the housekeeping help who could be returning to their own cottages nearby.

Alex went back to the bedroom where she had decided to start her search. Picking up a photograph from the dresser, she saw that it was of Raymond Bean, from maybe twenty years earlier, posed with his arm around an attractive middle-aged woman in a floral two-piece dress: Lucie Bean.

A second photograph caught her attention as it had been ripped in half, but left in its frame. What remained was the image of a young blond woman with her one arm extended, that must have been around someone else. The curvaceous woman was shown standing on a beach, wearing a modest two-piece swimsuit – a style that Alex thought was from the 1950s.

Another photo of the woman, from about the same time period, pictured her with a chubby infant on her lap.

Other photos were of Raymond as a boy; either pictured alone or with his mother. *Where was the father?* She didn't think that Lucie would have become pregnant through a brief, casual relationship. And Lucie was referred to as *Mrs.* Bean at the nursing home.

Opening the top left drawer of the dresser, Alex carefully lifted up a few lace-trimmed hankies and ladies' gloves. The top right drawer contained nylon stockings. *Or were they silk?* Some had seams going up the backs, which she knew hadn't been in style since the 1950s.

Opening the other drawers in the dresser, Alex found them packed with feminine clothing – mostly intimate apparel – scented from sachets of dried lavender. *Why were these things still here?*

Going over to the man's chest, Alex examined the photographs on top, first. One was probably Raymond's high school graduation picture, given the formal pose. He looked very much the same, except for being about thirty pounds lighter and with a full head of hair; but there was no mistaking the serious grey eyes, round cheeks and soft lips.

There was another torn photograph with about a third of the picture missing. What remained was of a pre-teen Raymond, wearing shorts and holding hands with his mother who was wearing a yellow sun dress. Both had tans and appeared to be relaxing on vacation. *Must be the same person torn out of this photo as the other one,* Alex reasoned.

Pulling open the drawers, Alex saw they all contained the usual men's apparel – socks, underwear, knit shirts. Nothing remarkable.

What *was* remarkable was that the room appeared to have been *shared,* given the equal number of men's and women's personal items. *But that wasn't possible, was it?* She looked over at the bed with more scrutiny, and blinked in disbelief. Crossing over to it, she ran her hand across the surface, which confirmed what she thought she had seen – there was a clear and definite depression on both sides of the bed.

Alex felt sick as she pulled down the bedding to better inspect the mattress. *Wait, what was that?* Walking around to the other side of the bed, she gingerly picked up a piece of silky pink fabric before realizing that it was a negligee. Closely inspecting the filmy garment, the scent of lavender wafted up – and stuck in her throat.

Dropping the lingerie, Alex forced herself to reach under and probe the contours of the mattress. There was no mistaking the fact that it had been hollowed out by two people of different sizes -- who must have *slept together* for several years.

Could there be any other explanation than the unspeakable – that Lucie and Raymond Bean -- mother and son-- had been lovers?

She had to get out of there to clear her head. Running back into the living room, she saw that the clock read 2:15. She had been in the cottage for an hour. She should go back in the bedroom to remake the bed, but she was too overcome right then.

Instead, she went over to the desk and pulled open the large center drawer. Right on top was a black hardcover book with corners and spine in red leather that she recognized as being an accounting book. Opening it, the familiar columned green pages confirmed its identity. Quickly perusing a few pages, there appeared to be a careful recording of income minus expenses all written out in the same small cramped handwriting. Without a comparison of the figures with receipts and billing statements, Alex couldn't imagine how anyone could tell whether or not they were accurate.

Feeling around in the drawer, she found another ledger book, this one with dark green corners and spine. Opening it to the first page, it was dated the first of the current year. Turning to the first page in the red-spine book, it also was dated the first of the current year. Looking across pages with the same dates in each book, she quickly saw that the items were identical, but that the figures were different.

This was how Raymond Bean was stealing from his employer and diverting money to pay for his mother's nursing home. It was the oldest trick in the proverbial 'book' – a duplicate set of records. Glancing down to compare amounts, item for item, she could calculate that the manager was inflating expenses for supplies and salaries by at least twenty percent, and decreasing actual income by the same percentage. *That's why the owner, Mr. Hall, thought that the place was such a money pit!*

Leaning back in the office chair, Alex wondered if she should just take both books with her, like she took Virgil Grimm's pornography. This was different, as Bean would be immediately aware of the theft. She would have to be prepared to publicly accuse the manager of embezzlement. Detective Tate couldn't obtain the books unless he got a warrant, which he said he couldn't do. She owed it to Tina Wrenn and the others to see this through. She kept out the two ledger books to take with her, but she had a lot of other things to look through before she was ready to leave.

Sitting down on the sofa, she picked up one of the photo albums. Opening it, she noted that all the photographs in this volume were black and white and held in place with glued-on corners. While there were some pictures of other family members and friends, most of them were of Raymond and his mother; pictured either singly or together. She found several more torn photographs that she thought must have included Lucie's husband; Raymond's father. *But what had happened to him? And why was he so despised?*

The second album contained colored photographs of a more recent vintage. Flipping through them, she couldn't find any more torn photos. *Apparently, Raymond's father was gone by then.*

Returning to the first few pages, she looked at the pictures that were mostly of Lucie and Raymond taken on special occasions, such as Christmas and on summer vacations where they posed against backgrounds of mountains, or sitting on beach chairs.

The last few pages held photos that had been taken by a so-called "instant camera," the type popular in the 1980s – photos that didn't have to be processed at a photography shop. The first few were of an embarrassed-looking Lucie Bean striking awkward "sexy" poses that showed her reclining on the sofa in a white terrycloth robe – opening it enough to reveal a bare leg in one, and dropping the robe off one shoulder on another.

Photos in the next few pages showed a different Lucie: a more glamorous, seductive woman wearing skimpy lingerie – bras and panties with garter belts that held up seamed stockings like Alex had seen in the drawers. Alex started gagging as she imagined Raymond directing his mother to assume the titillating poses.

But they hadn't really prepared her for the photographs at the back of the album: unmistakable evidence of incest between Raymond and Lucie. In all of them, the two smiled wolfishly at the camera to record their sensual pleasure.

For several seconds, Alex couldn't take her eyes off the unspeakably obscene pictures. Leaning back against the cushions, she closed her eyes to block out the images. Keeping her eyes shut, she tried to calm herself enough to think rationally to put everything back as she had found it, and to take some of the photos with her, along with the financial books.

Her reverie was stopped short by the sound of the clicking of the unlocked latch in the front door as it moved back and forth. Her eyes snapped open to see Raymond Bean standing in the doorway, staring at her.

"Can I help you, Miss Trotter? Or have you already found what you were looking for?" he asked politely, as though waiting on a customer in a gift shop. Alex's blood ran cold.

Chapter 40

The Confrontation

"WHAT ARE *YOU* DOING HERE?" she sputtered, cursing herself for asking an absurd question; not that she could have thought of anything better even if she had considered the possibility of being discovered, which she hadn't. At least, asking the question had given her a moment to absorb the shock of being caught, but she'd need more time to sharpen her senses to devise a plan of escape. Her life might depend on it.

"What am *I* doing here? Hah!" Raymond Bean snorted with a mirthless laugh. "That's a good one coming from an intruder! To answer your question, I guess you could say I was lucky to have had a flat tire or I might have missed your little visit, Miss Trotter." He flashed a mirthless smile.

The manager's mock cheerfulness was more terrifying to Alex than if he had been furious. What was he planning to do now that the proverbial "jig" was up? He must realize that neither one of them had to keep pretending anymore. And yet, he just stood there, grinning at her. She had to be ready for anything.

She already knew that he was a sexual pervert and a thief. The only question that remained was whether he was a killer, too.

His maddening silence was making her heart beat a tattoo against her chest. *Say something,* she thought. She reminded herself that she had better calm down and keep her wits about her. This was no time to panic – she needed all her facilities to be able to find an opportunity to get out of there.

The first thought that came to her was that she could charge into his midsection and bring him down. Then she could just run out the front door. She was younger and in better shape. She should be able to tackle him, even though he outweighed her by a hundred pounds. But what if she failed? What would he do then? She'd better not risk it, she decided. She'd wait to catch him off guard to give herself a better chance at success. Right now, what she needed most was to stall for enough time to work out a plan; or for someone to come by the cottage so she could scream for help.

"Actually, I'm not that surprised to find you here," Raymond said brightly, shocking her back to the present. "When I called the nursing home from the dock to tell them that I couldn't make it today, do you know what they told me? Yes, I can see that you do." At the question, Alex had gone limp, her face drained of blood. "They told me that *you* had stopped by to visit my mother yesterday. Now why would you want to do that? I asked myself."

"Tina had suggested it, telling me that your mother was in such a lovely –"

"Shut the fuck up! You were sticking your nose in my business! Just like in the bar last night when you asked, oh so innocently, 'Why haven't you ever married, Raymond?'" The falsetto voice he used made his words even more menacing. "Did you think I didn't know what you were doing? Do you think I'm stupid?" He paused, causing Alex to swallow hard and steel herself for what was coming next. "I can't hear you! I asked you if you think I'm stupid."

"No, of course not," Alex murmured, not looking up. "You're right. I have a tendency to ask too many personal questions," she added, lamely.

"Let's just cut to the chase," said Raymond, affecting a more business-like tone. "You didn't answer *my* question, which was -- what are you doing in my home going through my things?" As he spoke, he surveyed the room, squinting his eyes and deeply frowning. He ended his visual inspection with a sideways glance at his desktop on which lay the two accounting books.

Seeing this, Alex tried to divert his attention. "I - I was just taking a walk, and saw this cute cottage and wondered what it looked like inside. I tried the door and it was open, so I came in. I didn't know it was yours and . . ."

"LIAR!!" Raymond roared, pounding his fist on the desk causing Alex to jerk upright. Looking at her accuser, she was horrified to see the man's pale, doughy face redden and bloat with rage; the blood vessels in his neck thickened like rope.

"Don't play with me, missy. You had no trouble identifying my cottage in the dark the night Conrad Pierce was murdered. That was the first time you brought trouble to my door, and you've been nothing but trouble since then – you and that bunch of heathens you brought with you!"

Raymond's outburst had roused Alex out of her frozen state. Without thinking, she jumped to her feet, prepared for flight or fight.

As she took one step to get around the coffee table, Raymond screamed, "SIT DOWN, BITCH! YOU'RE NOT GOING ANYWHERE!"

Alex teetered momentarily, uncertain of her next move. She heard Raymond yank open the top left drawer of the desk. Reaching in, he turned towards her, a semi-automatic in his right hand. It was a weapon she had seen before but it wasn't a game anymore. Leveling the gun at her mid-section, Raymond noisily racked the slide that dropped a bullet into the chamber. He and the handgun were ready for business.

Alex crumpled onto the sofa; her resolve gone as she realized that she had probably missed her best chance of getting away. This would require a different strategy than just making a run for it.

"I said, you're not going anywhere," Raymond repeated slowly, in a quiet voice. He was no longer smiling.

"You can't just shoot me here in broad daylight with people around!" she protested, hoping she sounded more confident than she felt. "Besides, Detective Tate knows I'm here. He should be looking for me any time now."

"Oh, I don't think so," responded Raymond. "I just saw him leaving our dock in his launch after he had finished with his business at the Inn. I understand that you brought him out here late last night to arrest the Kerleys for buying cigars. I don't think he's worried about you being in any danger after your hysterics over nothing. He knows you're a troublemaker, too." he sneered.

"One of my group was murdered!" Alex countered, hoping to regain some ground by going on the attack. "And I have a duty to report anything that might have a bearing on the case. I think *you* might know something about that," she gambled.

"About who murdered Conrad Pierce? Is that why you broke into my house and looked through God-knows-what? He glanced down at the accounting books, again, looking perplexed. "If you know what's good for you, you'll start telling me the truth. It would be a shame if you were to have a tragic accident. I'm sure you'd be greatly missed," he added, luridly.

"An 'accident' like what you arranged for Ronette and Phyllis?" Alex rejoined, hoping she hadn't gone too far in goading him. It occurred to her that the longer she kept Raymond talking, the greater were her chances to survive. She was betting her life that he had the ego to want to brag about his exploits. Maybe she could keep him talking long enough for Tina to come looking for her; except that she had told Tina *not* to come looking for her, she remembered, miserably.

"Ronette and Phyllis are both whores!" Raymond screamed. "Ronette couldn't wait to fornicate like a mongrel in heat! And she a married woman, consecrated to another man. Phyllis Hanover isn't much better. She threw herself at Lawrence Livermore to steal him away from Nadine. I saw it all during the cocktail time, and later, after dinner. They're both harlots.

"The Lord God said that the loose woman who 'forgets the covenant of her God sinks down to death,'" Raymond quoted, loftily.

"That sounds like something from the Old Testament," said Alex, grateful for another avenue to explore. "Is that why Conrad Pierce was killed – because he *fornicated* with a harlot?" she suggested, hoping she hadn't been too obvious in connecting him to the murder.

"Of course not! You're so stupid! I don't know about Conrad Pierce, anyway. You think you're being clever, to get me to talk about that, but you've got another 'think' coming. You're not going to pin that on me!

"But what do you think you know about Ronette's and Phyllis' accidents?" he asked, backtracking. He sounded intrigued.

Alex was pleased to see that she was getting to him. Maybe, if she could provoke him into boasting about how clever he had been in endangering Ronette and Phyllis, he'd open up about his other crimes -- maybe even how he was involved in the murder of Conrad Pierce.

Whatever she could get him to talk about would buy her some time to figure out a means of escape. She really didn't think he planned to shoot her in cold blood; but she didn't want to dare him to pull the trigger by making a sudden move, either. At any rate, it wasn't the right time to try to make a break for it.

"What do I *know* about how *you* arranged for their accidents? To tell you the truth, I couldn't figure out *what* had happened for a while. I have to admit you were pretty clever." The manager beamed with pleasure.

"At first, I just knew that it didn't make sense for two people to have a near-fatal 'accident' on the same short outing; but I couldn't see *how* or *why* someone would try to hurt those two women.

"And then, when we went on the tram again yesterday, I found *this* on the floor – right where you fell -- and I realized it was yours." She had dug the dog whistle out of her shirt pocket and was dangling it by its ring, teasingly.

"I didn't even know what it was at first, but then it came to me. You made a big mistake by keeping it on you. Once I figured out what it was and that it belonged to *you*, it was just a matter of putting two and two together."

"It's just a dog whistle – why would that be suspicious?" Raymond asked, looking genuinely puzzled.

"You don't have a dog," she said quietly. Then paused to let it sink in. "And there are no dogs on the island." Raymond blinked in recognition of the logic.

"So, then I had to figure out another use for it," Alex went on, conversationally. "It came to me that if the whistle is in a *dog's* range of hearing, probably other animals hear in the same high range – like *horses,* for instance.

"To test my theory, I blew the whistle near a herd outside the Inn. They became fearful like the ones that stampeded over Ronette. That's when I knew for sure how you almost got Ronette killed."

"Fine," Raymond said, conceding the point. "There's nothing illegal about blowing a whistle. I couldn't *possibly* have planned where Ronette would end up, and in what direction the horses would run. I guess I didn't know my own powers. In the scriptures, the Lord once cast a spell over a herd of swine that rushed down a steep bank and into the sea where they perished, to prove his powers."

"Is that why you did it?" Alex asked. "To show how powerful you are? You didn't need much power to push Phyllis Hanover off the cliff."

"I don't have to prove anything to a bunch of spoiled, self-indulgent rich people. I was just trying to even the score. Every sinner must pay the price to have redemption. Think of me as an intermediary to exact justice here on earth to prepare people for the next life."

"Is that why you take money from your employees? Why don't you think that the punishment given to them by *actual* judges isn't adequate to pay for their crimes? Is that what you were trying to tell me last night when you referred to 'redemption money' -- that's what you take from all your employees to pay for your mother's care."

Raymond scowled, screwing up his mouth. "Oh, aren't you the clever little one!" he spat out. "I didn't *think* I left these accounting books out. Are *these* what you came here for?" he bellowed, holding up one of the journals. "Who put you up to this? You might as well tell me."

"No one. I came up with that myself." Alex noticed that while she had been explaining her whistle theory, Raymond had laid the gun on the desk, but kept his hand on it. She decided she'd better keep talking which seemed to distract him, even if she was laying out a case against him.

"First, I learned that nearly everyone you hired came out of prison," she started. "Now, why would you do that, I wondered? Were you a great humanitarian who wanted to give people a second chance? After I figured out that you caused the horses to stampede and that you pushed Phyllis, I knew that that couldn't be the case. Looking at how the employees could be a benefit to you, it finally came to me. You hired people you could *control* – people who didn't have good options if they didn't do as you said.

"I first noticed Tina's obvious anxiety all the time, especially when you were around. And then, there was Virgil

Grimm's gloominess, and Edna Butz' surliness. No one seemed to enjoy working here and they insulted the guests, and yet they've been here for years."

"You don't know what you're talking about," Raymond interjected. "They're grateful to be working here. Without me, they'd be out on the street."

"Without *you* they'd be able to keep their whole salaries," Alex countered.

"They are *earning their redemption*!" Raymond thundered, his face darkening again.

"By paying for your mother's care? You're nothing but an embezzler. How are you going to earn *your* redemption?"

"You don't listen, do you!" shouted Raymond. "I exact retribution for their sins! They should thank me for that. And Mr. Hall doesn't have any complaints about my management, so why should you?"

Raymond picked up the gun and waved it in front of her. "You must not take me very seriously, Miss Trotter. *I'm* the one who has the gun. *You're* the one who's about to be shot for breaking into my house. I have every right to shoot someone I discover in my home who is threatening my life. All I'd have to say is that I heard a noise in the bedroom, went to check on it and saw – what do they always say? – oh yes, a 'dark figure' coming at me and I shot in self-defense. Do you see how I'm in charge of this little game of 'Truth or Dare'?"

Alex's mind was spinning as she contemplated her options. Maybe he was bluffing, but she couldn't be sure – was he capable of cold-blooded murder? If so, did he really believe that he could justify shooting her? A 'dark figure'— *in the middle of the day?* Clearly, he wasn't rational, but that didn't mean he wasn't calculating. He was looking at his options, too, and, from his point of view, letting her go wasn't a possibility after all she'd accused him of.

The desk clock read 3:10. She had been there for two hours. Even though she had discouraged Tina from coming to look for her after two hours, as nervous as the woman was, surely, she would check on things at some point. Right then, Alex just had to keep Raymond talking to play for more time.

"Is that what we're playing, 'Truth or Dare?'" Alex asked, innocently. "If that's the case, it's *my* turn – tell me the truth. What happened to your father? In the bedroom I saw photos of you and your mother where someone else had been ripped out of the pictures. Was that your father?"

"It not your turn to ask me for the truth!" Raymond wailed, sounding like a petulant child.

"Yes, it is," Alex retorted. "Remember, I told you the truth about how I figured out how you staged the 'accidents' that happened to Ronette and Phyllis."

"Oh, yeah," Raymond agreed, sticking out his lower lip in a pout. "I don't like to talk about him," he complained, peevishly.

"Go ahead, Raymond; I'm listening," Alex cooed, mimicking a psychologist's mantra. She sensed from his facial moue and babyish speech that he had regressed back in time. She hoped that, in this vulnerable state, he would be willing to follow instructions.

"He was very handsome," Raymond said, wistfully, staring off into space. "He used his good looks to attract my mother who was also very beautiful. They liked to go to the beach – to show off their bodies, I think."

"Yes, I saw the picture of your mother in a two-piece bathing suit with her arm around someone – your father? – who had been torn away."

"That picture was taken on their honeymoon," Raymond said, nodding in response. "They were in Miami Beach. She often told me about how romantic it was. Their hotel was on Ocean Boulevard – fronting the beach -- and they ate out under the stars and slept on satin sheets in the bridal suite."

"That *does* sound Romantic," Alex agreed.

"After I came along everything changed, according to my mother. My father became jealous of me because I took her attention away from him. She saw me as an extension of their love, but he saw me as a rival. By the time I started school, he had found other women who offered him more attention and 'you-know-what' else. As I grew older, he picked on me, telling me that I wasn't what he had hoped for in a son – I wasn't athletic, handsome, or clever, like he was. My mother tried to make up for his rejection by lavishing me with affection. She was like an angel who would cradle me in her arms and tell me how wonderful I was, and how much she loved me.

"When I was fourteen, my father became more open about his affairs. Women would call him at home. At one point, my mother found him in bed with some tramp – their marriage bed! Mother was furious, of course, and told him to get out of the house and to never come back.

"When I came home from school, he was packing up to leave. As I walked into their bedroom, he screamed, 'There's your lover, Lucie! You don't need me in your bed as long as you have him. He can take my place."

"That's the last time I ever saw my father. He disappeared and never bothered with us again. My mother had to find ways to make enough money to support us. Besides the economic hardship, she missed having a man to love her. She was still a beautiful, sexy woman."

"And so, you became her lover, for real," Alex offered.

"That's right! She made a man out of me, and I was able to show her how much I loved her. There's nothing wrong with that."

"It's called *incest,* Raymond, and it's perverse. Your mother had no right to steal your innocence to satisfy her own sexual appetites and to stroke her ego."

"YOU SHUT UP! No other woman could be compared to my mother – certainly not you. You shouldn't have been allowed in her presence. The grief that she suffered by my father's unfaithfulness caused her to lose her mind. Sometimes she doesn't even know who I am. I miss the way she was. I miss being with her – her scent and the warmth of her embrace."

"So, you sleep with her lingerie," Alex spoke her thought out loud.

"It's all I have left. Now I know how abandoned *she* felt after my father left."

"Wait a minute! I just got it!" Alex blurted out. "Conrad Pierce *was like your father*! He was also a good-looking sensual man who left the woman who loved him once she was pregnant. Before he left Jennifer's mother, he had also been unfaithful to her. Like your father, Conrad couldn't accept Jennifer, as he saw her as a rival. The child would take his place as the center of his girlfriend's world."

During Alex's speech, Raymond had been breathing hard, sweat glistening on his face. "That morning in the study" he said, as though in a trance, "I was listening through the door when that brute told Jennifer that even if she *was* his daughter he never wanted to see her again. That she was *nothing* to him.

"She's a beautiful girl who has done well in life without him. How *dare* he turn his back on her after she went to all the trouble to find him!"

"So you killed him," Alex said, softly. "You killed *him* because you hadn't been able to kill your own father."

"Yes, I killed him. I knew how Jennifer felt when she pleaded with that monster to just admit that she was his daughter. She didn't want anything more from him. She didn't want to take his place with her mother."

"How did you have a knife? Where were the others who had been in the room with Conrad?" Alex asked.

"After I heard them in the study, I left and picked up the lunches from the kitchen for the tram tour. When I went back to the study to see if they were still going at it, only Conrad was in the room. I told him that he was a bum to have deserted his family like my father deserted me. You know what that bastard said? He said, 'looking at a queer like you, I can understand why your father left.'

"I had a knife from the kitchen to cut the strings on the lunch boxes. I drove that knife into his heart. I couldn't believe that he even had one; that he would die. But I was glad that I killed him. It's unnatural to leave your offspring, defenseless. And then, he continued his sinful ways by taking up with a loose woman right in front of his wife.

"The scripture says, 'the harlot entices the man with seductive speech, and he follows her, as an ox goes to the slaughter. He does not know that it will cost him his life!'"

Raymond leaned heavily against the door, his eyes closed, tears rolling down his face. He no longer seemed to be aware of Alex's presence as he continued to speak in a low, unintelligible mumble. From the tone, and the few phrases that Alex could make out, she thought that he was quoting more scripture about sinful behavior and its deadly retribution.

She waited until she was sure that his vision was sufficiently blurred for her to make her move. Then, muscles taut in preparation, she broke for the kitchen on a dead run. Two steps from the doorway she heard a deafening explosion and felt a searing pain in her left leg. The impact took her off her feet, and she crashed hard onto the floor. Getting up on her knees, she scooted around the corner and heaved herself into the bathroom. Bracing against the door she managed to reach up to turn the lock.

"You can't get away, bitch! You think I can let you go, now?!" Raymond's voice was a high-pitched shriek.

Inside the bathroom, Alex ignored her pain and slid on her own blood across the tiled floor over to the tub. She had to get to the window behind the curtain. She reasoned that she still had enough strength to climb out. Grabbing onto the plastic sheet, she ripped it off a few of its hooks to reveal the "window," which turned out to be a four-foot square of glass blocks. *Oh, damn! I've always hated those things,* she thought, angrily. *How can they even call them windows? You can't see through them, and you can't open them. And now they're sealing my tomb!*

For the first time that afternoon, Alex despaired of finding a means of escaping from the madman who had just confessed that he was a heartless killer. Hot tears stained her face as she hung her head in defeat.

Late Thursday afternoon

Chapter 41

An Unlikely Hero

"I KNOW YOU'RE IN THERE," Raymond sang out from somewhere in the distance. "Looks like we're going with the 'dark figure' scenario. You asked for this, you know. You could have minded your own business, but nooo!"

Still huffing from the exertion of wedging herself between the toilet and the tub, Alex looked up in the direction of the taunt, biting her bottom lip, in pain. Pulling down a towel that was hanging overhead, she wrapped it around her bloody leg as a make-shift tourniquet. At least Raymond Bean wasn't that great of a shot; although anyone could hit a person who was cornered in a bathroom, she thought miserably.

Backing up against the wall to minimize her exposure, she felt something hard under her right buttock. Patting her behind, she fingered the outline of a small box in her rear pocket. Listing over to one side, she wrenched it out to see what it was. Staring at it in her hand, it took her a moment to recognize it as the pager that Raymond had given her to call Virgil Grimm if she ever needed help at night. Giddy over the discovery and the irony, she doubled over in joy, barely able to suppress outright laughter. She wanted to call out her thanks to Raymond for making it possible to be rescued from him.

Her spirits buoyed with new hope and borrowed time, she wondered how she came to have the pager with her. She remembered that she didn't have it when Lawrence Livermore had found the snake in his bed . . . because she had left it in *these slacks* that she had on the night of the murder. It had just been dumb luck that she had been careless about keeping track of the blessed thing.

Now, what had Raymond told her about how to use it? Turning it on, she pressed the button he had shown her that would bring up Virgil's pager number. Opening it to the tiny keyboard, she remembered Raymond telling her that she could type up to twenty characters on each of four lines. Her fingers were shaking -- from blood loss, from fear, from excitement, from a shocking realization: only Virgil Grimm could save her now.

Why was Virgil Grimm's number the only one in the damn thing's memory? He would have been her *last choice* as a rescuer. Would have been — past tense. Now, she had to grateful that she could get a message to him. But would he even respond? She couldn't even think about that.

She typed in "HELP! RAYMOND BEAN IS TRYING TO KILL ME. HE HAS GUN. I'M IN BATHROOM OF HIS HOUSE," using all the available spaces and spelling out every word so that there would be no misunderstanding. She quickly read it back to herself before hitting the "send" button. *Not good grammar, but what can you expect from someone who has just been shot by a madman and has only a toilet for defense against being shot again?*

"Your message has been sent," was on the screen. Good. Now she just had to wait to for the convicted pedophile to come and save her from a deranged murderer. There must be worse scenarios, but she couldn't think of one right then.

"Why so quiet in there?" Raymond whined. "I know you're all right because I only grazed you with my shot." He paused. "Are you *mad* at me?" His voice rose in concern. He was just outside the door. "We were having such a nice chat before you decided to leave. You can't get away, so we might as well enjoy each other's company. You know, I've had very few visitors since Mom went into the nursing home. By the way, you didn't tell me about your visit with her, and what you thought of Whispering Pines."

Alex's jaw dropped open. The man must have lost all connection to reality to be talking like they were friends who had just had a minor misunderstanding. As bizarre as the situation was, she needed to encourage him to keep talking, so he didn't start shooting. If Virgil was willing to answer her call for help, it shouldn't take him too long to get there. Any other outcome was unthinkable, anyway.

"I thought the nursing home was beautiful and the staff was very kind," she began, struggling to keep her voice steady. "And I enjoyed meeting your mother. She was in good spirits and seemed well cared for. She thought I was Eleanor Roosevelt. Why do you suppose she thinks every woman is Eleanor Roosevelt?"

"She always admired Mrs. Roosevelt as someone who lived a full life despite having an unfaithful husband. She was an inspiration to my mother. Of course, my mother didn't have Eleanor Roosevelt's celebrity and money," he added, bitterly.

"You know your mother wouldn't approve of your imprisoning me in your bathroom, Raymond. Why don't you put the gun down on the floor and walk away so I can get out of here? We can keep what happened today just between *us"*

"Why should I believe you? You have every reason to lie, and no reason to tell the truth!"

Okay, he's crazy; but he's not stupid, she thought. "This isn't going to end well for either one of us this way, Raymond. You can claim that you mistook me for an intruder and fired a warning shot before you got a good look at me. If you put down the gun, now, I promise I won't dispute that. You know you can believe me. I'm bargaining for my life, here."

"Well you're not doing a very good job of it. Shooting you is irrelevant. You got what you deserved. But you made me say that I killed Conrad Pierce, so I can't let you go."

"You have a defense for that, Raymond. You can say that you acted in the heat of passion; which is true. It wasn't premeditated, so it's a lesser charge. You can even argue that you were not aware of what you were doing because Mr. Pierce had become, in your mind, your father who had rejected you. When he insulted you, you stabbed him as a reflex, without thinking."

"Because I was *insane.* That's what you're saying. Nice try, but I have no intention of turning myself in and going on trial. Not when all I have to do is to get rid of the only witness who could testify against me. You see how simple it is for me? That's why I said you have no bargaining chips."

Alex shook her head in exasperation. *Where the hell is Virgil Grimm? Did he find out that I broke into his room and stole some of his photographs? Did he look for his "Babes in Boyland" video and figure out that I took it, so I'm not worth saving?*

Alex was getting overheated and feeling sick to her stomach, and not at all sure that she had been able to staunch the bleeding from the gunshot. Raymond wasn't so crazy that he couldn't accurately assess his situation. In the end, he would probably get caught but, at that point, it wouldn't make any difference to her, since she wouldn't be around anymore.

Then she heard a muffled, thumping sound. *What was that?* From the front door? No, it was coming from the kitchen. No, it was behind the house. *What was going on?* Now it was getting louder. Was she imagining it? The pounding continued, coming from several directions; a steady thrumming all around the house.

"What's that? What did you do!?" Raymond shrieked.

"I sent Virgil Grimm a message with the pager you gave me, that you're holding me with a gun. Give yourself up. He must have gotten hold of the police. It's all over, Raymond."

"I'm not giving myself up without taking you out first!"

The rumbling continued, becoming faster and more insistent. Added to the banging, came voices yelling something in unison, but Alex couldn't make out what they were saying. A repetition of syllables. A chant. Then, they became louder, and she heard them yelling, "Raymond! Raymond!" like crowds calling for someone to take a bow, or make a speech. "Raymond! Raymond!" But in this case, Alex realized, it was a lynch mob calling for his head.

"Raymond Bean, come out mit your hands up! We've got you surrounded!" Chef Kasmarek's voice boomed through the front door. "There's no vay you can escape! Let Miss Trotter come out or vee'll break down this door!"

"Everyone's here, Bean! All of us you've cheated!" It was Edna Butz. "We've been waiting for this day, you son-of-a-bitch!"

"Alex, are you all right? Alex!" It was Tina Wrenn.

Alex didn't think she could be heard, but she screamed, anyway. "I'm okay! Be careful! Raymond has a gun!"

"Shut up!" It was Raymond, close by. "I told you, I'm taking you out first!"

That was the last thing Alex heard before the explosions outside the bathroom door sent singed missiles flying through the air, caroming off the walls, as the room filled with smoke and the smell of gunpowder.

Unable to resist looking at the door, Alex watched in horror as a hand reached through the splintered door and turned the lock. Rolling up onto her haunches, she prepared to launch herself at her pursuer with whatever strength she could muster.

Her thighs burned with the strain of tensing for one, two, three seconds. When the man fully entered the room, she leapt forward, seizing him around the ankles, driving him backwards. Her momentum carried her over on top of him until she came to rest on his stomach. "Oof!" she heard under her. Blindly jabbing with her fists, she landed one solid blow before her wrists were held down in a vice-like grip.

"Alex — you lunatic! It's Arlie Tate!" the man below her yelled.

"Wha?"

"Why don't you *look first* before you try to knock somebody out," chided the detective, wincing and rubbing his jaw.

Alex sat up on the policeman's chest, shaking her head in confusion. "Where did *you* come from? What happened to Raymond Bean? He was just trying to kill me and shot the lock out of this door to get to me!" She pointed at the shredded door as proof of her claim. "He fired like four times," she added, as though to substantiate the attack.

"One of those bullets was mine and ended up in Raymond Bean's temple," Arlie Tate advised her with his usual understatement. "Tina Wrenn called the station when you didn't come back from your latest 'Breaking and Entering' caper. She told me about his mother in the expensive nursing home, and the dog whistle, and all the rest. Since I was running out of murder suspects, I figured you might be onto something chasing down Bean.

"When I got here, all the employees and guests that Virgil Grimm had rounded up were outside the house. Grimm had worked the lock open, so when I heard the first shot, I rushed in and Bean took a couple of shots at me. That's when I took him out. He's dead. Now, would you mind getting off my chest?"

"Oh, my god! Yes, of course! I'm so sorry! I mean, thank you, Arlie Tate!" She flopped forward and gave him a kiss on his bruised cheek.

"Seriously," he groaned, "off my chest. My gun is digging into my ribs and I need to get up and take charge of this scene until the others get here. The medical examiner is bringing a first-aid kit, by the way."

"Oh, good," Alex said, sounding relieved. "For my leg."

"I was thinking about my *face*," Tate muttered. "That was quite a haymaker you landed on my jaw," he added, ruefully. "Anyway, you stay put until he comes, and I'll let everyone outside know you're okay. My people will take you back to your room after you've been treated, and someone will bring you your dinner. You've undergone quite an ordeal and you need to rest. I'll come back in the morning and you can tell me all about what happened today, okay?"

"I'd like to see Virgil Grimm, now," Alex said, on the verge of tears, "to thank him. He was a hero. I didn't think him capable of being a decent human being, but I was wrong."

"All right, I'll let him in for a minute, if only because it's the first time you admitted that you don't have all the answers. But, before you get too weepy in gratitude, you should realize that Virgil and the others saw their opportunity to get back at Raymond Bean. This was the moment they'd been waiting for."

"Oh, yeah," she murmured. "That makes sense."

"On the other hand, they didn't have to try to get in before Raymond killed you. Although, it would have made for a better case for whatever they planned on doing to him."

"Let's not over think this, if you don't mind," Alex said. "Just who wanted me dead, and when it would have been most advantageous. I'll just thank Virgil for coming."

"Yeah, whatever," Tate muttered on his way out the door.

Friday, April 19

Chapter 42

The Morning After

DETECTIVE TATE SET ASIDE his notebook and folded his arms to concentrate on Alex who sat across from him. "Just tell me, why did you have to break into Raymond Bean's cottage in the first place? I mean, what did you hope to find? And why didn't you just let me in on what you thought was proof that the man had tried to kill people? I thought we were working together on this."

Alex crossed her eyes and sighed in resignation before speaking slowly, with exaggerated patience. "I knew the financial records must be there that would prove Bean was cheating the owner and the staff. Beyond that, I hoped to find anything that might incriminate him of other crimes. I also knew you couldn't get a search warrant if you wanted to, which you didn't, because you didn't think his hiring felons was a big deal. I didn't tell you I was planning on 'letting myself in' to his place because you ordered me to stop snooping around."

Glancing down at her bandaged leg, she smiled to herself, satisfied with the medical examiner's work as well as her response. Wound care and a good night's sleep had been restorative to her health and spirit, evident over the past hour as she was giving Arlie Tate a detailed account of the previous day's events.

After having helped her walk down the hall and into the study, the detective had comfortably ensconced her on the sofa, propped her up with extra pillows, and had pulled up a chair to elevate her bad leg. Once she was settled, he had brought in a thermos of fresh coffee and a plate of cookies. A little different treatment from when she had been interviewed as one of the suspects, she noted.

"So, you thought I couldn't possibly see the importance of the evidence you had against Bean?" Arlie Tate asked, as though astonished.

"If you didn't make much out of someone running an inn with a bunch of criminals, how could I hope to convince you that a *dog whistle* was a murder weapon?" she asked, grinning smugly.

"Now *that* with the dog whistle was clever," said Tate, ignoring her putdown. "I *might* not have made that connection, myself," he shrugged, looking down to inspect his trousers and brushing off some unseen lint.

After tidying his wardrobe, he glanced up at her, having a sudden thought. "So, tell me this, since you're so smart — why do you think he wanted to kill Ronette and Phyllis? Surely, they weren't the worst guests who ever stayed at this hotel"

"Excuse me," Alex replied, archly. "Ronette and Phyllis weren't *bad guests* at *all*. According to Tina Wrenn, previous guests had met with so-called 'accidents,' too, thanks to Mr. Bean; but she wouldn't give me the details because she was afraid of losing her job if he found out she had shared her suspicions.

"Tina was the one who first suspected that Raymond was hiring people with prison records so that he could steal from them to pay for his mother's care. He threatened the employees that if they quit, he'd make it impossible for them to get other jobs; and with their pasts, they believed him."

"About Ronette and Phyllis . . ." Detective Tate inserted.

"As I told you earlier, Raymond Bean was first molested by his mother when he was *fourteen years old.* That sexual relationship caused him intolerable guilt, not only because it was against nature, but also, because he still loved his mother in spite of it, and in some, sick way, he even enjoyed it."

Detective Tate nodded impatiently, as Alex continued her recital.

"As time went on, in order to live with what he felt was unforgivable sin, he started punishing others for their 'sins of the flesh.' He couldn't condemn his mother, outright, and he hated himself for participating, so he sought redemption by making others pay for *their* behavior. Apparently, my group provided him with a lot of sexual activity that he found to be immoral."

"Like Ronette and Phyllis," Tate offered, grateful for the opportunity to bring the subject back to the two women.

"Raymond witnessed the sexual encounter between Conrad Pierce and Ronette on the porch that first night," Alex explained. "He was also aware that Lawrence Livermore was at first intimate with Nadine Rodgers, and then slept with Phyllis Hanover. All of that sex disturbed Raymond."

"I think he *envied* it," Arlie put in. "He's a paunchy middle-aged man who probably only had sex with his mother. He must have hidden the coral snake in Livermore's bed, to punish him for having so many women."

"Right," agreed Alex. "He quoted scripture to me about harlots enticing men who would then be slaughtered like oxen, as biblical justification that all the so-called fornicators in my group deserved to die."

Detective Tate pursed his lips and gazed off into the distance. "Back to the murder of Conrad Pierce. Bean confessed to you that he stabbed him, but are you sure he wasn't just trying to take credit for a successful murder? After all, he had failed in all his other attempts to kill people."

"I'm *sure* of it," Alex asserted. "For several reasons. First of all, remember, Raymond didn't want to admit to me that he had killed Conrad; it just slipped out, which he immediately regretted, and then decided that he'd have to kill me for knowing.

"Then, there's his revelation that Conrad Pierce reminded him of his father whom he hated and blamed for the onset of the incest with his mother.

"Also, we know that Raymond must have been listening at this door when Conrad and Jennifer were arguing the morning of the murder, because no one told him about the conversation that he knew all about.

"Raymond is one of the few people who was unaccounted for who *could* have been in this room to kill Conrad. No one saw him for several minutes after he picked up the lunches, which was about the time of the murder. Raymond said that he got a knife from the kitchen to cut the box strings, but he didn't have a knife when he got back on the tram.

"Lastly, when I went to his cottage to ask him to call the police when Conrad had been found murdered, he insisted on going back to the study first, to 'make sure the man was actually dead,' as he put it." She paused, letting the statement take effect.

"So?" Arlie asked. "He *was* dead, by then."

"I know. But don't you think going in the study by himself gave Raymond the perfect opportunity to make sure he'd removed any traces of his earlier presence? Like having the time to be sure he had wiped his prints off the handle of the knife?"

Arlie leaned back, nodding. "Yes, I do. Everything you've said is persuasive circumstantial evidence in addition to his confession. I've just been pushing you to examine everything carefully. I have no doubt that Raymond was the murderer, and his death will go down as punishment for all his crimes; including the attempted murders of Ronette, Phyllis, Lawrence Livermore, and the kidnapping and forming of intent to kill you."

Alex bit on her lower lip, lowering her eyes.

"You're the one who's responsible for bringing him to justice, but it was still foolhardy of you to 'let yourself into' his house, as you so quaintly put it. If you hadn't had that pager, or I hadn't come into the house when I did, you'd be cooling under a sheet in the morgue right now.

"Thanks for the image, Arlie. You really know how to make a girl feel special."

"Yeah, well. I said nice things about you to Barrington Hall."

"To whom?"

"The owner of the Grover Inn."

"Oh, right. I thought at first you were talking about a dormitory."

"Funny. I called him last night and told him about Raymond, and your part in bringing him down. He's coming here this afternoon to reorganize the hotel, and he wants to thank you in person. Actually, he was very impressed with what you did." Alex shrugged, modestly.

"So, is there anything else you want to add to your statement? If not, I'll have someone take this tape to the station and have it typed up and brought back for your signature. Right now, I need to get back to the cottage to make sure that all the evidence is collected before Hall gets here. He wants to see all those bookkeeping and personnel records, for instance."

Alex drummed her fingers on her chin, thinking, before she answered. "I just hope that Mr. Hall will be fair with the staff after all the abuse they've taken from Raymond Bean," she said, grimacing as she wiggled her bad leg to get back the circulation.

"As for my statement, I'd just like to add that I'm convinced Raymond Bean always acted alone. He never mentioned any employee helping him or even knowing what he had been up to."

Picking up the tape recorder, she spoke directly into it. "Lastly, for the record, Detective Tate was right in telling me not to investigate suspects on my own, and ignoring that advice almost got me killed." She looked over at the detective with a sly smile before continuing. "But I can't regret going into Mr. Bean's house, because I was able to find out who killed one of my people. But now that it's over, and we have all the answers, I think I'll stick to my day job."

Detective Tate smirked as he took the recorder from Alex and clicked if off. Leaning back against his chair, he ran his fingers through his thatch of sandy hair, studying Alex with a mixed expression of amusement and frustration. After several seconds, he stood and reached for Alex's hands to help her up.

"Uh, okay then," he murmured. "I guess that's all and you can go back to your room now," he added, sounding unsure how to end the interview.

As Alex came to her feet, the detective continued holding her hands as he faced her, but looked down at his shoes. Breaking the awkward silence, he said, finally, "I just wanted to tell you that I do think you're special, and I'm glad you didn't get yourself killed."

"Gee, thanks, Arlie," Alex said, rolling her eyes. "Don't get carried away with emotion."

"Look, I'm not a real smooth guy, you may have noticed. But I'm trying to say something here, and you're not helping. I mean, I *like* you and . . . oh, what the hell!" Bending down, he pressed his lips against hers, pulling her hands behind her in an embrace. A knock at the door caused him to quickly pull away, dropping her hands and tugging at his shirt collar, which appeared to have become too snug.

"Yes?" the detective asked in a lowered voice, turning towards the door.

"It's Holmes, sir. Brian and I are finished with the scene. Are you coming over? Do you want us to wait for you?"

"Uh, sure. Just a second. We were just wrapping things up, here." He shrugged at Alex, mugging a "that's one way to put it" look on his face.

Opening the door to the two lab technicians, he said, brusquely, "Good timing. Miss Trotter was just leaving. Miss Holmes can help you get up to your room," he added, speaking in the general direction of where Alex still stood.

Well, things are back to normal, Alex thought. She only hoped that her face wouldn't betray how stunned and giddy she felt after being kissed by Arlie Tate. She could hardly believe it had really happened. Later, she'd have the luxury of time to process what had just occurred, and what significance it had, if any, but right then she just needed to take her leave as quickly as possible.

"No thanks, Detective Tate. I can manage," she said a little too brightly for the mundane words. "I want to stop at reception, anyway, and talk to Tina." Then, unable to resist, she added, with the barest of smiles, "And thanks for everything."

Chapter 43

Wrapping up Loose Ends

ALEX FAIRLY FLOATED DOWN THE HALL, suddenly feeling no pain in her sore leg. Rounding the corner and heading toward the reception area, she saw the back of a woman she thought was Tina Wrenn, although this woman stood taller than Tina, and had loose hair falling to her shoulders, rather than Tina's tight top knot. As Alex drew closer, she realized that it *was* Tina, and that she was giving instructions to one of the housekeepers.

When Alex walked up behind her she heard Tina say, "I'd appreciate if you would go over the wood pieces in the front hall with some furniture polish, Mollie. They look so dull and lifeless. I think they give a very poor impression when guests first enter." The maid nodded in agreement, and started off, wheeling her cart in the direction of her assignment.

As Tina was still unaware of her presence, Alex cleared her throat to get her attention. Turning around, Tina's face lit up at the sight of her. "Oh, Alex! Thank God you're all right!" she exclaimed, giving Alex her second hug of the day. "And you look great! Honestly, no one would know that you were almost killed yesterday. You look like you just came from the spa."

"I've gotten a little pampering," Alex murmured. "But I was just thinking how different *you* look, Tina. What have you done to yourself? Let me get a good look at you. Stepping back, she eyed the young woman from top to bottom, taking in the long wavy hair that had been set free, the turned-up mouth brightened with red lipstick, and the stylish suit with a skirt that ended well above her open-toed heels; a makeover one would more likely see on a TV talk show than at the Grover Inn.

"Tina, you look great, but, more importantly, it just dawned on me what else has changed about you. This is the first time I've seen you when you weren't fidgeting or looking around, nervously. You're like a different person. And taking charge of the cleaning staff, no less."

"I have to admit I'm more self-confident and relaxed now that I don't have to worry about the guests getting killed off," Tina responded, without apparent hyperbole. "We all feel better now that we're free of Raymond Bean. I know I shouldn't be glad the man's dead, but he asked for it by trying to kill you.

"We just don't know what's going to happen, now, with the hotel, and with our jobs. Detective Tate told me that the owner will be coming here this afternoon, so I guess we're about to find out. I've never even met the guy, that's how interested he's been in this place. He's probably some crabby old man who doesn't want to be bothered with any of our problems."

"Arlie also told me that Barrington Hall was coming," Alex put in, trying out the familiarity of the detective's first name, as well as making it known that he had shared inside information with her. "Whatever happens, it couldn't be as bad as what you've had to put up with for so long.

"Anyway, what I wanted to tell you is how grateful I am that you called the police yesterday, and how smart you were not to have listened to me. I don't think I'd be here now if Arlie Tate hadn't been there to shoot Raymond, and Arlie wouldn't have been there if it weren't for you."

Tina's eyes shone as she took Alex's hand. "I knew when you weren't back by three o'clock that something had gone terribly wrong. I shouldn't have let you go without me, but as it turned out, I was able to do more from here than if I had been held at gunpoint with you."

Just then, the swishing sound of the opening and closing of the front door drew their attention as a tall, lean man, wearing a dark business suit and carrying a leather satchel, entered the hotel. His bearing, as he crossed the foyer with purposeful strides, gave him an air of importance, along with the quality of his wardrobe. As he came near, Alex and Tina fairly gaped at the man's good looks.

Tina, at first flustered by the unexpected visitor, found her voice and stammered, "May-may I help you?"

"Actually, I'm here to help *you,* Miss Wrenn," the man replied, managing to sound sincere in spite of the smarmy words. "I don't blame you for not knowing who I am, but I'm Barrington Hall, the owner of this hotel, and I know I'm way overdue in getting here and acting like one. Obviously, I'm here today because of what happened yesterday; actually, because of what I've learned has been going on for a long time. I hope to start to make things right."

"Oh, Mr. Hall, of course!" Tina exclaimed, beaming, in an attempt to cover her shock at discovering the man's identity. "I should have known. Detective Tate told me that you were coming, but you're so much . . . uh, *earlier* than I expected you to be. Here. Today." She gave Alex a sideways look, daring to be contradicted.

"Oh, and this is Alex Trotter, who you must know all about," Tina said, placing her hands on Alex's back and pushing her forward. "We're all grateful for what she did, and relieved that she's okay," Tina added.

Barrington Hall's face broke into a smile, revealing even white teeth that fairly sparkled against his tanned face. "Miss Trotter. You are one remarkable woman," he asserted, taking her right hand in both of his. The two women instinctively peered down at his proffered hands, checking on whether he was wearing a wedding ring, and seeing that he did not.

"You're one of the reasons I made sure I got here today – I heard you'll be leaving tomorrow morning. I wanted to meet you and thank you for your tremendous act of courage, of course, and to let you know that you're welcome to stay here, as my guest, anytime you'd like. I know that you might not want to come back for a while, maybe a good long while, but I hope in time you'll allow us to show you what a first-class inn the Grover can be."

Alex heard a soft whimper behind her, and felt a poke in the small of her back. "That's very kind of you, Mr. Hall, but you should know that in many respects this already *is* a four-star hotel, thanks to the staff whom I've seen take excellent care of the guests, despite their low wages and threats from Raymond Bean. And you should also know that, if it weren't for all the employees who came to my rescue, particularly Tina, here, who called the police on a hunch, I probably wouldn't be here today."

"That's the same story I heard from Detective Tate," Barrington Hall III said, craning his neck to include Tina in his remarks. "Which reminds me; I need to meet with him at the former manager's residence."

Alex started at the casual reference to Raymond Bean as the "former manager," as though he had just lost his job, rather than his life in a violent, bloody shoot-out only the day before.

"Miss Wrenn, it was a pleasure meeting you," Hall said, shaking her hand and giving a little bow. "I'd like to meet with you and the rest of the employees at, say four o'clock, if you'd let them know," he said, consulting his watch. "I should be done by then."

He looked at the two women and smiled. “Maybe I can have dinner with both of you this evening. If you don't have plans.”

“That'll be nice. Thanks,” Tina calmly accepted, causing Alex to stare at her in amazement.

“Yeah, sure. Fine,” Alex murmured.

While Barrington was going over the books in Raymond Bean's cottage, Alex was meeting with the remaining members of her tour group to answer questions about the manager’s life, and to explain his violent demise. As Alex finished recounting how he had been responsible for all the dirty tricks that week and the murder of Conrad Pierce, the sound of high heels was heard coming down the hallway. As the staccato grew louder, they all looked up in shock to see Ronette standing, teetering, in the doorway.

“Ronette,” Alex called out. “Uh, we didn't expect to see you. Come on in!”

“Hey, everybody!” Ronette called out, walking in without hesitation. “I was told y'all were in here talking ‘bout Raymond Bean. Ain't that somethin’? When I was in my cell, I overheard the police going on about how Raymond had been stealing from the Inn, and that he was such a pervert and everything. I knew only a mother could love that man!” She laughed a deep, throaty laugh. “He wouldda fit in well where I come from!” She laughed again.

“Ronette, are you back here, now?” Alex interjected, not wanting to hear any stories about incest for the time being, especially ones that Ronette found amusing. “I mean, you're out of jail?”

"I'm here just to pick up the rest of my stuff. I guess y'all heard about that little business with Wade and the ceegars. That man! He's always trying to better himself, you know? But sometimes he's not too smart. Well, he aint never too smart.

Anyway, my cousin Sherrie bailed us out, not that I'm going to stand trial, since I dint do nothin' but be with my husband, that a wife's s'pose to do. Anyway, I gotta get goin' as the police lady is waitin' to take me back across. It's good to see y'all, though. This was a real nice week— I mean, aside from the stampede, the murder and our being arrested. Well, I'll see you, then. Bye-bye, now!"

After her departure, there was a stunned silence for a few seconds until Phyllis said, "She's a real character, isn't she? You can't help but like her, though. I'm glad she was with us, and I wish her well. I really do." Others chimed in with similar remarks as Alex stood to say that maybe it was time to end the meeting and go upstairs to relax before cocktails.

* * *

DINNER THAT EVENING turned out to be a celebratory event with everyone toasting Barrington Hall's future success with the Grover Inn. The whole staff was staying on and would receive twenty percent raises, retroactive to the first of the year. This news most certainly explained Edna Butz's new attitude, seen by her cheerfully taking orders, encouraging substitutions, if desired, and then serving each plate with a sincere wish that the meal would be enjoyed.

Tina received congratulations on being promoted to the position of manager. She would continue to receive guests at the front desk until a replacement could be found, along with a couple of porters to better assist the guests.

Barrington advised Alex and Tina that Lucie Bean would be allowed to stay on at the nursing home, by turning over only her social security, as she had already paid the required minimum to have her "life care" contract honored. When Lucie had been told that her son Raymond had died, she had only nodded and asked if she could watch *Golden Girls,* as the show was just starting.

The owner assured Tina that he would be in close contact with her by phone, as service was coming to the island; and he would be visiting more often, although he had every confidence in her to capably run the hotel.

* * *

IT HAD BEEN A FITTING END to all that had transpired that week, but Alex went up to her room that evening feeling disappointed and dissatisfied. She hadn't seen or heard from Arlie Tate after their little romantic interlude early in the day which had stirred feelings in her that had been left unspoken and unresolved. She had to admit that she had become quite fond of the man, even if he had frustrated her in her efforts to find the killer. In the end, he had saved her life, and then gave her the credit for bringing Raymond Bean to justice.

Thinking back, she realized that she had been intrigued by him all week; from the first moment when she misjudged him as being incompetent and backwards, to when she realized that he was a step ahead of everyone, including her. He was a complicated guy whom she had just begun to appreciate, and now she'd probably never see him again. Would he really allow their friendship, their relationship, to end with an interrupted kiss? What would have happened if Needra Holmes hadn't knocked on the door? She hadn't even had a chance to tell him that she was leaving the first thing in the morning.

Anyway, she needed to pack up her things and get some sleep. She thought about clearing out the dresser, including Virgil Grimm's pornography she'd have to take home with her to throw away. She could just imagine explaining the photographs and the tape to security if they searched her luggage. *No, Officer, these aren't mine. I stole them from the pedophile I later called to rescue me from his boss who was trying to shoot me in his bathroom. Oh, never mind-- I'll come with you.*

She would be traveling home with Jennifer, David, and Nadine; flying from Jacksonville to O'Hare. David had told her he'd pick up her bags in the hallway at about seven to take downstairs for Virgil Grimm to load into the van for their drive to the ferry.

With a full day ahead of her, Alex decided she'd go to bed and not dwell on Arlie Tate anymore. What was it that Scarlett O'Hara had said when she first realized that she was losing Rhett Butler? Oh, yeah. "I can't think about that right now. If I do, I'll go crazy! I'll think about that tomorrow."

Saturday, April 20

Chapter 44

Leaving Bedford Island

EARLY THE NEXT MORNING, Alex woke up in a dark mood following a fitful night's sleep. After quickly showering, she pulled on the same long-sleeved shirt and slacks that she had worn coming down to Bedford Island. And, just like then, the southern Georgia heat and humidity made the clothes stick to her like Saran wrap, which didn't improve her disposition.

Looking at herself in the mirror, she made a disparaging assessment: her face was puffy, her eyes were reddened, and her hair had frizzed out to an unprecedented volume. Tugging at her mane to see just how far she could make it stand out, the thought struck her that she resembled a certain old-time television star: of course, Roseanne Roseanneadanna was *supposed* to look ridiculous. She pushed her hair back down and shrugged at the slight improvement.

By 6:45, Alex had pushed her two suitcases out into the hallway for David to take down, giving her some time to kill. Not feeling like going down to the dining room, as she wanted to neither eat nor socialize right then, she flopped onto the easy chair to review the week and get her thoughts together. The past seven days had been anything but relaxing as she had anticipated. Still, despite the tragic and near-tragic events, she had done her job and, at least, the people who worked at the Inn were better off for her efforts.

Then her mind went back again to Arlie. After a rocky beginning, they had become friends, and even partners, in a way. Two days ago, Arlie had rushed in to save her when he heard Raymond Bean's first shot, knowing that Raymond had the advantage of position. Yesterday, he had expressed his affection for her. You would think that the man could have at least said good-bye, she thought, sadly.

Breathing a deep sigh, she raised herself up off the chair, shouldered her carry-on bag, took a last look around the room, and headed out the door. Making a slow and stiff descent on the stairs to the first floor, she found that no one else was around. She knew that Margaret and Chloe were leaving later, meeting Chloe's fiance in St. Annes to claim the body of Conrad Pierce and to make arrangements. Lawrence was traveling with Rosemary and Phyllis, and would spend a couple of days in Washington D.C., and the Bertholds were catching a later flight back to Knoxville.

Walking past the empty reception desk, Alex smiled, thinking of Tina Wrenn's transformation from nervous wreck to doyenne of hotel management. She felt like she had made a friend of Tina. And Tina had the decency to say good-bye.

At the front door, Alex saw that her suitcases were still sitting there, waiting to be carried out to the van. As hers were the only ones, she thought she might as well take them outside onto the porch, where she could sit and wait for the others. Checking her watch, she saw that she still had fifteen minutes before they were scheduled to depart for the ferry.

Grabbing hold of her two bags, with her carry-on hanging around her neck, she backed into the heavy glass door using the suitcases as battering rams. Halfway through, the wheels became stuck in the grooves of the threshold, infuriating her. Pushing against the door as ballast, she yanked up on the handles with all her might just as the door gave way, catapulting her and her bags through the air en masse until, just as suddenly, she and the hurtling pile lost inertia and crash landed.

"Aaargh!" Alex heard from somewhere nearby. "How many times are you going to flatten me when I'm just trying to help you?" a disembodied voice asked.

Alex, dazed, got up on one elbow, unable to see anything as her carry-on had landed on her stomach, in front of her face.

"Ow! That's my collarbone you're digging your elbow in!" the voice complained.

"Arlie? What happened?"

"You seem to be in a better position to answer that this time. I thought I was opening the door for you, when you suddenly threw your luggage at me and jumped onto my chest. Again."

"My luggage got stuck in the doorway. You took away the resistance and made me lose my balance. And where have you been? You get all lovey-dovey ... well, sort of ... and then you disappear on my last day."

"I had to finish processing the crime scene and file reports to justify my actions. Besides, *this* is your last day, and the last ten minutes of it. Do you want to spend the remaining time hollering at me while we're stacked on top of each other like mating narwhals?"

Alex managed to shove one of the cases out of her way to allow herself space to roll off Arlie and sit on the floor. Pushing her hair off her face, she looked down at him, laughter bubbling up. "We do get ourselves into pretty ridiculous situations, don't we? And no, I'd like to spend our next few minutes the way we spent our last few minutes yesterday. You're maddening, Arlie Tate, but I would like to see you again, if that's even possible."

Arlie sat up and stroked her cheek with the back of his hand. “I think we can arrange that. I wouldn't mind visiting Chicago, and maybe I should go along on one of your trips. From what I’ve seen, you could use a police escort.”

“Sorry to disappoint you, Detective, but you can expect only smooth sailing on any of my trips in the future. I’ve never been involved in any murder investigation before.”

“Oh, yeah? Well, as nosy as you are, I don't imagine it'll be the last time,” he said, smiling and reaching for her.

ACNOWLEDGMENTS

Many thanks to my sister-in-law, Carolyn Carlson, whose vacation at the Greyfield Inn on Cumberland Island off the coast of Georgia was the inspiration for this book. I used many details of that island in writing about the structures and ecology on Bedford Island, and used the Greyfield Inn as a model for the physical description of the Grover Inn. Of course, the real Inn is well-managed and everyone on Carolyn's trip remained in good health.

I would also like to thank my friend and college roommate, Kandy Higinbotham, who encouraged me to write this book and sent me a story about a reclusive sociopath who was the inspiration for Virgil Grimm in my story.

I'm grateful to my friend Paul Buie who voluntarily read my manuscript and gave me his enthusiastic review, while advising me of some misconceptions about the Coast Guard.

I appreciate that my brother, Robert Carlson, a retired graphic artist, spent many hours working on a cover design until we were both satisfied with the artwork and lettering.

Finally, I would like to thank my husband Jim who made constructive comments after patiently reading through every rewrite, and was uncomplaining of the amount of time I needed to complete this project.